Conviction

A Dominion Novel

By Lissa Kasey

Conviction : A Dominion Novel
2nd Edition
Copyright © 2015 Lissa Kasey
All rights reserved
Cover Art by Simone Hendricks
Published by Lissa Kasey
http://www.lissakasey.com

Please Be Advised

This is a work of fiction. Names, characters, businesses, places, events and incidents are either the products of the author's imagination or used in a fictitious manner. Any resemblance to actual persons, living or dead, or actual events is purely coincidental.

Warning

This book is licensed to the original purchaser only. Duplication or distribution via any means is illegal and a violation of International Copyright Law, subject to criminal prosecution and upon conviction, fines, and/or imprisonment. This eBook cannot be legally loaned or given to others. No part of this book can be shared or reproduced without the express permission of the Author.

A Note from the Author

If you did not purchased this book from an authorized retailer you make it difficult for me to write the next book. Stop piracy and purchase the book. For all those who purchased the book legitimately: Thank you!

JAMIE
(a Dominion Short)

USING THE weights at the Y wasn't the same as using them at the gym, mostly because the few guys in the weight room were more casual lifters than the two guys with me. Rick and Michael looked like the bodybuilders they were: bulging muscles, veins, and necks rounder than their heads. No matter what Seiran said, I was not nearly as obsessive or large as my workout buddies. I curled 40lb dumbbells, they did 60lbs, but I could see how that would intimidate a small man like my brother, who could only do 15lbs on a good day. Nothing wrong with that, he was fit for his body type.

People stared, though. We always stood out. I sometimes convinced myself it was the muscles and impressive sets that made everyone stop. Other days I wasn't so sure. Rick and Michael wore super tight shorts and tanks, outlining every well-defined ridge of their bodies. I was in running pants and a T-shirt just loose enough to cling. Sei didn't like all the muscles on display. They made him nervous. Or maybe it was just the way Rick and Michael joked and teased him like he was their little brother too. They bitched at me for walking on eggshells around the kid.

JAMIE

Said I acted different. But they didn't know what Sei had been through.

I put the weights away, wiped everything clean, and stretched a little before heading for the shower to wash off the sweat. Neither Sei nor Kelly was in the locker room yet. I'd probably have to drag them out of the pool. The second the sky had dropped its first snowflake of the season in the Twin Cities, the two had been perpetually at the pool. It was the one amenity that Gabe's building didn't have. At least not an enclosed one that could be used during the winter.

Rick and Michael headed to the track to go around again. They'd only met me here today so I wouldn't have to be in the weight room without a spotter. Admittedly I didn't meet them as often. What used to be four or five days a week was down to two, and that was only if I was sure Sei was busy elsewhere.

I had lunch planned with the boys, so we had to get cleaned up and downtown before the lunch crowds swarmed. Sei would freak if we were shoved into a corner surrounded by noisy, smelly people. Large groups and small places always made him twitchy. The last few months of heaped-on shit hadn't changed that. I'd been pushing Gabe to convince Sei a vacation would be nice. Get Sei's mind off the past, and maybe ease some of the never-ending tremor that often ghosted through his limbs.

After the shower, I yanked on a clean pair of black pants and a T-shirt. The rest would just make me sweat, so the button-up would have to wait until I got the boys out of the water. I had to pause in the doorway of the pool room because Kelly was squatting with his back to me. The lithe muscles of his legs strained, and the tiny Speedo did little to cover that small, tight butt of his or the lean length of his back and strong shoulders. The line of his neck was mostly hidden by his bleached blond hair, which was cut in a sort of skater punk versus surfer do. The strands looked darker wet, clinging in an almost taunting way. It begged to be brushed away from his tanned neck.

I swallowed back a moan when he shifted his weight and dropped to one knee. His strong hands worked at Sei's back, massaging the probably aching muscles. Sei had been attacked by a rogue witch a couple weeks ago and had really hurt his back. The doctors said he would heal. I knew spinal bruising took a lot of recovery time. The injury could have been so much worse. He could have been paralyzed. The thought made me shudder.

JAMIE

Sei relaxed into Kelly's hands, a long sigh releasing the tension like a cork had been pulled. Most of the time it was me who did the massaging, but I couldn't begrudge Kelly the right to touch him. They were best friends. I found them curled up together asleep on the couch more often than not, or even in one another's beds, though Sei never looked at Kelly with more than a friendly smile, and he seemed to be okay with that. It wasn't sexual, but it was a bond. Sometimes I had to fight the compulsion to separate them, usually after I had some horrible realization about how security in the building sucked or that someone could get to them in the pool if I wasn't around despite the security Gabe hired to discreetly follow them around.

There was a time or two I admitted to worrying about Kelly's motives. Sei had been betrayed before, countless times. But nothing in Kelly's eyes ever said calculating killer or even sociopath. Which is what he would have to be to have fooled us all. So my worry began to expand to Kelly too, watching and protecting him to keep my little brother from experiencing heartache at the loss or betrayal of another friend. Never mind the fact that my body had other ideas as to why Kelly needed watching.

Kelly was carved like the runner—and swimmer—he was, lithe with strong shoulders and narrow hips. His arms were toned, not muscled like Rick or Michael or even close to my definition, but no one would have thought he was anything but fit. Without a shirt and mostly naked, there was no denying just how *fit* he was.

I sighed.

I would not lust after my baby brother's best friend. It just wasn't right. Kelly was one of the few people Sei had ever trusted in his whole life. The two talked like magpies, only shutting up long enough for Gabe or me to get food into them. There was no hesitation when they were together. They got into everything and Sei did things no one expected him to ever try. Like swimming in a public pool where there might be germs.

Getting Sei to open up to others was more important than whatever my stupid body demanded, especially since I wanted to curl around a man more than ten years my junior. I was the grown-up and had to act like one.

"Jamie!" Sei called, seeing me. He was sprawled on his stomach across a lounge chair that had been covered in towels. He wore board shorts and a T-shirt. I noticed the tear on the side of the shorts and mentally noted I'd have to go online to order him a new pair. The tear was low. Near the knee and only minor, but I'd either fix it or replace it anyway. I was a little surprised he hadn't noticed it already and insisted on changing.

Sei's smile lit up the room. There should have been the noise of other children, swimmers, and chatty parents. But Gabe donated a sizable amount of cash to keep the area closed and clear for Sei to play. Kelly plopped down in the chair beside where Sei was sprawled out. Sei rolled over instead of trying to push himself up. "Good workout?"

"Yep. You guys have fun swimming?" I sat carefully on the end of the Sei's lounge chair, picked up his towel, and rubbed his head with it. His trunks were still slightly damp, but his skin appeared mostly dry. Drops of water hung from his short dark hair. He had thick, silky hair that anyone who cared about hair wanted to have. I knew he missed the length. Sei spent hours brushing my hair. I even let him braid it in interesting ways just because it was nice to have time close to him, even if he only did it 'cause he missed his.

I wondered, not for the first time, if he'd grown up brushing his mother's hair, which had been long and straight until about three years ago. Sei hadn't even begun to grow his hair long until he graduated high school.

"Kelly did like a billion laps," Sei said, interrupting my wandering thoughts, then took the towel from me and flung it around his shoulders as he got up.

Kelly wrapped his towel around his waist and stretched. "The water was so nice."

"Warm," Sei said. His weight had dropped low enough that he didn't have enough fat to insulate his bones. I was working on that, feeding him as much as I could and wrapping him in blankets when he wasn't in Gabe's lap, at school, or at work.

"You two better go get ready. We have to get to lunch." I grabbed up their bag of water stuff and followed them to the locker room.

"I just need to shower off the chlorine." Sei headed for the shower, stripping out of his trunks and shirt on his way to the back of the tiled shower stalls. Kelly followed suit, and I couldn't turn around fast enough to not see his toned ass and the white outline of his tan. Shit.

"I'll be out here," I told them, trying to ignore their banter and laughter as they showered beside each other. The three of us shared a locker, so I pulled out all their stuff, lined it up on the bench, and then checked the rack by the shower for fresh linens. Gabe or I usually called ahead when we knew Sei

Jamie

would be coming so they could clean things, put extra attendants on duty, and clear the pool area. Gabe joked about buying a building and turning it into a private pool just for them. The idea had merit, like better security and little chance that someone had peed in the pool before we arrived. But Kelly did occasionally use the track and the weight room to work out. And Sei followed him like a little duck from place to place. So anything Gabe did would have to be more than just a pool. Maybe I could convince him to buy a gym. Go in on it with him. It would give me something to do as I got older, bored with nursing, or Sei didn't need me anymore.

"So you'd really go to a game with me?" Kelly asked Sei as they were leaving the shower. I didn't dare turn their way for fear of what I'd see. My mind filled in lots of blanks for me to go with the round little ass Kelly had and his warm, golden skin. The two were close in height, only a few inches separating them, but Kelly was broader in the shoulder and more defined.

I needed to stop thinking about him.

"Yeah. I'll go. I can't promise to understand it, but hot men running across a field in tight pants, sure." They had to be talking about football. As far as I knew, the only football happening right now was college games, since the Vikings had already tanked their season, but it was Kelly's favorite topic. I heard the sound of clothes rustling. Maybe if I thought really hard, I'd imagine something other than Kelly dressing. Of course he'd slide his pants up those lean legs, hop in to straighten them, and snap the jeans up over his crotch before pulling the shirt over his head and smoothing it over his flat stomach...

"Jamie?" Sei touched my arm gently, something he didn't do often, but it brought me out of my fantasy. "You okay?"

"Of course." I glanced over him, making sure he was dressed warmly enough for the cold.

"Ready to go?" Kelly asked. At least he was dressed too, even if the jeans he wore were a little tighter than I thought was stylish right now.

I was more ready than he could know. I picked up their things and led them to the car, letting them chatter away behind me. If I breathed and meditated, I could brush it all off. The image of Kelly's ass wasn't burned in my brain. It would fade. I'd seen a lot of asses in my lifetime. Why was his any better than any of the others? I sighed again and stuffed our bags in the trunk of my car, got in front, and started it.

JAMIE

"Want me to drive?" Kelly asked. He slid into the backseat beside Sei, but made a motion to open the door and get out.

"No. I'm good." I needed something else to focus on other than the blond man in the backseat. Maybe after lunch I'd call an old friend of mine who liked to wrestle and didn't mind taking care of a little wood. Christ, I was feeling like a teenager. And hungry. At least it was lunchtime.

The restaurant was quiet when we pulled in just after 11:00 a.m. The host seated us in a booth with views of the whole room, which I appreciated. Sei and Kelly sat across from me, ordered veggie egg rolls as an appetizer, and continued talking. It would be okay. I could handle it, though my gut churned as I stared out at the room. Watching people and making sure Sei was secure always made me feel normal. It gave me purpose. Though I was a little on edge, like a slightly overwound spring. Maybe I should have just done some boxing with the guys instead of the lifting. My overactive libido was probably because I hadn't been spending as much time in the gym.

Between looking after Sei and my studies, time simply wasn't on my side. How long before the scale would start inching up? I hadn't checked in weeks. *Shit.* I was probably already up ten pounds, maybe as much as fifteen. Had my clothes been tight? Rick and Michael usually noticed, but they hadn't said anything. Were they just trying to be polite?

Silence brought my eyes back to the young men sitting with me. "Huh?" I asked, since both of them stared at me with questioning gazes.

"You're kind of spacey today," Kelly remarked.

"Yeah," Sei agreed. "What's wrong, Jamie?"

"Nothing. I'm not sure what you mean." I hated to see that worried look in Sei's eyes. He had enough issues without adding mine.

"Okay. What are you going to order, then?" Sei prompted, holding up his menu.

Thankfully I'd gone over the menu online before planning on coming here and knew what I was getting. "The chicken with peppers and rice."

"I totally figured him for the steak," Kelly said to Sei.

Sei's face crinkled up in a look of distaste. "Beef is so bad for you." Which was why I wasn't getting it—not because it was bad for me, but because Sei believed it was

Jamie

bad for me. "The tomato avocado sandwich looks good."

"I'm getting the steak." Kelly smiled at us both. "I promise not to keel over from a heart attack before lunch is over. Jamie could probably use the extra protein too, since he lifted today. The extra iron will help his muscles build and repair too."

Sei looked my way with a raised eyebrow. "Maybe you should get the steak."

I searched his face and words for any sign of disgust or judgment, but there was none. "Yeah, okay."

Sei's smile lit up the table. Kelly winked at me and returned his friend's grin as we ordered and passed off the menus.

When the food came, I cut into my medium-well steak, loving how the juices ran out onto the plate. How long had it been since beef had crossed my palate? The first piece melted in my mouth. I stole a glance toward Sei and Kelly, fearing I'd find them watching me in a disapproving way. Food was fuel, not pleasure. *Fuel*, I reminded myself.

They were engaged in conversation about a Magic Studies class. Kelly occasionally glanced my way, throwing sweet smiles in my direction. Did he know he was flirting? *Was* he flirting? The only people who usually looked at me like that were flirting. Fuck, I was out of practice.

I went back to my steak, enjoying food for the first time in ages. Not that I didn't like the things Seiran made, but he made a lot of rabbit food: lean proteins, super grains, veggies, and fruit. It was healthy and all whole foods, which weren't bad. But I'd been secretly adding more healthy fats to his diet. Even making him chocolates with coconut oil and almond butter. He needed the omega-3s to help his mental balance just as much as I did.

Kelly pushed the last of his steak toward me when Sei grabbed the dessert menu. They picked out some monstrous chocolate flowing cake and ice cream mix of which I had only two spoonfuls of. Half of Sei's sandwich sat on his plate, taunting me more than any sweet treats ever did. How much time would I have to spend in the gym tomorrow if I ate that sandwich on top of the steak I had? The waiter came back, and Sei asked to have the sandwich boxed up. I paid for lunch despite their protests and we made our way to the car. If I were lucky, my stomach wouldn't growl until after I got up to my place and could have a protein shake.

A text chirped on my phone just as we pulled into the condo. I dug out the phone

Jamie

while I pulled their stuff out of the trunk. The words made my stomach clench. My mom was asking for a visit. I swallowed back my sigh and headed inside to put everything away. Kelly and Sei found their way to the counter, books on magic spread out. Sei took his role as a mentor to Kelly pretty seriously. He had a few new titles to study himself, since I'd given him some of my favorite books that had been gifted to me by our father. They were old and probably outdated, but were better than a lot of the highly edited Dominion-approved texts.

"Sei, I have to go out for a bit," I called to him after a minute. "Need anything?"

"No. Bye, Jamie. Be safe."

Kelly waved to me as I made my way out the door. Gabe wouldn't be up for another few hours, so there really was nothing to stop me from seeing my mother. She really wasn't as bad as Tanaka Rou. Logically, I knew my sister Hanna would make a better mother; after all, I'd raised her to care about others. None of that stopped the dread from filling me as I got in my car and steered it toward my mother's house.

I pulled into the driveway of the suburban house and had to take a deep breath. Was this ever going to get easier? Finally I got out and approached the door. My mother threw open the door. Her deeply bronzed skin looked like she spent hours every day sun tanning, but it was her natural color, just like mine. Her strawberry-blonde hair contrasted beautifully with her dark Native American eyes. Her mother had been a delicate Swede and her father a Native American warrior with weathered skin and eyes that told the tales of generations. I missed my grandfather suddenly. Odd since I'd barely known him—my mother's father had been a kind man. I was thirteen when he passed away less than a year after my father was put to death. My grandfather had never looked at me with judging eyes.

"Momma," I said and wrapped my arms around her in a gentle hug.

"Come in, come in." She wriggled free of my grip and led me into the house. "Have you put on weight? You always were such a big boy. How about I make you some green tea? That's supposed to help you lose weight and gain energy."

I flinched. It really wouldn't matter how I answered, she'd do it anyway. I sat down at the kitchen table while she made tea. The steak I had for lunch threatened to come back up.

"Have you seen your sister? She's positively glowing. I've been telling her for

JAMIE

years that a baby would do that for her. I'd all but given up on having grandbabies."

"Hanna is excited for the babies. So is Sei."

"Smartest thing that boy ever did," my mother mumbled.

"Don't start, please." She gave me her disapproving look. I gave mine right back. "You wanted me to visit."

"Millicent has a lovely daughter..."

"No," I interrupted before she could continue. "No setting me up with anyone." Hanna was fulfilling the obligation to have a baby and continue the Browan family. The responsibility had really never been mine. Being a male child born to a Dominion family always sucked. We were mostly invisible unless a union could be made with a *good family*. At least I hadn't been first wave like Sei had. Or an only child. I needed to call Hanna and thank her again just for being born.

"You need a strong Dominion girl to take you in hand. Spending all that time with that Rou boy isn't making you any friends. If he weren't Pillar, Hanna wouldn't be having his baby. So sad Tanaka was only left with that boy. He's so flamboyantly gay too. She couldn't even find a girl who would be willing to marry him."

"Sei is what he is. He's strong and I don't just mean powerful with magic. He's dealt with more shit than anyone I know, his mother being part of that shit. If she'd just let him be who he was, he wouldn't have half the issues he does. Not that he'd be any more willing to marry a girl since he does prefer boys. And with all the snobby witches in the Dominion, I'm beginning to agree with him." The silence of the room made the blood pounding in my ears all the louder. Had I really said that out loud?

"Are you telling me you're gay?"

Technically, I was pretty sure I was bisexual at this point in my life, but whatever. The older I got, the less labels mattered to me. "If I get to choose who I spend the rest of my life with, it will be someone I love. Not someone who can have my child or is a good union between families. And before you say anything, yes, I'd like to have children someday. But Sei, my baby brother who I adore, has proven that not everything has to be the way the Dominion wants it to be. If I have kids, I will not allow boys to die or be cut. They will be raised to learn about their powers, about the Code, and with a healthy knowledge of magic in

JAMIE

general. They will be respected for who they are, not discriminated against because of what they are. Their parents will love them no matter what sex they are born. Gender is nothing but a stereotype."

My mother's face was blank, and she sat so still I worried I'd really shocked her into having a stroke. Finally she said, "You think I don't love you?"

"Honestly, I don't know. Sometimes it seems like it. Other times I really don't think so. I'm Dominion born and you didn't stay with my dad because you had me. Though I'm not sure why you kept me."

She frowned at me.

"I'm just tired of trying to please everyone." And I realized in that moment that I really was. Sei's and my battles weren't really all that different. Sure, he was pressured in the limelight by a tyrannical mother and mine was more subtle, but it was still discrimination, hate. I was tired of caring for people who hated me just for being me. *Fuck.*

I let out a long sigh and my stomach grumbled, reminding me of other wars I was still fighting. It was time to pick my battles. This one with my mother was one I obviously wasn't winning. I got up from the chair. "I really need to go."

"Don't leave angry," my mom said and grabbed my arm.

"I'm not angry. I'm just tired." I leaned over and kissed her on the forehead. "We can't always live for others. Sometimes we just have to make a choice for ourselves. Sorry, Momma." I left with that, getting in the car and heading back to the condo. The drive gave me time to stew in my own misery for a while. Was I angry? Did I have a right to be? She'd done her best, though I often wondered if appearances mattered more to her than the happiness of her children. Wallowing in my own misery was not going to do anyone any good. Maybe I'd go up, take a nap, and then see if I could shove more food in Sei. There had to be something I could do to eradicate the dark circles that still lingered under his eyes.

After parking in the underground lot, I made my way upstairs, taking the actual stairs all the way up to my loft without stopping. Maybe if I could work up a sweat, I'd work off some of the steak I ate. The flight should have winded even me, but I arrived without a drop of sweat and still breathing normally. Damn.

The place looked so orderly, kitchen untouched other than the blender that I used several times a day for protein shakes. The

JAMIE

living room sat empty with a large-screen TV that I never turned on and a brand-new leather sofa that saw dust bunnies more than my ass. I mounted the stairs up to the loft, kicked off my shoes, threw myself on the bed, and tucked a pillow over my head to block out the light. Sleep must have taken me fairly quickly, because the next thing I heard was the sound of soft voices talking below and moving closer.

The soundproofing to the loft could have rivaled a bomb shelter, so I knew the noise wasn't coming from neighbors. Then a dark head peered up over the edge of the loft. Sei rewarded me with a sunny smile. I moved the pillow and tucked it under my head. "What are you doing up here?"

He climbed the rest of the stairs up and leaned down to grab a few things from Kelly, who followed him. They had a tray full of food. I tried to get up, but Sei pushed me back down.

"Rest. We made you dinner."

The idea of eating in front of them made my heart pound in fear as my mother's words from circled through my head. Had I put on weight? What did they always tell me in therapy? Weight was just a number. I couldn't control how other people saw me. Yet the idea of Sei and Kelly perceiving me with the horror and disgust the world dropped on overweight people made my heart hurt. "I can meet you guys in the kitchen. Did you eat?"

Kelly set the tray in front of me while Sei stacked the pillows up behind my back. The plate was heaped with eggs, golden and fluffy, three peanut butter banana muffins, and a glass of milk. Everything smelled so good my mouth watered, and I felt like a buffalo for even thinking about eating it all.

"I knew you weren't feeling well," Sei told me. "You should have said so. I made eggs 'cause they should be easy on your stomach, and the muffins are flourless, just like you like them." He touched my forehead. "You feel warm, but you always feel warm." His face scrunched up like he was thinking. "I can get you an icepack if you want. Or more blankets." He glanced around the room, probably looking for my spare bedding, which was actually in drawers under the bed. "Maybe from downstairs?" He picked up the fork and stabbed some eggs and brought them to my lips. "Eat, please."

"No kidding." Kelly said. "Have you been eating anything other than protein shakes? There is nothing in your fridge." He cut the muffin in half and added some butter and honey to it. "You looked a little shaky today after you came out of the weight room."

Jamie

I swallowed half the eggs and devoured a muffin, but was unwilling to continue and make a pig of myself despite the gnawing hunger clawing at my gut. Sei blinked at me from where he sat near my legs as Kelly pulled open another muffin. "Don't you like it?"

"It's great, Sei. I'm just full."

"That is a lie." Gabe came up the stairs and leaned against the rail. His green eyes looked at me in challenge. I wanted to throw something at him, but that would only make Sei suspicious. He raised a brow at me, a question. Did I want him to tell them? I shook my head. Not yet. Maybe someday, but not yet...

Sei looked between us and then finally back at me before lifting another bite of eggs to my lips. "Jamie, eat."

And so I ate every last bite. After the last of the milk went down, I was finally satisfied, but not overly stuffed. None of them looked at me with any disgust or judgment. They all just looked concerned. Gabe took the tray away, and Sei curled up next to me on the bed, his stomach pressed to my hip, head on my chest. "Are you still hungry, Jamie? I can make some more eggs."

"No. I'm good."

"Sleepy?"

Actually, I wasn't. He'd never sat so closely without twitching nervously or having to do something with his hands, like braid my hair or flip through a magazine. It was nice. Even Kelly was fawning over me with concern. "No."

"Movie time," Kelly said. He got up and tugged me out of bed. The three of us stumbled down to my unused sofa where Gabe was messing with the wires of the TV and DVD player, which I'd never plugged in.

Finally the movie was going, and I realized it was the kid's movie, *Meet the Robinsons*, which was all about being accepted for who you are. It was one of Sei's favorites. The two boys curled up next to me, one on each side, Gabe sat on the far side of Sei, and we settled in to watch the movie.

Only when it came to a close and both Sei and Kelly slept peacefully against me did I realize the movie meant something to me too. Sure I was different, and unlike Sei, I didn't have a terrible past of people abusing me. But right this moment, I had a family who accepted me for all the flaws I had. I felt myself smile and fight back tears for a moment. So maybe Sei wasn't the only one with self-esteem issues in the house. I was pretty sure they were all okay with that.

Jamie

I crept away from the group to the kitchen, wondering if there was a mess to clean up. But of course since it had been Sei cooking, the place was spotless. There really was no food in the fridge. Not even frozen chicken in the freezer. How had I let that happen? I closed the fridge to find Gabe standing beside it, a business card held out in front of him. A very familiar business card.

"It's not that bad," I protested quietly.

He didn't speak, just swept his gaze over the counter which was filled with jugs of protein powder and a very well-loved blender. When had it gotten so bad? Sei's kidnapping maybe? The gunshot? I shook my head. I couldn't blame anyone else for this. I sucked in a deep breath and took the card. My therapist could help get me back on track, before things got worse.

"Do I need to check the closets?" Gabe murmured quietly.

I shook my head. No. I couldn't let it get that far. Not again. Not when Sei was finally in my life and he needed me to look after him. He and Kelly were curled up sharing a blanket now. I had Kelly to take care of too. And soon there would be babies. I had to be strong for them. Work on this. I typed the number into the phone.

Chapter One

Kelly

BLOOD SPATTERED down, pouring over me in a hot rush, leaving spots of black in my sight and filling me with dread. The weight of him pressing against me increased as he fell—I couldn't hold him. I wasn't strong enough. I tried to catch him, but his mass dragged us both down. Landing on top of him, I could only stare into his honey-colored eyes until the light faded from them. The scream began somewhere deep in my throat and found its way to freedom just as those eyes turned to blank pools of darkness and he seemed to dissolve beneath me.

Someone shook me, called my name. I turned and prepared to fight. But instead of the demon I expected, light flooded my eyes, forcing me to blink away tears and the nightmare. Sei knelt on the edge of my bed, worry etched on his face. Light poured from the lamp on the nightstand. Sweat dripped off me, my heart pounded like an African drum, and I could barely breathe. Spots sparkled across my vision, warning me I wasn't getting enough air.

He reached into the bedside drawer without hesitation and brought an inhaler to my lips. A couple huffs and several seconds later, the pain in my lungs began to ease. The tightness gripping my lungs and my heart began to seep away like a fist unclenching.

"Sorry," I whispered, my throat hurting. How long had I been screaming?

"Wanna talk about it?" His voice was like dark chocolate, deep and rich, belying the wide sapphire eyes and pixie haircut that made him look so young. People used to mistake him for a girl sometimes when he had long hair. Until he opened his mouth to talk. There was no thinking the voice was female. And now that his hair was short, his Adam's apple was more prominent, and his few months of struggles had leaned him out, giving him muscle tone he'd not had before. I'd only known him personally for a couple of months but found it hard to imagine life without him now—Seiran Rou, earth Pillar, practically witch royalty, and my best friend.

"No." The idea of voicing the fears chilled me to the bone. Like somehow it would make them really happen.

Originally, the dreams of Jamie's death had been just memories of him being shot in the parking lot when Sei had been kidnapped a few weeks ago. The bullet had nicked his lung, but until the medics had come, I'd held my shirt to the wound while blood poured over my hands. He'd lost a lot of blood, which slowed his recovery and added fuel to the nightmares. Unfortunately, the dreams had evolved, and I couldn't tell Sei that I kept having nightmares of his brother dying in new and horrific ways. He had enough issues.

Sei flicked off the bedside lamp, then shoved me over, yanking the blankets over us both. He snuggled up against me, much like I imagined a real lover would have, and let his body heat calm me.

We weren't lovers. Never had been, though I'd once had a crush on him. As the nightmares became more frequent, Sei stayed less and less with his actual lover, Gabe, simply because he believed I needed him more. And at that moment, he was probably right. Though I couldn't help but feel bad for taking the two away from each other when they had finally overcome some commitment issue Sei'd had.

I wrapped my arms around him, catching the scent of honey clover and pulling it deep into my lungs. It was a distinctly Sei smell, probably because he was an earth witch. Jamie was an earth witch too, but he smelled more like musk and pine—winter in a forest. Both were comforting, and before meeting them I never realized that witches had individual smells. Now that I was in the

CONVICTION

Magic Studies program at the U, I realized that witches of all flavors gave off a scent within their element. The more pronounced the smell, the more powerful the witch. It was something I planned on writing a paper on in the future.

Sei curled around me, his pajama bottoms and a tank top pressed against my skin. He never seemed bothered that I often slept just in boxer briefs. Tonight, the soft cotton of his top was like a life preserver holding me together. I gripped it and held him close. If I could have stripped bare and hugged him against me without him thinking I wanted sex, I would have. Sometimes it wasn't about the act, it was just about comfort. Sei had been abused enough in his life that he almost always expected everyone to want sex from him. I was still working on convincing him otherwise, which was funny because there was a time that's exactly what I'd wanted from the infamous Seiran Rou.

For two years I had wondered how to get close to him. At the time he was the only male in the whole world studying magic at university level. A lot had changed in the past few weeks. And now I was also studying magic with a handful of other men. His struggle had changed Dominion laws and paved the way for equality, though there was still a long way to go.

I'd never tell Sei that I used to search for him in the crowds at my track meets. He'd been an unreachable idol, strongly facing the crowds of opposition. When we'd met a few weeks ago, I realized just how hard his life had been. Yet he kept going, no matter what life threw at him.

Sei attended all the track meets. I knew now it was because he longed to be part of it but hadn't been allowed. He hadn't shown up to any of the swim practices, for which I was grateful. That would have been awkward and embarrassing since my erection would have been too obvious to hide.

My affection for him had changed, though, deepened, even while morphing into something completely nonsexual. He was still sort of my cheerleader and role model. He had love I could only dream of and had gotten through a past that would have destroyed lesser men. I wasn't crazy enough to want to be him, but I hoped that I was at least as strong as him.

He shifted in my arms, turning to face me, and brushed his fingers against my face. Was I crying? What the hell? Sei pressed his cheek to mine and whispered soft words. "Nothing's going to hurt you, I promise. I'll take care of you."

He was three inches shorter and probably forty pounds lighter than me but never hesitated to be the protector. Sei seemed to believe that his being two years older meant it was his job to take care of me. As I fell asleep to his reassuring words, I hoped I'd someday get to return the favor.

THE MORNING came sooner than necessary. The light through the window said it was going to be a cold Minnesota day. Solstice was only a little over a month away, and my new little family would be taking its first vacation together. Skiing, snowshoeing, and maybe a little cuddling by the fire were on the menu for the weekend.

A winter getaway had been my idea. Sei was less than thrilled since he hated the cold. Jamie's eyes twinkled with that merry spark that I'd come to learn was excitement, and Gabe wanted to get Sei away from the city for a while. So we were going on a snowy weekend trip.

Before bed last night, I'd packed, planning to sleep in, since we weren't hitting the road until midday. It appeared Sei had the same plan, as he slept soundly beside me. The door to the apartment opened, though, and the heavier footsteps meant Jamie. Gabe, who was a vampire, wouldn't attempt to enter our sunlit place at this time of morning.

Jamie moved around the condo for a few minutes before finally peeking into my room. I glanced at him, trying not to disturb Sei. Jamie wore a white T-shirt and tight black jeans. His long strawberry-blond hair was swept back in a ponytail. His arms bulged with the definition of a bodybuilder. He had friends who were larger, almost scary at their size. Jamie wasn't quite that big. He could still fold his arms across his chest or wrap someone in a hug without crushing them. His wide shoulders tapered down to a slim waist; legs that could run a marathon showed off that he had been a model. Still could be if he wanted to. I probably had every line of him memorized. And since my best friend was asleep, I looked my fill.

Jamie didn't flinch when he saw Sei with me. Jamie and I had never talked about it, and Sei wasn't the kind of guy who shared a lot with anyone. It wasn't the first time he found us in bed together. In fact, Gabe had walked in us more than once. The first time I was sure he was going to hurdle me across the room for touching his boyfriend, even if it was in a nonsexual way. But Gabe had just shrugged and asked if we needed anything: food, blankets, therapy. Most of the time the answer was no.

CONVICTION

I was pretty sure I wasn't the only one hoping the vacation would change things. Maybe I could sort out whatever was causing the nightmares. Maybe Sei would realize that opening up to other people wasn't so bad. Since we had two cabins rented, one for Gabe and Sei and the other for Jamie and me, we'd be bonding, but not stuck in each other's pockets the entire time.

"Do you want me to make breakfast, or wait for Sei?" Jamie whispered.

Breakfast, I mouthed to him.

He nodded and left the room, heading to our kitchen. The clock next to the bed read after seven. I wondered if Sei had packed yet. Extracting myself from him was a practice of patience and flexibility. He sort of clung, wrapping arms and legs around me like I was a giant pillow. I wondered if he did that with Gabe too.

After easing my way off the bed, I tiptoed across the room to open the door. I glanced back, grateful Sei was still sleeping peacefully. Hopefully this vacation would be a good change for all of us, though the only one who seemed to be haunted by nightmares anymore was me.

In the kitchen, Jamie chopped a couple of Granny Smith apples and sliced a stack of homemade cinnamon bread. I sat down at one of the barstools to watch him. He mixed the bread and apples, adding a handful of raisins, then layered them in the bottom of a glass baking dish before pouring an egg mixture over the top. It had to be some sort of egg bake, and since a notebook was open beside him, the recipe was Sei's.

"If you're going to sit around in just boxers, you should turn the heat up," Jamie said, though I don't think he'd glanced up at me at all.

"I'm not cold." And I wanted him to see me, even if he wouldn't go there. He'd looked me over more than once in an appreciative way. But my mild flirting never went anywhere. I guess it was sort of taboo to date your brother's best friend, or your best friend's brother.

"Everything okay with you and Sei?" he asked after he loaded the dish into the oven.

"We're good." Did he think Sei was cheating? "We're not having sex if that's what you're asking."

"I didn't think you were." He leaned against the counter, his eyes meeting mine for a second before flashing away. "You both know I'm here to help if you need me, right? With anything. Gabe too. If you're not comfortable talking to me."

"Yes." Except if what I needed was him. Pretty sure he wasn't going to say yes to that.

I grabbed a magazine from my stack in the holder on the edge of the counter and flipped through it, trying to ignore what I really wanted to say. Would the nightmares stop if he was mine? If it was his arms I slept in at night instead of Sei's? Could he ever even see me as more than just Sei's best friend? Or something other than just another kid he had to take care of?

Jamie had a strong hero mentality. I got that, even if he treated us like kids. He escorted us to school or out shopping, got between us and anyone he viewed as a threat. He was like Captain America or something, fighting for the greater good, walking old ladies across the street, and rescuing kittens from trees. It was sort of annoying to have that much intensity aimed at you. I knew it bothered Sei. He'd always been very independent. But it was just how Jamie operated.

I purposely hid the fact that I had asthma from Jamie so he wouldn't freak out about it. He'd likely insist that I give up sports, and there was no way that was going to happen. I could only imagine how he'd react if he knew about my dreams. But really, what could be done? I knew enough about the psychological mind to understand dreams were just issues we tried to sort out while we slept. The question of what the issue was had to be solved first.

At this point I had a theory. Jamie had changed since the shooting. He'd always been the silent, stoic type, but he'd treated me like family. Now he held himself apart, like he was waiting for me to turn on Sei too. I knew it wasn't just me. He didn't trust anyone who got close to Sei. Were the dreams about the death of his trust for me? Seemed like a lot of blood and pain for such a simple concept.

I didn't know how long I'd been staring at the same page, because it had gone fuzzy. The heavy weight of Jamie's stare burned into my shoulders, bringing my eyes up. Again he looked away, checking the oven instead. The smell of the concoction began to fill the room with the sweet, homey scent I'd come to love. The coffeepot gurgled, reminding me I hadn't had my first cup yet but had been up for almost half an hour.

While I filled my mug and took the first heavenly sip, Sei appeared in the kitchen. His hair stood up in a hundred crazy directions, sleep lines etched across his face, and he rubbed at his eyes.

"Coffee?" I asked him.

"Tea, please," he replied.

Jamie poured him a cup and handed him a bottle of raw honey to sweeten it. Sei settled in beside me at the counter, sipping his tea and staring at the food bubbling in the oven.

"Hungry," he mumbled into his mug. His stomach growled, echoing the sentiment.

"It's almost done. Did you pack yet?" Jamie asked.

Sei nodded. He leaned over and rested his head on my shoulder. I suddenly felt really bad for waking him up with my nightmares. Maybe the trip would help since he'd be with Gabe the whole time. But I cringed to think of what would happen if I woke Jamie up. This was going to be an interesting vacation.

Jamie finally pulled breakfast out of the oven and set it out to cool. Mornings were always simple like this: homemade food, good friends, coffee, and a sense of peace. Now if I could translate it to the rest of my life, things would be good.

By the time we'd eaten, worked out, showered, and gotten the car loaded, it was after 11:00 a.m. Gabe had rented a special SUV with heavily tinted windows so he could travel during the day. He met us in the parking garage, kissed Sei like the two were honeymooners, then crawled in back by the luggage and wrapped a blackout blanket around himself, just in case.

Jamie drove. I sat shotgun, and Sei sat in the back near Gabe, whispering things to him. With only a handful of stops, the trip would take six hours. Of course that depended on the weather. Every news channel predicted a cold but fairly clear few days for us. The piles of survival gear Jamie had packed meant he was ready for the worst, and having loaded up my own, I guess we were on the same page.

I didn't remember falling asleep halfway through, though the cold, blowing snow that filled my head woke me with a start as we drove into the parking lot of the lodge. I really hoped it wasn't an omen of things to come.

The lodge looked like something out of a magazine of luxury log-cabin homes. Thick wood beams spiked out of the ends, one side broke off in a display of windows that covered two whole floors, and I could see a fireplace large enough to park our SUV inside. A garage stood across the parking lot, looking very unlike the lodge. But the doors were small, meaning it was more for ATVs or snowmobiles than cars.

We parked near the front door just as the last light of day streaked in red and orange lines across the horizon. By the time we had keys in hand and everyone on the snowmobiles, the moon, which had been visible for hours, was a calming crescent.

"I'll show you the way and bring your luggage along," said the owner, whose name was Hans. He looked like anyone's uncle in flannel and a duck-brown Carhartt coat. He handed each of us a rubber bracelet that looked like one of those fitness trackers. "Trackers, just in case the weather gets bad. Wear them until you check out, please."

We all clipped on our bands. It had a digital display that read the time and temperature. I wondered if it had those heartrate type of monitors in it too. I suppose being up this far north it was wise to have a way to find us if there was a major snowstorm.

"Do these link up to the ranger station, or just here at the lodge?" Jamie inquired as he put his on.

"Just here at the lodge," Hans said. "Though I'm sure the rangers could look them up if they needed to." He gave us a reassuring smile. "We've never lost anyone for more than a few hours."

Sei flinched and clung to Gabe's arm.

"We're not gonna lose anyone," I told Sei. "We're sticking together this weekend. Family fun, remember."

He nodded, but his frown didn't fade.

Our luggage was loaded into a large sled that was attached to Hans' snowmobile. He revved the engine and took off slowly into the dark, headlights leading the way. I clung to Jamie, letting him drive, and enjoyed the feel of his hard body against mine while I watched as Sei hid his face in Gabe's shoulder. Though we kept the speed down, it had to be a new experience. Since his mother wasn't exactly the camping kind of person, Sei had limited experience with some of the most normal parts of life, something we were all working to change.

The brisk air had me checking my pocket for my inhaler a half-dozen times. Cold and asthma didn't mix well, though the tightening of my lungs was more in my head than real. Sei's anxiety disorder was probably starting to rub off on me.

When we finally slid to a stop beside a duo of cabins, the chill had really descended. Hans opened the doors for us and even started a fire in each cabin before unloading our things and waving good-bye for the night. We all gathered in Sei and Gabe's cabin, drinking hot cocoa to ward off the chill and playing card games. By the time I decided I was tired enough for sleep, it was after 1:00 a.m., and Sei slept curled against Gabe on the bed.

Jamie got up and stretched. "We'll do some skiing tomorrow. It's dark early up here, so we won't be out more than a few hours."

Gabe nodded and stroked the hair out of Sei's face. "I rented a room at the lodge for the weekend too. I'll take him back tomorrow night. He seems to think we're lost in the wilderness. Dinner and a warm bath will help."

"I like this wilderness. It has indoor plumbing," I told them, pointing to the toilet. No showers and the water was pumped in, but anything was better than whipping out essential anatomy in the snow. Heading for the door, I glanced back beyond Jamie, who followed. "Night, Gabe. Tell Sei when he wakes up that we'll see him in the morning."

"I will."

The cabin I shared with Jamie was identical to Gabe's: two beds, though they had only needed one. We would be using two. The fire made the place feel solid and warm, safe. I stripped out of everything but my boxer briefs and crawled into the bed farthest from the fire. The chill in the sheets made me shiver, but I warmed up fast enough.

Jamie moved around a while longer, the little sounds he made lulling me to sleep. For the first time in weeks, I didn't dream of his death.

Chapter Two

Jamie

Kelly slept fitfully, making small noises of distress that gutted me. I'd been tempted to wake him more than once, had even sat down on his bed and laid a hand on his shoulder. He seemed to still when I touched him. But he might think it a little odd if he woke up with me in his bed, so instead I paced the room.

When Sei had fallen asleep earlier, I realized that finding the two of them in bed together a lot of mornings had nothing to do with Sei's past and everything to do with Kelly. Neither one of them spoke, though, no matter how hard I prodded. Gabe wasn't sure either, but he thought it was some posttraumatic stress from the shooting. A crazy vampire had bitten Sei and forced him to shoot at Kelly and me. The day was pretty vivid in my memory too, though I recall getting foggy pretty fast after the gunshot.

I'd parked the car near the door to Gabe's condo and got out. Kelly slammed his door shut on the other side. No sooner had I clicked the locks, than Kelly lifted a hand and pointed.

"Isn't that Seiran? And who's that he's with? He's not supposed to be going anywhere without one of us, right? Not with his hands all bandaged."

I turned in time to see Sei pushed into the passenger side of the car. Neither the car nor the driver—who was wearing a very unfashionable ski mask—were familiar. "Fuck," I muttered and began fast walking their way. If Sei was just going off with some friend without telling anyone, I was going to be pissed. "Stay by the car," I told Kelly, glancing back his way. Then the gun fired.

The sound echoed an oddly hollow boom, and it missed me. The second shot, however, did not. Fire ripped through my side, doubling me up, and stars exploded, blanking out my vision. I lost a few seconds of consciousness I think, because suddenly I was on the ground facedown, smelling salted pavement.

"Jamie!"

For a minute I thought it was Sei calling my name. That somehow he'd gotten free of the car or maybe I'd been overreacting to seeing him with a stranger. But whoever it was touched me, rolled me over, then looped his arms under my armpits and hauled me backward into the cold shelter between a couple cars. The cold pouring off them chilled me to the core. A shiver started in my toes and rolled up my body in waves until my teeth chattered. The man beside me pressed something into my side that made me growl a sailor's curse. My stomach threatened to rebel.

"Stay with me, Jamie," the familiar-but-not-Seiran's voice told me. He sounded sort of far away, though I could feel him touching me. He spoke on a phone for a minute, giving information, answering questions. I could only make out pieces of the conversation. Someone was hurt. I should have gotten up, tried to help. What if someone was shot? I was in training to be a nurse, dammit.

I must have been struggling, because he pressed harder on the wound in my side, and I fought to breathe through the pain. The sparklers across my sight faded slowly, bringing me back to the bright but frigid day with Kelly curled around me. His face dripped with tears and blood. Was Kelly hurt? My heart raced and I tried to reach for him.

"No, don't move. Damn you!" Kelly scolded and held me in place with a strength that belied his size. Liquid began to fill one lung, and I gasped, choking on the blood filling my throat. Fuck, I was shot. Yeah, that explained the pain, numbness, and disconnect in my head.

"Are you hurt?" I asked Kelly. "You're bleeding."

"It's your blood. Not mine. You were shot, remember?"

A horrible idea crossed my brain. "Seiran?" I gasped and hacked out a bloody cough. Oh fuck, that hurt. Please let Seiran not be lying dead in the parking lot just feet from us. I tried to see around Kelly, but something in my side ripped and the world went black. All I heard was Kelly's sobbing cry of "I'm so sorry."

I'd recovered from the bullet, and Sei had been kidnapped, not shot. Once I'd come to in the hospital, I'd laid into Kelly about making me think Sei was dead. He didn't understand why I would have thought that as he'd said nothing about Seiran. Not even the fact that he'd been the one to shoot me and was in the car when it drove away.

Either way I'd been weak that day. Kelly had dragged me to cover under a hail of bullets—he insisted it had only been two. I'd done nothing but bleed. I hadn't even been able to help search for Sei. Gabe was nearly murdered and Kelly went stalking into the wilderness on his own to bring Sei home. I'd failed them all.

Kelly grew fitful again, turning and mumbling in his sleep. I put on my fitness watch, set it to vibrate and wake me in just a few hours, then curled up beside Kelly on his bed. We all needed this trip, not just for a vacation, but for a chance to heal. I needed to help my little brother smile again. And if I could calm whatever storm was growing inside of Kelly, that would be okay too. At least then I'd be useful. I closed my eyes and listened to Kelly breathe. When the tension left him, I finally dozed.

Kelly

SEI'S SOFT laughter woke me the next morning. I must have slept hard, because I actually felt rested for the first time in weeks. Sei labored over the cooktop, flipping pancakes and sipping tea, while Jamie sat in a chair near the fire. They never seemed to have a lot of alone time to bond, so I hesitated to let them know I was awake. Jamie spoke quietly but seemed very engaged. He was laughing and animated like I'd never seen him before. His laugh made my balls tighten up, and fuck if I wasn't already hard.

"So I'm staring at the door and the handle, which is in my hand, wondering how exactly I'm going to get out of the bathroom without looking like an idiot. After like two minutes I thought I'd have to start screaming and pounding on the door for help since I left my phone at my desk."

"So what did you do? Did someone find you?" Sei's eyes were wide.

"I pushed the handle and the mechanism together, tried to shove it in far enough to turn. The metal must have connected with something, because I was able to catch the handle on something and pull the door enough to shove my fingers in there and pry it open."

"That's so crazy. I can't imagine being locked in the bathroom. I would have freaked out."

"I *was* freaking out. There were no windows and someone must have had bad burritos for lunch 'cause it stunk." Sei grinned and Jamie continued, "My face must have been bright red when I walked out. Thought everyone could see that I'd broken the bathroom door handle and gotten locked in." Jamie shook his head. "It was a very different walk of shame."

"Did anyone else get stuck?"

"I don't know. I used the garbage can to prop open the door and put the handle on the floor beside the door as a warning. But from now on, I'm taking my phone with me to the john with maintenance on speed dial. I can just hear the call now. 'Yeah, Bob? I'm stuck in the bathroom again. Bring your plunger.'"

Sei laughed loud enough to ring around the cabin. He glanced back at me. "Sorry, Kelly. Didn't mean to wake you."

"Been up for a few minutes, so no worries." I grabbed yesterday's T-shirt and pulled it over my head, glad it was long enough to cover me to midthigh. Hurrah for winter layers. The morning wood wouldn't bother Sei, but Jamie might take offense if I flaunted it. "What's for breakfast?" I asked as I pulled on some sweats and yanked the bedclothes into a presentable form.

"Blueberry cream cheese pancakes." Sei didn't even look back my way while he flipped another in the pan. "Sausage on the side or eggs?"

"Sausage. The eggs will be too much for me."

"'Kay." He dished up a plate with four large cakes and two links, then passed it over to me. All-natural butter sat beside him on the small workbench and several types of jam. No syrup. The smell made him nauseous. I'd learned of Sei's super sense of smell before we'd even become roommates.

Living with him made life interesting, because even some soap smells set him off into a sneezing fit.

I was pretty sure it was the cat side of him, and not because he was a level-five earth witch. My sense of smell was normal and I was a level-five water witch. All the Dominion authorized textbooks said our spirit animals wouldn't bleed through, but that was bullshit right along with the idea that we weren't supposed to change on the new moon. It was either ride the power high or let it smash you to pieces like a boat stuck near land in a hurricane. Maybe if I had some weird side effect of my animal I'd feel differently. Mostly the Dominion rules seemed archaic and uninformed. I wondered if they were written by very low-level witches who didn't really know how spirit animals worked for a witch.

"You still sleepy?" Sei asked. I realized I'd been staring at my plate and the display of sauces for a minute or so.

"Sorry. Thinking too hard." I picked up the marmalade and applied it liberally before settling in to eat my food.

"None of that. We're on vacation," Jamie told me. "Lots of snow and fun to be had."

"Snow does not equal fun," grumbled Sei. I suspected his cat might feel differently, but Sei the human hated the cold.

Jamie swabbed at his plate with the final bite of pancake, speared the last few bits of egg, and swallowed, cleaning his plate just before Sei dropped another two on his plate. The silence of the room made me feel like my heart beat too loudly. Jamie stared at the added food, a trail of emotions crossing his face. A month ago the tension wouldn't have existed. But I didn't know how to fix something that I hadn't broken.

Jamie had a food thing. That's all Gabe would tell me. He also begged Sei not to push, but Sei gave back to Jamie all the brotherly caring bullshit Jamie doled out. That included extra food, special meals made just for Jamie, or random pretty drawings he'd drop into Jamie's lap like a little kid. At least Jamie let us see the mixed emotions now instead of just brushing us off.

I finished my last few bites of food, watching Jamie take careful precision in eating the eggs. Sei wouldn't start a fight about it. Jamie would never actually explain what was going on in his head and why he only ate when no one was around. And while I suspected I knew what it was, I didn't have any right to butt my nose in his business. I wasn't his boyfriend or even his family. Just close enough to worry.

In the bathroom I cleaned up and got ready for the skiing we'd be doing by adding layers that breathed and would keep me from sweating like a pig. At least the morning wood was gone. That was a complication I really didn't need on this trip. The clock read after ten, so I'd slept late. Sei looked rested, though still a little on the thin side. He ate a single pancake and a half a sausage link before declaring himself done. Pushing him never helped, so I started digging out all my snow gear. If I packed a few protein bars, I'd probably be able to get both of them to eat them later. Jamie glanced up once or twice, but any time our eyes met, he looked away.

"You guys ready to have some fun in the snow?" I asked.

Sei shook his head but put on his gear.

Jamie's grin was genuine. "This is gonna be great, Sei. I promise. The sun is shining bright. You can soak up some vitamin D and breathe the fresh air."

"Cold air," Sei grumbled.

I checked my phone for the weather. "It's almost thirty degrees. Not all that cold. Once we get moving, you won't feel it." He couldn't hide his nervous frown. He clenched his hands into fists, but I noticed the tremble. Anxiety, not physical illness, I reminded myself. Sei was strong. His brain was wired a little off, but he could handle anything we threw at him. Hopefully we could teach him what it meant to relax and just have fun for once. It would have been better if Gabe had been able to come with us today, but vampires and sun didn't mix. He'd be around as soon as it set. Jamie and I would just have to do for a few hours.

An hour later, I watched Sei balance precariously on one foot while Jamie helped strap ski boots to his feet. The expression on Sei's face was almost laughworthy. I remembered his horrified expression when I'd first asked if he wanted to go cross-country skiing. At the time he'd been going through so much, and he'd shrugged off the trip. Things that turned out to be a voice in his head that was an old lover turned vampire who wanted to control him and a psycho therapist who was experimenting with vampire mind powers. But over the past few weeks the suspicion and fear in his eyes had begun to fade. The only voices in his head now were his and Gabe's. And he got this tiny little smile that tugged up the corner of his lips when Gabe spoke to him that way.

"Ready, Kelly?" Jamie inquired, putting his hand on my shoulder.

"Oh yeah, sorry. Sort of daydreaming."

Sei barely moved, his eyes wide like he were about to take his first steps.

Jamie stomped into his own skis, grabbed his poles, and motioned us toward the path. The trees lined the path like skeletons caked in snow. But the day was brisk and not overly cold. The perfect day for an outing like this. "Use the poles to push yourself, Seiran. Once you get moving, it will be easier," he instructed. "I've mapped out the route. It's safe and pretty easy."

"Like this," I whispered to Sei, sliding up beside him and using my poles to push his skis in the right direction. I shoved one foot forward, then the next, demonstrating how to do it.

"I don't think I'm meant for skiing," Sei mumbled through all his layers.

"You'll be fine," I assured him.

"Maybe if I have some more tea."

"Not till later," Jamie told him, his voice taking on the big brother instructional tone. "I have everything, don't worry. I've got lunch, your pills, tea, a cell phone, and your book reader if you need a break. We'll be fine. We're not going that far." He pushed himself ahead of us and skied down the trail.

Sei experimentally slid one ski forward, and it moved, making him quickly correct it by shifting his other foot to keep his balance. He floundered with the poles but remained upright and moving, slowly, but moving. I set my pace to his. At this rate we'd get a block or two in an hour, and that didn't bother me at all.

"Have you ever been sledding?" I asked. Maybe we should have started with something easier. Every parent took their kid sledding once, right?

"I'm not an outdoorsy kind of guy," he answered. Which would be a no.

Jamie slid back to our side, easing his pace with little effort. "Except when he turns into a lynx. I bet he's used those big paws of his to slide down a hill or two. He goes all nature man and even eats bugs."

"I do not!" Sei cried. "I play with them but never eat them."

"Gabe says you love centipedes."

"They're icky. But they have so many legs moving kind of like a wave..."

Sei's new moon counterpart was something of a legend. I'd heard he could do it, even seen some of the aftereffects, but had never experienced his change. Mostly because mine came at the same time as his, and we were very different animals. He could also change on non–new moon nights. I'd never tried, since most said it couldn't be done. But he could. The last time he'd changed I'd found him cowering in a closet of a farmhouse, human in form but cat in thought. Sometimes, it felt like he hadn't come back all the way. He had lapses in memory of things that were completely normal and human. Often his gestures and reflexes were more cat-like, the turn of his head or the way he stared up at nothing making me think there was something he could see that I couldn't.

"We can rent snowshoes. There might have even been some in the cabins. They'd act more like your paws do when you're a lynx, but they're harder as a human. You have to lift your feet. Sort of like lunge squats," I offered. If Sei wanted to play as a cat this weekend, I was okay with that too. So long as he stayed close. I know sometimes I just liked to swim to get all the crap out of my head. Why wouldn't Sei just want to run and play?

"What do you turn into?" Jamie inquired, eyes flashing with curiosity. Since the Dominion, the ruling body of magic, didn't approve of new moon transformations, it wasn't something we talked about. "A fish?"

CONVICTION

I brushed my blond hair out of my eyes, shoving it more firmly under my hat. "A dolphin. Once a mammal always a mammal, I guess. My parents have an indoor salt-water pool. But it's pretty limiting." Of my whole family, only my mother and I could change. I wondered what it would be like to change in the ocean for once, see millions of fish, swim in the vast wide blue. Earth witches seemed to have more options. But maybe, like Sei, when tempted with the greater expanse of the ocean, I'd be lost in my other shape too. "I wonder if there are any air witches that turn into birds. Are there bird mammals?" I shook my head at the questions popping up for which none of us would have any answers. The Dominion needed some overhauls in the education department. "It's sad that the three of us will probably never spend the new moon together. Must be fun for you and Sei to run. What's your counterpart?"

"He's a bear." Sei said it like it was a "duh" moment.

I suppose that made sense. Jamie was a big guy, midthirties, over six feet, covered in muscles—not fat. Though, other than his long blond hair, he didn't seem all that hairy. But maybe he was a manscaper. If that was the case, I'd have liked to see him more natural. I liked a man with hair. Maybe I could get him to give up some of the manscaping. But since he was my best friend's brother, no matter how interested I was, searching for stubble was out of the question even if it would have given me a valid reason to be staring at his body.

"Lynx don't like bears much. Sei kind of goes all the way, and it upsets him when I'm around. When he does play with me, he's actually kind of mean." Jamie glanced at his brother. "Has sharp claws and likes to jump out of trees onto my back. Gabe usually follows him. Keeps him away from the road and stuff." Jamie sounded a little sad about the topic. "What about you? How many days do you change? What's it like to be underwater for long periods of time? Do you feel like a real dolphin, or do you retain your humanity?"

Sei slapped Jamie's shoulder. "Stop. You're like a cop giving him the third degree. Creepy, Jamie. Jeez." He hit a minor hill and seemed to be stuck. He reached again for Jamie, who was closer, but I pulled up behind him and nudged his skis enough to help him over the hill. "Just ignore him, Kelly."

"I don't mind." Catching Jamie's eye, I winked at him. "He can give me the third degree anytime. 'Sides, the Ascendance talks about it all the time." Sometimes the group

Conviction

was more refreshing than the Dominion since they actually were real about things like new moon transformations. But the Ascendance was made up mostly of untrained men. I wondered just how accurate any of their ideas and experiences were. At least the Dominion had rules that tried to keep people from getting hurt. The Ascendance seemed to have the whole ends-justify-the-means attitude.

The haunted look that crossed Sei's face made me want to smack myself for bringing it up. The Ascendance reminded him of Andrew Roman, who had a never-ending quest to make Gabe's life miserable and, through him, Sei. Roman was one of the leaders of the Ascendance, and though he seemed to want equality for male witches, he wanted more to kill Sei just to make Gabe suffer.

"Sorry," I whispered, feeling like the biggest ass in the world.

"For what?"

"Bringing up crap that hurts. It was thoughtless."

Sei shrugged.

"Anyway, I can I change all three nights of the new moon. I think I'm still mostly me. But I'm always in a pool, so it's not like I can swim around the ocean floor and get lost chasing fish or exploring coral."

"That's cool," Sei said. "Have you ever been to the ocean?"

"Yes, but not gone in as a dolphin. My mom has always said it's not a good idea."

"You might not come back?" Sei prodded.

"I guess. There would be a lot to see in the ocean. Things to do that I could never dream of. Probably like you in a new forest."

Sei nodded. "Yeah. I always want to explore everything. Search every tree for owls or birds and the trunk for mice and bugs. It's a different world as an animal." He waved at the forest around us with its towering pines. "And not so cold."

The forest always *felt* more alive when I was with Sei, like every little hiding thing looked at us waiting, expecting. Would the ocean do that? "Maybe next time we'll go someplace tropical. See if the ocean has as many wonders as the forest."

Sei frowned. "You can't leave me, Kelly. No swimming off into the sunset to be with whales or whatever."

I reached over and gave him a quick one-armed hug. "Not going anywhere."

"Hey," Jamie interrupted, probably to change the course of his brother's thoughts. "Let's hook up the rope. Me in front, Sei in the middle, and Kelly, will you go last?"

"Sure." I leaned in and latched a cord to the belt on Sei's snowsuit. Jamie could no doubt pull us both with little trouble, but Sei and I liked to do as much for ourselves as we could. Jamie was hot personified, if you liked the muscular sort, which I did. He could have doubled as the bare-chested guy on the cover of a romance novel. The idea made me laugh.

He raised a brow at me.

"Just thinking that you could be on the cover of some of Sei's favorite romance novels."

He tugged us forward, but I did catch the red flush of his face.

"Oh my God, you have, haven't you?"

He shrugged. "I did some modeling when I was younger. We all start somewhere."

I grinned and even Sei flashed me a smile. We both knew Jamie was no muscle-headed moron. He was smart and resourceful as well. He was going to be getting his RN certification in just a few weeks. He had a degree in sports medicine and did some heavy-duty investing. He just spent most of his time trying to help Sei rebuild some of the strength lost in weeks of healing. I admired his devotion and wished my own blood family were closer.

Jamie knew when to step back and let us do our thing, most of the time at least. But I was so going to tease him about the romance covers in the future. "You'll have to show us some of your covers."

Jamie shook his head.

Sei gave me a pleading look that told me he wanted to see badly. I'd be looking them up on my phone when we got back to the cabin later. I nodded and winked at him.

"If you get tired, let me know. I want to make it to the picnic grounds for a late lunch. There's a fire pit up there that will be nice," Jamie told us before taking off down the track and yanking us along. Sucking in a deep breath, I put my body to work to keep the larger man from pulling our weight.

The picnic area had to be only a little more than three miles away, which on skis, shouldn't take us that long. Three hours later we slid into the park, and Sei nearly collapsed in front of the fire. He'd been pushing hard to keep up, and his hat was a sweaty sponge to prove it. He'd be really sore tomorrow.

His hands shook when he tried to pry off the gloves to warm his fingers by the fire. At least the bandages were gone, even if the shake wasn't. Maybe we'd asked too much of him. He'd only been out of the hospital a few weeks. Jamie too.

"You okay?" I asked Sei, sliding in close. I pulled a fresh hat from my bag and took his soggy one, swapping them out so Sei's head wouldn't get cold. We definitely should have done something easier for the first day, sledding or maybe building snowmen. A few miles of cross-country hadn't seemed that strenuous an idea. Sei used to run seven to ten miles a day. He was only up to three since his injury, but running was a different set of muscles than skiing. And running on an indoor track in nothing but shorts and a T-shirt was a lot different than cross-country skiing with forty pounds of gear.

He nodded. I glanced to Jamie, who pulled supplies out of the bag he'd had strapped to his back. His bag had been almost three times the size of mine. He probably had a tent in there somewhere if Sei were to mention that he wanted to be out of the wind.

"I have tea, Sei. I need you to eat, please. We'll rest a bit before heading back."

We all sat on a snowy log bench and ate quietly in the relative warmth of the bonfire. Hans had told us their maintenance guy came around a lot to tend it. I was glad he didn't pop out of nowhere and scare us. Sei was already in bad shape. The tremor that had started in his hands moved all the way to his legs. To anyone who didn't know him it looked like a nervous twitch. He didn't often get that bad.

Sei downed his sandwich, half a protein bar, and half the thermos of tea without commenting. I didn't know whether to point the tremors out by asking if he was cold or tell Jamie we should call for a ride back. Only Gabe could calm the shake when it got this bad.

Jamie didn't look concerned. Instead, he held up a bag of marshmallows, a pack of graham crackers, and some chocolate bars. "Anyone for a chocolate fix?"

I laughed as Sei's eyes lit up. "Sugar is good."

We found sticks to dangle the marshmallows near the flame. It took only a few seconds before the heat crisped up the outside into a dark shell with gooey insides. The chocolate oozed out of Sei's s'more as he stuffed one end in his mouth. The oversized bite had him looking like a happy chipmunk.

"Good stuff?"

"Heaven," he mumbled through full cheeks.

I bit into mine and tasted the sweet chocolate and sugar rush. Jamie nibbled on the edges of his, eating it much slower than either Sei or I. He seemed to be silently laughing at both of us.

"What?" I demanded.

He leaned over and rubbed his thumb along the edge of my mouth, which came away with chocolate on it. "Saving that for later?"

Heat burned my cheeks. "Maybe."

When he stuck his chocolate-covered thumb in his mouth and sucked on it, the warmth left my face and fled right to my cock. I shifted a little to keep my pants from biting into my erection. Sure, he had a habit of touching me, but I'd honestly begun to think it was just from the lack of affection he showed Sei, since Sei wasn't a touchy guy. That little display, however, had not been brotherly at all. But maybe he didn't realize how erotic it had been. He was straight, after all. And most straight guys I knew were pretty clueless.

I wasn't quite sure how to read the small smile on Sei's face. But if he was going to ignore Jamie's weird behavior, I could man up and brush it aside too. For now at least. If Jamie wanted to play, I was game.

He grinned at me like the walls he kept up weren't there for the first time in weeks, then glanced at his little brother. Finally Jamie looked away from both of us. When he turned our way again, his calm mask was in place, like it had never slipped. I swallowed a sigh and stared into the fire.

The sun was starting to set, though it was only around four in the afternoon. We had hoped to be back before dark, but there was no way that was happening now. A phone rang in Jamie's pack. He dug it out, checked the ID, then flipped it open, saying, "He's fine."

"Is that Gabe? I'm okay. Just tired." Sei sipped more tea. We wouldn't have enough for a return trip. I nudged him to finish the rest of the protein bar. He nibbled at it.

Jamie just listened to Gabe for almost a minute and a half before replying, "Okay. See you soon."

"Jamie..." Sei began in protest.

Jamie put the phone away. "Gabe is riding one of the Ski-Doos up as soon as the sun sets."

"I'm okay."

"It's his vacation too, Sei. Gabe wants to spend more time with you. He made reservations at the lodge for dinner. He just didn't expect us to be out this long." Jamie patted Sei's arm. "I'll get Kelly back, and we'll find dinner on our own." We had a cooler of meals—mostly Sei's recipes—ready to heat up and serve.

Sei sighed. "We should all go to the lodge. You guys could probably use a fancy dinner too."

"Fancy dinners are for dates," Jamie told Sei. "Consider tonight a date night."

"But Gabe and I don't have to date. I'm already a sure thing," Sei protested. "I don't get him at all."

Which was so untrue. Sei knew that Gabe was a born romantic and existed just for him. They both looked at each other as if the other hung the moon. The romantic dinner would serve the purpose of getting Sei to the lodge without him losing any personal self-worth for being too tired to do it on his own. They'd have a quiet night in and Gabe would use the excuse of sex to massage the soreness out of Sei's muscles. We really shouldn't have pushed him so hard.

The last of the fading light vanished, and we soon heard the buzz of a snowmobile roaring up the path, lights glaring in the distance. Some of the tremble left Sei's limbs and some of the tension in his shoulders relaxed when the machine eased to a stop a few feet from us.

Gabe stepped off and grabbed another helmet from under the seat. He handed the second one to Sei. "Skis off. Jamie will bring them back."

Sei glared warily at the skis as though he were still unsure how they worked. Jamie leaned over and unsnapped them, then started packing up all the supplies. I gave Sei a one-armed hug and helped him step around the skis to get to Gabe, who plucked him up off the ground and held him close.

Gabe kissed Sei lightly on the lips, and they shared a look that made me swallow back a groan. Sure, I had never really been in love with Sei, but there had to be someone out there to look at me like that, right? Was that too much to ask? I, at least, thought this should have been a romantic ski vacation, even if Sei didn't.

"Can you guys find your way back okay?" Gabe asked, adjusting the strap on Sei's helmet. He got back on the machine, sitting forward so Sei could wrap his arms around him from behind.

"We'll be fine. It's not far," Jamie assured him.

CONVICTION

With a nod, Gabe and Sei took off. I felt bad about being happy to see Sei go. But it was my fault he was so tired. I shouldn't have suggested this trip. It could take him years to heal from all that happened in the past few weeks.

"He's fine. The tremble is 80 percent anxiety, 20 percent exhaustion. I could have carried him back if I needed to. He's still under a buck twenty," Jamie pointed out.

I shook my head at him. No way was I going to let go of the guilt that easily. Family took care of family, even if they didn't always agree with each other. I'd failed last time. It would not happen again. "He's been through so much. I should have realized he wasn't ready for something like this. He gets that faraway look in his eyes, and it's like he's not even there."

"If the Dominion would support him like they are supposed to, he wouldn't have so much power cycling through him. That's what makes him distant, unless Gabe's around. When he's close, I'm sure he's just listening to whatever internal waves they have going from the focus bond now. Without him, the earth can be very distracting. Gabe has been working with Sei to let it just flow through them instead of always pummeling Sei with energy. It will take time and practice.

Most Pillars have a group of witches around them to help support the transition and bleed the energy into. A coven to support them." Jamie strapped the extra skis to his back, then slid toward the path that would lead us to the cabins. "You ready?"

I nodded and followed. "I'm surprised Sei didn't want to stay in the lodge." He was sort of high maintenance. He had this compulsive showering thing that was almost as bad as his kitchen OCD.

"He thinks people are staring at him. And I suppose sometimes they are. He *is* the first male Pillar in history. If I didn't know him, I'd want a look too." He shrugged. "They will sneak in, have a warm bath, and make it back to their cabin before morning." Jamie wasn't even breathing hard, though he pushed fast enough to make me strain to keep up. "Do you want dinner at the lodge or the cabin?"

"Cabin." Watching all the couples together at the lodge would only grate at my loneliness. At least Jamie was friendly company. And the heavy wet feeling of the air told me snow was coming. "There's going to be snow."

Jamie adjusted his hat, glanced at the sky, and nodded to me. "Wasn't supposed to be any on radar this weekend."

I shrugged. "Minnesota. What can you do?" It then occurred to me: the path we'd taken to the picnic area had been sort of roundabout. "You planned to wear him out so he'd let Gabe take care of him, didn't you?"

A ghost of a smile touched Jamie's lips. "Don't know what you mean." I couldn't keep the grin off my face as I pushed on, looking forward to getting back to the cabin and out of the cold.

Chapter Three

By the time we slid to the door, the snow had already begun blowing fiercely. Inside, I set the skis aside and stripped out of the snowsuit, wrapping myself up in the heavy down blankets of my bed. The fire had dimmed to almost nothing, but throwing a few more logs on, we got it roaring again.

"I have sandwiches or chili," Jamie told me, digging around in the cooler. "Sei's recipe for both, so the sandwiches are little on the odd side and the chili is extra spicy."

"Sandwiches." It would take longer for the chili, and I suddenly felt really tired. The little adventure shouldn't have worn me out. Maybe all my time at school was cutting too much into my workout time.

Jamie grunted in reply.

"He puts chocolate in the chili," I said, mainly just to keep the quiet of the room and the increase in blowing wind from outside from getting to me. "Did you know that? It's tasty. Never had a recipe from him that I didn't like. Never eaten so many vegetables in my life, though, or tried so many new things." Curling up under the warm blankets made my eyelids heavy but didn't stop the shivering. I ate the sandwich Jamie gave me and then an apple.

The wind howled like something alive, whipping past the cabin so hard the walls and roof creaked painfully and then everything was deathly still. The crackling fire was the only noise other than our faint breathing. Pressure built up behind my eyes, like a headache was coming. Only I'd never felt anything like this before. A pulsing edge of pain was driving in from a distance. My senses tingled with energy.

"Did you bring a weather radio?" I asked Jamie.

As far north as we were, cell reception was spotty, especially when the weather got bad. We had plenty of wood to last a whole winter if we needed. Food, not so much. We'd only packed for three days. Jamie could change and hunt, but nothing much would be outside in bad weather so the pickings would be slim.

He dropped the radio into my lap. I flicked it on, grinning like a fool. The guy must have been in Cub Scouts or something. And since he turned into a bear on the new moon, that just made me laugh like a lunatic.

"Share the joke?"

I wiped at my eyes and waved a hand at him. "I think I'm just tired. It wasn't that funny. Sorry." Tuning to the first weather station I could find, I listened. Six to eight inches predicted overnight. That was doable. Forty-mile-an-hour wind gusts, not so much.

"Sounds like we're in for a blizzard. I hope Sei and Gabe got to the lodge okay." My feet tingled like they were frostbitten, little needles of pain shooting through each toe and across the arch. And my hands began to throb in rhythm to the pulses in my feet. *Fuck.* The cabin wasn't that cold. What the hell was going on?

I checked my phone for updated weather stats, but it wasn't catching a signal. Dammit.

My knees shook like Sei's often did. The little bit of skiing I'd done shouldn't have tired me enough to feel this cold. "Maybe the chili would be good. Heat me up from the inside out. I don't know what's wrong with me. I just can't get warm." I rubbed my arms and shivered.

"Is the blizzard affecting you like the earth affects Sei? I know he can feel a quake even if it's a half a world away. Gets really shaky when one's coming. No pun intended."

"I can usually feel a storm long before it starts. This one sort of rode up quick. Didn't even see it on the news this morning before we left. But the water in the air is heavy, cold, and strong." Suffocating. I gripped my inhaler, though I didn't need it. I couldn't recall a time I'd felt a storm front this strong. Every once in a while there would be a prickle of something far in the distance, but never a full racing down the highway Mack truck of power like this was.

Jamie handed me a cup of tea that steamed and smelled sweet. "The chili will take a while to warm up. Drink some of this. It should calm you. Water inside, just like earth inside for Sei."

"Sure." I sipped the tea, used to the flowery bitterness, hoping it would ease some of the stiffness welling up in my limbs. Picking up a book, I wondered if I could focus enough to take my mind off the storm. The wind-sailing book had the advantage of being about warm weather and clear blue water. I flipped through a few pages, examining the waves and trying to center my thoughts on the warm thoughts of ocean stretched out around me. But ignoring the pounding cold was harder than I thought and I kept rereading the same sentence, unable to comprehend what it really said. I finally got up, threw another log in the fire, and sat down on the rug by the hearth.

The heat rose in waves from the fireplace. Could have burned the chili in there in a minute or two, I was sure, instead of the slow simmer on the stove where Jamie stirred it. My teeth chattered. Even sitting this close to the blaze, all I could feel was the cold wind—like I'd been dunked in a tank of ice water and dropped in a snowbank. It numbed everything from my toes on up. I closed my eyes, focusing on the moisture in the air, tried to give its fury some calm. Sadly, the water was just along for the ride, and I had no power over wind.

I tried to read again using the firelight. Got through three pages when a huge gust of whatever was playing with water and wind ran through me like a cold-edged blade. I couldn't stifle the gasp. Goose bumps rippled across my skin. And I sucked in a deep breath, choked on it and coughed hard, trying to clear my lungs.

The fire flickered, then died with a hiss as a huge drift of snow slapped onto the woodpile from the chimney above. Outside the wind howled an eerie echo around the cabin—calling me. Something was wrong. A darkness pulsed through the air, dangerous, waiting. I'd never felt anything like it before, yet my magic recognized the malice.

I leapt to my feet and rushed into my coat, boots, hat, and gloves. We weren't safe here. The water magic rolled through me in waves with the force of a battering ram. Panic rose in my gut. Too much power hammered into the elements tonight. We were in danger. We had to go. Escape the storm. Get free of the power.

"Where are you going?" Jamie asked as I bustled passed him and out the door. "It's not safe out there. I'll get the fire relit in a second." He was already dragging the wet logs from the fireplace and replacing them with dry ones.

"Gotta get to the lodge. I have to tell Sei it's not normal. It's wrong. The storm is wrong." I rushed out into the snow, not waiting for his reply. Ice pellets smacked me around in an icy Jack Frost grip. There was nothing happy holidays about this blast. The white flurry blew from every side. I stumbled through the deepening snow toward the spare Ski-Doo. Already the drifts were knee high, and I fumbled forward through the darkness. We'd left it on the other side of Sei and Gabe's cabin. If I could get the sled, Jamie and I had a chance.

Another gust hit me hard enough to knock me back into the snow. The swirling flakes blew too heavily to see more than a foot in front of me as I struggled to get up. Which way was the other cabin? Hell, which way was the lodge? I moved toward something in the distance, hoping it was one of the cabins.

"Kelly?" Jamie's voice sounded so far away. The raging wind made the words roll from different directions.

"Jamie?" I called back, trying to make out his location. Another step and I sank farther into the snow. It hadn't been this deep just an hour before. How fast was it coming down? We'd have more than five feet by morning if this kept up. Panic rose up my spine, sending flaring warning signals across my brain. My heart beat so hard I feared it would burst, and I struggled to breathe. I reached for my pocket, but found it empty. Crap. I'd left my inhaler inside.

I kept moving, shoving my legs through the snow though they felt like lead icicles. I should have put my snowsuit back on. But I had to get to the lodge. Sparkles popped around my vision, cold burned my lungs. I had to tell Sei it wasn't normal. Something kept muttering in my head, "It's not normal. Run."

I stumbled again, falling face-first in the snow. I floundered to the surface, fighting the snow and my body for air—drowning in the weight of whiteness. Over the years there had been a few close calls. A bad muscle cramp could take out the best swimmer. The cold, however, far outranked the heavy weight on your chest of water when it filled your lungs. Water killed you quickly, painfully. Frigid temps like these sent pain through your limbs, slowly took your consciousness, and finally, your life. The stinging cold had nearly succeeded in taking me into the abyss when strong arms yanked me upward and began dragging me out of the snow.

I couldn't recall ever hearing Jamie curse so thoroughly. He held me in an iron grip, pausing a moment to haul me up over his shoulder before wading back to the cabin. I buried my face in his jacket, the world fading in and out as I prayed he somehow knew how to get us safe again. "Tell Sei," I grumbled. Darkness overtook me for a moment.

The opening creak of the door woke me. And the heat of the billowing fire hit us. I swallowed hard and shivered. The world floated around me in a haloed haze of color that blinking didn't peel away. My eyelashes were frozen.

"That was a damn fool thing to do," Jamie growled at me and started pulling off all my wet clothes. I tried to protest when he pushed my wet jeans and boxers down and pressed himself against me, wrapping his meaty arms around my torso.

Fire! He was like being pressed to hot coals! I struggled against him, but his grip was too firm.

When his warmth didn't ease the trembling, he stripped down, leaving his boxers on, wrapped the down blanket around us, and sat us in front of the fire. Had I not been freezing to death, I'm sure I would have embarrassed myself in the arms of a very attractive and mostly naked man. His warmth began to soak into me.

"S-sorry," I said. "Have to tell S-Seiran. S'not natural."

"We have to get you warm first. What's not natural?" He rubbed my fingers and blew on them. "The cold rushing to your heart could be lethal. Let's get you warm."

"Storm," I mumbled into his chest. "Not natural." And I had my face pressed to his left pec, just inches from a tasty-looking nipple. His bulging biceps, veins winding their way artistically down them, shoulders strong enough to carry a ten-point buck with ease, and sculpted abs gave me something other than the cold to focus on. He didn't have a six-pack, but an eight-pack. He could have been on the cover of a men's health magazine. So nice. "I like looking at you," I mumbled.

"You're loopy now too."

I longed to count the defined muscles beneath all that sun-kissed skin. His dark nipples looked like bits of coffee with a dash of cream. How would they taste? Would his skin be salty or sweet? The cold made me shake and my brain sluggish enough to keep from reaching out for a lick of those mocha buds. Would he push me away? I sighed.

"What do you mean the storm isn't natural? We're in the middle of nowhere in northern Minnesota. Storms happen all the time. Bad ones. Lots of open land for them to build up over." Jamie's voice rumbled from his chest where I rested my face. I couldn't make out his tone because his body heat made me sleepy. "Feels like a storm to me."

"Not natural," I repeated. Magic or not, something out of the ordinary was happening. It twisted and writhed outside the door like a living being.

"How?"

"Lots of pressure letting go, but no buildup."

"Like an earthquake?"

I shrugged. Wasn't the earth always under pressure? "Feels like a living thing."

"All magic is a living thing. Pretty sure that's in one of your beginning Magic Studies classes. Is this different than a bad rainstorm?" Jamie seemed to be searching my face for something.

I shrugged, glad the feeling was beginning to return to my limbs. Needles poked into my skin all over. I wondered if I had frostbite. But the fury outside still beat at me hard enough that I clung to Jamie, not caring if all my fingers or toes fell off. The water in the air almost seemed to call for help as it was frozen and tossed about fiercely. I gasped as another shot of power rolled through me. "Talk to me, please."

Jamie sat silently for a few seconds before saying, "I'm not much of a talker. That's more Gabe's thing. Maybe you should talk. Tell me why I find Sei in your bed most mornings now?"

I sighed, not really wanting to get into the issue. "I'm having nightmares, that's all."

"From when Sei was kidnapped?"

"Yeah. When you were shot. There was a lot of blood. And Sei got taken away. It was like my heart was ripped in two. He wakes me up from the dreams, curls up with me, and I sleep better. It's no big deal."

"You sure it's not something else? You were in love with him once."

"Nah. It was a crush. I get that now. It was a fantasy. I dreamt of taking care of him before I even knew him. But I could never be what he needs."

Jamie shifted my weight in his lap and pulled the blanket tighter around us. "You're a nice guy. Happy, smart—with the exception of running out into a snowstorm—and solid. You're not bouncing from relationship to relationship, job to job. Sei needs those things in his life, even if it's not in an intimate way."

"I wish I'd approached him years ago. Maybe it would have stopped all the stuff from happening. Maybe Sei would be better on the path to healing. I shouldn't have followed the crowd and kept my distance. He just seemed so different." I settled deeper into Jamie's embrace, enjoying his heat and feeling my body light up in a somewhat embarrassing way. "I want people to stop trying to hurt him. He needs a chance at a normal life. I thought this trip would be a chance to show him normal. A little time outdoors with people who cared about him, and lots of snuggling by the fire. But he totally hates the outdoors. Or maybe just winter."

Jamie was silent for a while, thinking it seemed. "It's probably my fault he hates the outdoors," Jamie finally admitted.

"Why do you say that? Because of the dog incident?" Sei's memory was spotty. We had all begun to label things as BM, DM, and AM, Before Matthew, During Matthew, and After Matthew. His life before meeting the man who would abuse him for several years was a patchwork of horrible events. His time with Matthew was untouchable by anyone other than a therapist and Gabe. No one brought it up unless they wanted a very moody Sei. After Matthew he became self-destructive until he met Gabe—who really was the key factor in turning Sei's life around. But the most infamous BM memory was the accidental drowning of a puppy Jamie had brought Sei.

"No, this was actually before that." He sighed. "Shit, all I ever did was hurt him."

"That's not true. I'm sure you were just trying to be a big brother."

"And failing miserably. I raised Hanna, you know. Mom was protective of her. She's a Dominion girl, that's how it goes. But she really didn't do things like make meals or help with homework or make sure we got to bed. By the time Sei was born, Hanna and I were pretty self-sufficient. My dad helped a lot while he was still alive even though she wasn't his, but then he passed and it was just us. Sometimes there wasn't enough money to buy food and Mom would just forget." Jamie frowned. "I learned to steal at a very young age," he admitted. "Got caught and then learned to work. Earned money doing errands for people in the neighborhood. The Browan family is nowhere near as wealthy as the Rou family. I was really mad at first, about Sei. My dad told me about him. That he would be born soon. And there was so much going on with the Dominion. Lots of anger in the news. I didn't understand it at the time. All I knew is that there was going to be another baby. I kind of thought that he'd be given to me to take care of like Hanna had been. I worried about how I'd feed him. Then my dad brought me to Tanaka's house the first time."

"Mansion," I corrected. I'd seen the Rou house once or twice. Even been in it once when Sei asked me to sit with him while he waited to do a short interview with reporters about being Pillar. The entire thing had been staged, back-dropped by the Rou wealth and power.

"Yeah. We drove up and I was in awe. And inside it was so... rich. Like a museum or something. Tanaka was polite and very formal. She barely moved from the chair, but was round with child. She and my dad spoke. I don't remember about what really anymore. I just remember staring at her belly and thinking there was a baby in there, and he was going to be born to all this privilege. He'd never want for attention, food, or love. Tanaka loved my dad. I could see it on her face. She also kept touching her stomach like she was trying to comfort Sei while he wriggled around inside her."

"She does love him in a sort of psycho kind of way," I admitted. Sei's mom could have won years' worth of worst-mother awards. I'd sort of always believed that parents were just there to support their kids no matter what, but that was because of the family I had come from. Sei's mom seemed to believe that the more trials he went through as a child, the stronger he'd be as an adult. But a kid shouldn't have to work to survive their childhood.

Jamie nodded. "She did love him. Does, I guess. When he was little, she protected him from everything. Even me."

"I can't imagine you ever being a danger to him."

"I was mad," he reminded me. "Jealous of this kid who was being born to everything and had all that I ever wanted. And then my dad died. He told me to take care of Sei. Protect him and help him become a good man. He'd watched me with Hanna, so he knew I could do it. But I didn't want to. I wanted to hate Sei. My dad died because of him—now that wasn't really the truth, the Dominion had a dozen reasons to kill him—but in my mind that's what it meant. Sei killed my dad."

"What changed? Did you just overcome your anger because your dad wanted you to?"

Jamie's eyes widened in shock. "No. God, no. Does Sei think that?" He frowned. "Shit. No. The change happened when I held him in my arms the first time. He was hours old. Tiny, with giant blue eyes, and a thatch of black hair in a stripe across his head like a Mohawk. The birth had been dangerous for Tanaka. She'd ended up having her uterus removed. Too much bleeding, I think. I don't remember all the reasons. My father's death had been hard on her. And now she lost any chance of ever having another baby. I held Sei in my arms, looked at her tired face and thought maybe I could have him. This tiny bright-eyed baby could be mine. I wanted him. I wanted to give him everything, make him smile, laugh, teach him how beautiful the world could be. And protect him from all the pain I knew would come his way."

"But she wouldn't let you take him."

"Nah. Sei was all she had. Her career was troubled. She was a Rou, but had shirked the rules to be with my father and then kept Sei instead of aborting him the second she found out he was a boy." Jamie sighed. "She did try. When he was little she gave him everything."

"What changed?"

Jamie was silent again for a minute or two. The wind outside blew stronger and I shivered against him. His story was nicely distracting. I hoped the storm blew itself out soon.

"Was it the dog thing?"

"No, before that. Don't tell Sei. He doesn't need to remember. I told him we didn't see each other until that incident. It's better if he just remembers it that way. All I ever did was cause him pain."

"You spent a lot of time with him, then?"

He gave a half shrug. "Until he was five." Jamie was quiet again. "It's better that he doesn't remember. Hell, I think Tanaka may even have put a spell on him to keep him from remembering. I played along because it was better for Sei."

I wasn't sure about that, but I also didn't know the whole story. "I won't tell him. I promise."

He let out a long sigh. "He was five. Tanaka had just gotten the job as assistant Regional Director for the Dominion. It was huge for her. But she had less time for him. I spent a lot of time babysitting him. Would sneak food from the Rou house home just to feed Hanna. I convinced Tanaka to let me have a little campout with Sei and Hanna in the Rou yard. We set up a tent, literally twenty feet from the back door. It shouldn't have been a big deal."

"Something went wrong." My gut clenched. "Was Sei hurt?"

"Hanna had told one of her friends at school, who told another friend, who passed it on to parents, so on and so forth. It shouldn't have been a big deal," he repeated. Obviously it had been. "But Tanaka was on the news as the face of the Dominion. There was talk that soon she'd be the Regional Director. The unrest from the execution of my dad and the others was still fueling occasional riots. There had been death threats. I didn't know about it at the time. I wasn't much more than a kid myself. It shouldn't have been a surprise that people snuck onto the property—they'd obviously been watching us—to try to kidnap Sei."

"Fuck," I couldn't help but curse. "Blackmail?"

"With a death threat." Jamie nodded. "We were all sleeping. Hanna curled around me, Sei at my hip." He sucked in a deep breath, staring off into space. "It happened so fast. Sei screamed and grabbed at me as they dragged him away. They hit me hard. I remember passing out briefly and waking to Hanna sobbing beside me, telling me they'd taken Sei." He paused and swallowed hard. "My dad gave me his power when he died. I'd never really used it. Worked my body hard in the gym and doing chores to not do the things the Dominion preached against. But that was the first time I'd changed."

"Became a bear."

"Yeah."

"And not on the new moon."

"Nope. I only vaguely recall the pain. I know it didn't take long. Minutes, maybe even seconds. Hanna screamed, and I tore out of the tent searching for Sei. I think that was the only time the bear was more in control than me. Sort of how Sei loses it. We tracked them. Tanaka's land is huge and they'd come through the woods on the opposite side to hide their vehicles. I caught up with them before they could get there."

"You saved him?"

"I killed his kidnappers. I still only remember pieces of it. Though in the end I stood over Sei, covered in blood and gore, bellowing my victory as he sobbed in terror."

"Shit."

"Yeah. From that day forward I was only allowed to see Sei with heavy supervision. He had guards with him everywhere. No more babysitting or backyard camping trips. Tanaka could have had me killed for changing like that and murdering three people, but instead she gutted me by taking Sei away." He sighed and shifted me so I was more firmly in his lap. "She made him forget me. One day I came by to see him and he just didn't know me. That was after the puppy thing. I still hate her so much for that. But I understand it."

"You did what you had to."

"Terrified him. He should have grown up camping and hiking and communing with the earth. Instead he was in a gilded cage, trained to be the unseen prince of the Dominion. After the puppy thing, she refused to let me see him at all. Sent him to military school."

We both left that terrible fact and all its outcomes untouched.

"But he turned out okay. Mostly. He met Gabe."

"I think that's what saved him. Gabe saved him," Jamie admitted. "I wasn't strong enough."

"Hmm." I looked up at him. His blond hair tickled my bare shoulders. "Does it ever bug you to see Sei and Gabe together?"

"No. Gabe treats Sei like he's the most important person in the world and at the same time doesn't let him get away with anything. I can't think of anyone who'd have a better handle on Sei than Gabe."

"That's not really what I meant, but okay."

"What did you mean?"

"Like what they have. Can you look at it and not want it for yourself?"

"Love?" He sounded surprised. "Doesn't everyone want love?"

I shrugged. "Wanting it and having it are two different things." For a guy who was so messed up in his perception of the world, Sei sure had a lot of great things going for him. I had a handful of siblings, and while my mom wasn't upfront and angry about me being gay, most of my siblings were. Jamie obviously had no problem with it. "You're a great big brother."

He laughed hard enough that we both shook. "Sei calls me a stalker. Says I'm creepy 'cause I pay too close attention to him. He hates when I dote on him."

"Gabe does all those same things. Sei's view of the world is a little skewed."

"Yeah. We're working on that. He allows it from Gabe because he's giving Gabe sex. It's an exchange. He can't figure me out because he's waiting for me to demand something from him."

"That's fucked-up."

"I'm not saying he doesn't love Gabe. He does. He just doesn't know how to show it." He got up, lifting me like I weighed nothing, and carried us to his bed, which was closer, before burying us both beneath a mound of blankets.

"And this bed's just right," I laughed, cramming myself up against him. He was all carved muscle and big-boned perfection. He didn't complain that I was naked and rubbing all over him. He just wrapped us up in the blankets like a burrito. At least I wasn't shivering as bad anymore.

"Watch it, Goldilocks. Or I'll tell the world you're not really blond."

"The horror," I groused at him. The teasing made me smile. "I'm blond. Just dirty blond with chemical help to be blonder." He laughed. "And protected by the big bad bear."

"You really are loopy." He rubbed my back in calming circles. "Sleep. I'll keep you warm until the storm passes. Then maybe I can get something warm in you."

My gut clenched again, along with my balls, his words giving me so many bad ideas. "Clueless," I muttered at him.

"Hmm?" he asked.

I shook my head. At least with Jamie acting as a barrier, the storm didn't pound as hard at my magic. It sort of persistently knocked around the edge of my psyche, or natural shield, as the Magic Studies 101 textbooks would call it. Whatever the power was, it was strong.

I wrapped myself around him, basking in his heat and praying he didn't cry straight-boy foul and push me away. He settled into the pillow and closed his eyes. His even breaths helped lull me to a deep, dreamless sleep.

Chapter Four

Jamie

THE PANIC of not being able to find Kelly for those few minutes in the blizzard had brought the bear in me to the surface. I didn't let it out. Not like Sei did. Strong emotion made it hard to control. It was even harder because it wasn't a power I was born to have. That was the trouble with the inheritance ceremony. Just because someone could give you power, didn't mean you could handle it. I could have shifted and gone out to find him in the snow, but would the bear have just killed him? I wasn't about to take that chance.

But not changing and rushing after him was like being shot and knowing Sei was being taken away all over again. The fear and sense of helplessness was not something I handled well. If not for my nurse training, I'd probably have been a puddle of panic on the cabin floor. There was a fucking blizzard blowing so hard outside that visibility was less than a foot in any direction. I tried to not think too hard on the feelings. Kelly was becoming family, after all. I had always had a strong desire to take care of my family.

Lying with his naked body pressed beneath mine made me want very unbrotherly things. I'd slept beside him last night, blankets separating us. Now they bound us together. His trim form, toned long legs, strong shoulders, and flat stomach had my mind wandering in inappropriate directions. I teased him about not being blond. He was dirty blond, hair bleached lighter and his pubes black like a lot of blonds I knew. He definitely trimmed and I wondered if he ever waxed. He'd probably be pretty sexy bare. I shouldn't have been studying his pubes, but staring at his face only made me want to trace the lines of his cheekbones and jawline. His lashes lay dark and heavy against his cheeks, hazel eyes hidden from me, but his color was finally returning.

At least I kept my hands in check. He needed comfort, not my big paws molesting him. No matter how hard I tried to pretend what I felt for him was the same as what I felt for Sei, nothing about him said "brother" to me. If I'd met him at a club, I probably would have pursued him. Maybe even fucked him into a bathroom wall and left with a good memory. That couldn't happen with Kelly. Not when he was my little brother's best friend. Some lines weren't meant to be crossed.

When the fire had gone out, he'd fled with a look of terror on his face. I'd been confused, slow to understand what happened and why he'd just rushed by me and out into a storm. He'd been shivering by the fire moments before, the tremble in his limbs and wide eyes a familiar but unnerving sight. That very same shake had haunted Sei for months. Watching it build was a slow study in torture. I thought keeping him calm, acting normal, making him food would help. But just like with my little brother, I didn't know what caused it so I had no way to prevent it. As a soon to be registered nurse, I knew a lot about medicine and illness. But what was happening to them wasn't biological. Maybe I should have studied psychiatry instead. Or magic. Often I suspected it was the power that got to them the most.

Kelly shifted in his sleep, making a little pained sounds that echoed through the room and were a stab in my chest. I relaxed my grip on him, fearing I was hurting him. After he'd fallen asleep, I'd searched him from head to toe for any signs of frostbite. He'd been clean, but the tremor returned each time I stopped touching him. Now I held him tightly, like sleep could steal him from me again.

The wind outside blew strong enough to make the cabin creak, and snow piled to the edges of the two windows. I stopped checking when the white flakes built midway up. Listening for the sound of Gabe and Sei's snowmobile returning or the phone vibrating letting me know they were safe at the lodge kept me awake. Gabe's strong sense of survival would keep them at the lodge—I hoped. He'd keep Sei safe at all costs. I had faith in him.

If sleep would find me, I'd have faith that I could keep from seducing the man in my arms.

Chapter Five

Kelly

Waking up in the heat of someone's arms was heaven. Even Sei's embrace hadn't been this sweet warmth. The handful of boyfriends I'd had in my life had been quick one-night trysts followed by a "Good-bye, see you tomorrow in class" sort of thing. But feeling someone warm beside me was definitely a step up from lonely morning wood. And oh, did I have wood—even worse than yesterday when I'd woken to Jamie's laughter. And sadly there was no shower to disappear into to rub one off.

Jamie leaned against my back, his arm wrapped around my waist. His hard length said he was happy to be there, and I was more than thrilled to be so entwined with him. But I was pretty sure he'd freak out if he woke up with a stiffy pressing into my butt like it wanted to dig a new channel. And what a stiffy it was.

I tried to ease out from under his arm, but it was like trying to move an anchor without a pulley. *Crap.*

Well, what the hell? It wasn't like he was going to throw me out in the snow. I wiggled my butt back, caressing his erection with my ass cheeks, and ground into him. It damn near tripled against my backside. Holy crap, he was huge!

He'd kept his boxers on last night when we'd cuddled to get me warm. Now I was dying of curiosity. I leaned back into his chest and tried to turn as much as I could. "I can take care of that if you'd like." *Oh please say yes.* Even if it was just a hand job, I'd have memories to get me off for months.

He opened a groggy eye at me, staring like he didn't understand, but his expression was an open book of sleepiness and lust. I rubbed against him again. His face turned beet red, and he leapt away from me, taking the blankets with him.

"Shit. I'm sorry." He hurriedly stuffed his legs into his jeans. I hoped he didn't zip up too fast and catch something.

"No hardship on my end." I stretched and felt the air with my magic for moisture. It was heavy and strong outside but no longer being whipped around. How much snow had fallen? The fireplace still blazed, so it hadn't blocked the chimney.

I reached down to my bag and pulled a clean pair of boxer briefs over my still wanting cock. No need to torment the guy. "Don't mind the wood on my end. I don't think I've ever slept with a guy as hot as you. Even if it was just sleep."

Jamie was silent for a minute, then said, "Seiran thinks I'm gross."

I blinked at him, knowing Sei did not think anything close to that. "Huh?"

"He thinks I'm gross because my muscles are too big. He says I smell sometimes."

"Everyone smells sometimes. Plus Sei's got that super sniffer thing. He can smell me across the room. Never try to fart around him and hide it. It's not gonna work." I grinned at him. Jamie still didn't look convinced even with my attempt to lighten the mood. "You've got way too much brother worship going on. No one should change who they are just to please someone else. Not even their little brother." And besides, I happened to like big muscles and the smell of a man after a good workout. "You have friends bigger than you. I think he just worries that you would do something unnatural to get bigger."

"I would never," Jamie protested.

"I know that, and you know that. Does Sei know that? I think if he knew more about you, he'd be less apprehensive around you. Have you thought about maybe sitting down with him and having an actual conversation?

Answering questions he might have about you? Sei's never been good with anyone focusing just on him. I haven't even known him that long and I know that."

He deflated, shoulders drooping. "I just want him to be happy."

"And when you're smelly, he's not happy?"

Jamie shrugged, looking very young. Sei wasn't the only one who'd had a crappy childhood. I was beginning to think Jamie needed therapy as much as Sei did. I crossed the room and wrapped my arms around him in a gentle hug. "Sei loves you, even if he doesn't express himself well. Whether you have muscles or are smelly. He's just not good at showing it. He feeds you and worries about you. That's love from Seiran. Let him feed you more and we're all golden."

He stiffened at the mention of food.

"Wanna talk about it?" I prodded.

"No," he said very firmly.

"You should talk to someone. Even if it's not me. I know you try to hide it from us, but Sei has noticed too."

Still he said nothing. For a moment he almost seemed to be forming something he'd voice, his chocolate brown eyes a bit watery as he stared across the room thinking hard. He let me hold him for a few seconds before pulling away, looking uncomfortable and trying to put his mask together. I watched the transformation, wondering how I could get him to break out of that protective shell more often.

Finally he said, "What do you want for breakfast? We have chili and sandwiches."

"How about we get wild and crazy and eat them both?" We would need the energy to get back to the lodge, and Jamie needed the distraction.

"Okay." He put together the food with that soldier-like concentration that he had whenever doing domestic stuff. When the chili was reheating, he pulled on the rest of his clothes and ran his fingers through his long blond hair. He wove little braids through the front parts and must have noticed me watching because he said, "Braiding it keeps it out of my face. And when it's cold like this, I like to keep my hair down for warmth."

I nodded like I knew what it meant to have long hair. Mine had never gotten longer than a Beatles shag. While I'd left most of my hair products at home—Sei often teased me about the sheer volume of them, I still ran some oil through it to keep from having total hat hair by the time we got the lodge.

The tracker they'd given me read after 11:00 a.m. once we were finally all suited up and ready to go. Had Sei and Gabe made it back last night? Sei hadn't come knocking, and I really hoped they were okay. The cell phones blinked red with no signal. Even the weather radio stopped working.

"Shit," I heard Jamie mutter, so I looked back to him. He'd opened the door, and the snow was piled to nearly the top of the frame.

"I've only seen that happen on TV."

"Happens in New England a lot from lake-effect snow."

"No major lakes around here unless you go up north to Duluth. You spend a lot of time in New England?"

"Mom's got family out there." Jamie shrugged and began to dig through the random chests and storage until he pulled out a pair of snowshoes, then dug around until he found a second pair. "How good are you at snowshoeing?"

"We'll find out, won't we?" It was going to be a long trip. I packed up some clothes in my bag. "There's like five and a half feet of snow out there. This is insane."

"Which is why we need the shoes. Be sure to put your suit on. I'm going to go check the other cabin." He bundled himself up and climbed out the door, creating a ramp up to the top of the snow. I hurried to douse the fire and gather anything I could carry easily. When he returned, he pulled off his goggles and snow mask. "They didn't come back last night. Must have seen the storm and stayed at the lodge. Let's get going. The temp is dropping, and we don't have enough food for more than a few days of this."

Once Jamie had most everything strapped to his back and I was bundled in my snow gear, we headed for the lodge. He had an old-fashioned compass since the satellite GPS wasn't catching a signal. We seemed to be pointed in the right direction, so I wasn't worried. I wondered if the trackers they'd given us were working at all. Would they send help if we waited? The sad truth was that I didn't have a lot of patience, so I followed Jamie out into the snow.

The trek was a lot like a scene out of a disaster movie. We picked our way carefully along the top of the snow, surrounded by what looked like Christmas trees. I was sure they were probably just the tops of old pines. Some had such large drifts of snow blow against them they looked like hills instead of trees as we trod by.

The temperature dropped, sucking the last bits of moisture out of the air. I was oddly tired despite the heavy night's sleep I'd gotten. I recited my picks for this year's fantasy football league in my head a couple hundred times, trying not to concentrate too hard on watching Jamie move. He trudged through the snow like some sort of survivalist pro, seeming to know when the snow was too soft or even if the path would become too difficult to navigate. Before my stomach had a chance to rumble with hunger, he handed me jerky and a handful of trail mix. He even stopped twice to rub my arms and blow warm air into my face. If I hadn't felt so drained, I would have kissed him the last time he'd gotten that close. I wanted nothing more than to lay down in the snow and sleep, but he kept us moving.

When the lodge finally came into view, my legs were numb trunks of weight. The cold air made my face ache, and I was sure I had windburn. The massive wall of windows was a dream come true—like some hallucination of Heaven in the distance. I could almost see waves of heat pouring from the building.

The snow had blown up against it and we probably could have walked right up to the second floor, but we made our way around to the entrance, finding it surprisingly clear. I'd never been so grateful for heat than I was the instant we stepped inside and were hit with a blast of the fire's warmth. I sank to my knees, body tingling all over as the warmth began to thaw my limbs.

Jamie dropped to a knee beside me, rubbing my back. "We need to get you in a warm bath. Fuck, you're frozen."

"Clueless," I grumbled again. A warm bath with Jamie...

"Jamie! Kelly!" Sei ran through the lobby toward us.

Jamie stood to strip off his snowshoes and gear. Sei threw himself at him, giving him a fierce hug. Jamie held on a little longer than most would have, but they didn't often hug, so I wasn't about to get in their way.

Sei let go and turned to me, his expression filled with concern. He gave me a hug too, helping me back to my feet. "Are you okay? The hotel owners have been trying to reach someone to help all day. The radios are blocked, and the phones aren't getting a signal. We were going to send search teams out looking for you."

"We're fine, Sei," Jamie said. "Nothing some food and a warm fire won't fix." He glanced behind his little brother at a pair who seemed to follow closely behind Sei, and had a hard time keeping the frown off his face. "Who are your friends?"

They looked a little alike, one male and one female. Both had rich brown hair and dark blue eyes. The woman was delicate and prim, like she was used to having people do things for her, and the guy was tall, wiry, with tattoos visible at his neck and wrist. He had a rough and ready stance that seemed to ask for trouble. He reminded me of someone I once knew, but I couldn't place the face. Neither seemed the type of people that Sei took up with.

"Cat and Connie. They were renting cabins too but came back for dinner last night. When the storm hit, we all decided to stay here," Sei said. He wrung his hands and looked around the lodge. "Most everyone is here. Just you guys were still out there. I knew you should have come back for dinner with us. Gabe was already distracting me before we even realized the storm had started." A tremor appeared in his hands. He clenched his fits at his sides the second he noticed it. "I was so worried." He hugged me again.

"Catherine," the woman said.

"Constantine," the guy told us. And the name brought it all back. High school boyfriend. Gangly Con had grown up into a troublemaking player. He wasn't the muscular model like Jamie or an exotic beauty like Sei, but his spiked hair and colorful ink gave a wildness to him that just didn't mesh with the guy I used to know. Fuck, those were memories I didn't need. I returned Sei's hug, squeezing him fiercely before letting him go to play stranger to a man who'd cast me aside years ago.

"I'm Kelly, and this is Jamie." I shook Con's hand like I didn't know him. We had not ended on good terms. Was the girl his pretend girlfriend? If so, he hadn't changed much.

Jamie had already dismissed them. His concern was all for Sei. He dug out a thermos and handed it to his little brother. "We should get lunch. You need to eat. Have you taken your pill? We need to get Kelly warm and fed too."

I grinned at being looped into his overprotective push to feed his brother. I'd eat. Even if I wasn't hungry. But I'd also make sure Jamie ate too. We'd both probably burned a week's worth of calories on the hike to get there.

Sei clutched Jamie's sleeve. "We can go now." He seemed more skittish than usual, but being alone at the lodge, since Gabe couldn't travel around freely, would do that to him. I was actually sort of surprised he'd left the room. Sei rarely went out in public without one of us at his side. "Your tracker showed up about a half an hour ago. I was watching it in Hans's office. Wanted to go out and meet you, but Hans insisted I stay in here."

"We're good, Sei. Fine. Just hungry," I assured him.

"We have free rein of the kitchen." Cat skipped ahead of us. "Follow me."

Con smiled at me, a simple lift to the edge of his lips. That smile had been lethal in our younger days. He wore that after we jerked each other off in the locker room between practices. To this day I still didn't know how we got away with it without being caught. Jamie followed Cat toward the kitchen with Sei at his side. "I'm gonna try to get us a room," I called to Jamie.

"Thanks. I'll grab you something warm to eat." They vanished into a far doorway that I assumed was the kitchen.

"Kelly Harding. You're looking sunny as usual. Still bleaching your hair, I see," Con remarked.

"Tanning booths. They're all the rage. Didn't you hear? It's winter in Minnesota." I snapped up my bag and headed toward the main counter. Hopefully they had a room. All four of us in Sei and Gabe's room would get crowded and awkward fast. When together, Sei and Gabe rarely stopped touching each other. For Gabe it was tiny reassurances that Sei was still in his life. For Sei it was just to be sure Gabe was real and still wanted him.

The comment about my hair irritated me. Con had always been that way, hadn't he? Judging. I liked my hair the way it was, mostly bleached blond and semi-spiked. I combed it flat when I needed to look professional, so it worked for me. Sei never complained about the color or the fact that our bathroom often smelled like bleach. And the tan was mostly natural. I was just darker skinned than a lot of the guys I knew. Well, except Jamie. But I think his coloring came from his Native American grandfather.

I threw Con a frown. What a way to ruin a vacation, running into an ex. A woman smiled at me from behind the counter. She was midfifties with graying hair pulled back into a bun and happy crinkles at the corners of her eyes. She held out her hand to me. I took it and shook a greeting. "Louise Gossner," she said. "Hans's wife. I'm glad to see you boys are okay. We were worried. Hans is still trying to reach the county sheriff to find out when the roads will be plowed. No one saw that storm coming, else we wouldn't have rented the cabins out to you boys."

"We're fine. Just hoping you have another room?" I pulled out my wallet to grab my credit card, but she waved it away.

"The only empty room I have is a single king. I won't charge you. You've already paid for the cabins." She pulled out two regular keys and handed them to me. "Give one to the other boy. The one with the big brown eyes."

"Thanks, Mrs. Gossner."

Pocketing a key, I turned around, only to run into Con again. He tilted his face down toward me, stepping into my space like he was going to kiss me. I stepped back, putting distance between us. "What, man? You made yourself clear years ago."

"I'm out now. Don't you think that fate is giving us a second chance?"

"No." I stomped up the stairs to my new room, Con on my heels.

"So you're into muscles now? Gym bunnies?"

"I'm into anyone not you," I told Con, then opened the door, stepped inside, and slammed it in his face. My heart thudded in my chest while I waited for his footsteps to move away. Shit, that had been unexpected. I shouldn't have felt anything for him anymore. He'd really fucked me up in high school. As if high school hadn't been hard enough.

I learned fast to keep my head low and out of trouble. The one other jock I'd fooled around with had beaten me up when one of his friends jested about me looking at him funny. Hadn't seemed to matter much to the guy the night before when he had his cock in my mouth.

Con had been a whole other world of trouble.

We panted, coming down from the quick hand job in the back of the shower after training. Con had a dragon tattoo outline that wrapped from his navel all the way around his back and up to his neck. It would be badass when it was finished. I traced it with my fingers, though all that really mattered was that his skin felt good against mine.

"Come over after dinner," he said.

I'd climbed the tree beside his window a hundred times. Tonight would be different. We'd been together a whole year as of today. And though we talked about it a lot, we'd never done it. "Did you get the stuff?"

"Yeah. I'll make it good for you, I promise."

The shower was good for me. Hot water pouring down on us. His firm grip still massaging the two of us together, and me pressed to his warm skin. I liked what we had so far. "I've read it hurts."

His lips pulled up in that hot smile that made me want to go down on him then and there. We'd only have a few more minutes before someone else entered the shower, and our game would be over. "I'll take care of you." He leaned in and kissed me, all lips and teeth and exploring tongue.

"Okay," I said when he pulled away. My heart pounded, and I had to say it. "I love you, Con."

"Love you too, K."

I shook myself out of the memory. That night had been all about romance. The sex hadn't been all that great. It had been important because I believed I loved Con. He had wanted it bad. I'd been okay doing what we'd been doing. But we'd been together a year and I caved to the pressure.

We took classes together. Ate lunch together, camped, fished, and later fucked as much as we could. He'd always been a bad boy and a player, but I thought I could keep him on the straight and narrow. I had believed he loved me. How naïve I'd been.

I unpacked my things and headed into the shower, determined to wash him from my mind and warm up my toes. Somehow I didn't think burying the memories again was going to be as easy as I had imagined. Losing him had hurt. First loves were often that way.

Chapter Six

Jamie

I KEPT an eye on the entry area until Kelly disappeared upstairs, keys in hand. I didn't like that the tattooed guy followed him, but Kelly's reception of him had been chilly at best. I trusted him enough to think he'd be okay by himself for a few minutes. The tattoo guy might have come off as dangerous, but I had a feeling Kelly could take him without much effort. I'd watched Kelly in the gym enough to know he was strong and fast.

The kitchen was a disaster. To say Sei freaked was an understatement. I didn't expect the cleanliness that Gabe required in his home or his bar to be extended to places outside his reach. But the counters filled with dirty dishes waiting to be washed and the stained grill had Sei gripping my arm tight enough to hurt.

"No, no, no," Sei said over and over, looking over the horror of the kitchen. It wasn't a health code violation, but it could have been cleaner. I didn't much like the idea of eating anything that would come from that grill either. He began opening cupboards, probably looking for cleaning supplies. I wrapped my arms around him and dragged him back toward the door.

"Let me find us food," I told him.

He gaped at me.

"Trust me." I made him face away from the kitchen, toward the door.

"What's wrong with him?" Cat asked. She grabbed my arm and batted her overly made-up lashes at me. I didn't need her kind of trouble.

"Thanks, miss. I'll see to our lunch." I put her off, hoping she'd go away. She did stop touching me at least.

I headed to the fridge, found some fresh eggs, and asked for a microwave and a bowl. The bread could have been better, something more natural than the cheap white the lodge had stocked, but it worked for an egg sandwich. I feared opening the microwave to heat the egg. What if it was splattered with food goop? Even if Sei didn't see it, *I* was likely to have a cow about it. Sei's neat-freak tendencies must have been rubbing off on me.

At least there was fruit and blocks of cheese. I made a small plate of both and shoved Sei into a recliner by the fireplace. Kelly hadn't returned yet. I glanced up the stairs. That guy Con wasn't doing something, was he? The idea made me frown.

I did end up cleaning the microwave before cooking the eggs and returning to Sei's side. He took his pill and ate, nibbling at the sandwich and a piece of cheese. Sei could probably eat all the carbs he wanted. His body seemed resistant to the idea of building up fat, no matter how hard I tried to put weight on him. He needed another twenty or so pounds to actually be on the low end of healthy. "I can find you something else if you want," I told him and turned to go back to the kitchen and see what I could dig up.

Sei tugged at my sleeve. I turned his way and gave him a faint smile. He watched me with worry and curiosity that I wasn't used to. "Stay."

I nodded and returned to my place beside his chair. Another glance up the stairs and still no Kelly. What was taking him so long? Wasn't he hungry? I hoped he hadn't fallen asleep in the bath and drowned. The thought made me frown harder.

"You okay?" Sei asked me.

"Fine," I promised. "Just wondering where Kelly is. He should eat too."

"He probably wanted to shower first," Sei said, eyes still focused on my face.

Did I have something on my face? Smell? *Shit.* I probably did. I'd been pushing hard to get us back to the lodge. "Maybe I should go up and shower. Sorry." I pulled away from him.

Sei shook his head. "Don't leave me, please."

I'd never thought I'd hear Sei utter those words to me. Shock stilled me and I stopped, just standing over him, trying to understand what he needed and how I could get that for him. "What?" I finally asked.

He shook his head, looking away, but then his eyes darted back in my direction.

Did he think something was wrong? "You can talk to me, you know."

He just gave me a sweet smile and stole a grape from my tray. "It's okay, you know," he said after a minute.

"What's okay?"

He smiled, glanced at the stairs, then back at me. "You can go check on him if you want. I'll wait here."

"Who, Kelly?" I shook my head. He was fine. He had to be fine. I had to convince myself he was okay. If I thought for one minute he wasn't, I'd be up those stairs faster than lightning. Of course, that would leave Sei down here alone, vulnerable. I hated that feeling. Ever since that day he'd been taken from our tent...

"Will you tell me what's going on with you and Kelly?" I wondered if either of them was giving me the whole story.

"Nothing's going on."

I wanted to ask why I'd found him and Kelly sleeping together a half-dozen times in the past couple of weeks, then, get Sei's take on his best friend's behavior, but Sei would probably shut down on me, I didn't want to lose our progress. "I just want to make sure he's okay."

"He's okay. Just dealing with stuff. That's all."

"Like you were dealing with stuff?"

"I'm okay." He glanced my way again. "We're okay." After a moment he shrugged. "We're working on it. How about you? You working on it too?"

And that was the bomb, wasn't it? Kelly had admitted that they both noticed something I tried to hide. The food thing... Well, it had been an issue for a long time. I'd had therapy. Could mostly handle it. Some days were harder than others. "If I talk, will you promise to tell me something if you need to get it out? You won't just tuck all your emotion in like your mom taught you and pretend you're picture perfect?"

He snorted an annoyed laugh. "I'm far from perfect."

I sat on the edge of the arm of the chair. "We all are. So you really wanna know?"

Sei studied me for a minute. "Only if you're ready."

"Is there ever a good time to admit you have major issues to someone you care about?" I let out a heavy sigh. "I am—was bulimic. I have a body dysmorphic disorder, which is a fancy way of saying how I see myself is not how other people see me. I've had years of therapy."

"But you don't throw up anymore," Sei clarified. "I heard that can cause heart attacks."

"I haven't done it in years. Sometimes I'm still tempted, but I've got the tools in my arsenal to talk myself out of it," I admitted. "And people to call if I can't."

"And the hiding-food thing. You don't want any of us to see what you eat." He nudged the uneaten half of his sandwich my way. I picked it up, took a bite, and chewed thoroughly, thinking about what to say that didn't sound stupid or like I distrusted them.

"It's all in my head," I finally said.

Sei gave me a sideways frown, tilting his head and squinting at me.

"No, really. I think that people are judging me by what I eat. Sure, some people probably are. My mom does every time I see her. But most are too self-absorbed to care. So it's all in my head. There are some things I can't do. Like I can't step on a scale. It freaks me out and I do crazy things to myself when I do. I've got a great therapist and medical doctor who help me through my yearly physicals." I paused and looked over him for any more doubt, but he just looked worried. "Really, I'm okay. I have bad days, but most of the time I'm just me."

"And you have a little brother that likes to cook," he said.

"A little brother who is a fantastic cook."

"I'm sorry," Sei said.

"Why? You didn't make me this way."

"I've said not nice things to you. I didn't mean them to be so not nice, but Gabe says I need to think harder before I speak. 'Cause sometimes I hurt the people I love without trying."

My heart skipped a beat. Sei had just admitted he loved me. I sucked in a deep breath and tried to keep from jumping out of the chair, grabbing Sei in my arms, and squeezing the stuffing out of him. "You love me?" I finally asked quietly, afraid of what he'd really say.

"Yeah. Duh. You're my brother, right?" He frowned at me again. "You sure you're okay from the walk here? Did the cold mess with your brain or something?"

I laughed and gave in to the need to hug him, but just leaned forward to give him a light squeeze instead of the bone-shattering hug I craved. "I'm tired, but I'll make it. However, I think as soon as the roads clear, we should go home."

He shook his head. "It's our vacation. We're supposed to do family stuff."

"And you hate the cold and snow. We should have gone somewhere warm. We can have as much fun in Gabe's kitchen with you cooking, me watching, and Kelly studying. We just work that way."

"If we went someplace warm, I couldn't spend much time with Gabe."

But Kelly wouldn't be trembling like a willow tree in the wind, and Sei wouldn't have that tight set to his shoulders when he thought people were staring at him. Which that tall tattooed guy was doing now as he stood near the stairway. Gabe could have rented an island or something.

Sei caught my look. "They're Dominion, you know."

"Don't seem your type."

"Nope," Sei agreed. "Cat sure seems to like you."

"Not a chance in hell."

He grinned and picked at the fruit.

The main lodge door opened, and Hans came in looking cold and distressed. He stopped at the counter to talk to his wife for a few minutes. I caught the words "sled" and "frozen." That didn't sound good.

I brushed Sei's shoulder. "How about you go and nap with Gabe for a while. You look tired. Drop the fruit and cheese off with Kelly so he has something to nibble on. He's probably napping himself."

"I *am* a little tired," Sei admitted, then stretched and yawned.

I walked him to the stairs, watched him disappear toward the rooms, and then I headed for Hans. If we had a chance of getting out of here, I would do what I could to make that happen.. With Kelly and Sei safe

CONVICTION

upstairs, I could search for a way out of the hills and valleys of northwest Minnesota and back to where I could guard them with ease. No one was coming in the dead of night to steal them away from me. I was no longer afraid to let the bear out and would do what I must to protect them.

Chapter Seven

Kelly

AFTER WASHING away the day from my skin and dressing in clean, warm clothes, my stomach rumbled. Sei knocked on the door just as I was slipping into my shoes. "Hey," I said when I let him in. He handed me a plate of fruit and cheese. "Thanks. I'm starving." I stuffed a couple pieces of cheese in my mouth. "Where'd Jamie go?"

Sei shrugged. He looked exhausted. "I'm gonna go curl up with Gabe. Jamie said you should nap too. After you eat."

"Yeah? And you're all about listening to Jamie now?"

He gave me a sleepy smile and left. Well damn, had Jamie taken what I said to heart and already sat Sei down for a talk? I hoped so. A glance back at the bed and I contemplated taking a nap. A nap sounded really good right now. But Jamie probably needed one as badly as I did.

I found my way back down to the lobby, thankful Con was nowhere around, and tried to find Jamie.

"You need anything else?" Mrs. Gossner asked.

"My friend Jamie?"

"He's out looking at the snowmobiles with Hans. None of them will start, and we can't find Ron. He usually does all the maintenance."

I wondered if the sleds had been full of gas before the storm hit. If they'd been low, the lines could have frozen. Or maybe the batteries just needed a boost.

The lodge looked so empty. No one was gathered by the huge fireplace or in the dining area. The entry was clear of coats and boots. I expected to see people lingering, talking, or even hanging out in the oversized chairs reading. Even Con and Cat had vanished. To their rooms maybe? How many other guests were trapped with us?

The sun setting in the distance meant it had to be close to four in the afternoon. Gabe would be up soon. The cold that had gotten to me yesterday didn't seem to be rearing its head yet. Maybe it was just a fluke.

I crossed the lodge and headed out the door, hoping to find Jamie and learn just how stranded we truly were. Being at the lodge made the storm seem less intimidating. There were strong walls around us and a decent food supply. Having other people affected helped too. There would always be someone more reasonable ready to help if needed. Facing another bad storm just didn't seem as big of a deal. I hoped I was right, but feared something was just starting.

The garage door was shut tight against the increasing wind, so I had to rush across the very snowy lot. Good thing I'd put my Docs on before coming down. The cars were just heaping mounds of snow where it had been blown over them. I couldn't imagine how bad the roads were. Out here in the great open north, whiteout conditions were a real threat. Hopefully the sleds worked and we could get to a ranger station for supplies if needed—or rescue.

The wind groaned in crazy bursts through the barren trees, throwing loosened snow at me the whole way across the lot. I stepped inside the garage and shivered. The lights were on and it was warm, though not the friendly heat of the fires at the lodge.

Jamie hunched over one of the sleds, hands wrapped somewhere in the core of the machine. Hans peered in the gas tank of another. "It looks like they all were," he said.

"Shit" was Jamie's reply.

"What's wrong?" I asked.

Jamie glanced back my way. "You shouldn't be outside without a coat."

"I'm inside now." I gave him a mischievous smile.

"You're almost as bad as Sei." His tone made it sound more like approval than a complaint. Like he was trying to be angry with me and failing miserably.

I moved up beside him and stared down at the sled. The metal glistened with condensation, and frost covered a good portion of the lines. "That doesn't look good. Water in the lines?"

"Yeah. All of them," Hans answered. "Never seen anything like it."

The uneasy feeling the storm had left me last night came back in a quick shudder. Having never lived in a hurricane state I couldn't relate to that—the raw power of the storm. If I could imagine, and my imagination was really good, whatever had hit us last night had been somewhere along the lines of a low-level hurricane of snow, the force of the wind, water, and pressure creating a whole soup of bad.

I refocused on the lines, and when I looked up, Jamie was watching me curiously. "What?" I asked.

He shrugged.

"Are the radios working yet?" Maybe I should have grabbed my coat. The temp in the garage couldn't have been more than forty degrees.

"We got a short CB message through to the ranger station, but no response." Hans pressed his hat down farther over his gray hair. "Can't find Ron anywhere."

Jamie got up and shrugged out of his coat, handing it to me. I shook him away. "I'm fine."

"You're shivering."

"You need that more than me. There's more of you to heat."

He growled, much like the bear he became on the new moon, and wrapped the coat around me. "What is it with people not taking care of themselves? Doesn't anyone train their kids to be self-sufficient?"

When he put it that way... "I'll run in and get my coat."

"Take that one with you. Just bring it back when you come in again. It's only two or three degrees above freezing." Jamie went to the next sled, digging into the engine like an old pro. Was there anything he wasn't good at?

I turned away, letting myself out but making sure the door was firmly shut. I hurried across the frozen lot, wind blowing at me hard. Jamie's ginormous coat only helped ward off the chill a little. In the few minutes since I'd left the lodge, snow had blown heavily around the doorway. I yanked on the doors, expecting it to fly open so I could dart inside, but they wouldn't even budge. My shoulder stung with the force of the unrewarded pull. *What the hell?*

Tugging harder, I tried pushing and pulling both doors. Neither moved. The huge wooden slabs didn't have any glass to look through, so I pounded on them. Was it the cold, or had someone locked us out? I followed the wall around the opposite side of the house to see if there were other entrances. They must have a fire exit or something. Maybe a delivery entrance.

The right side of the building didn't have as many trees, so the drifts of snow towered above me, pressing against the building. I picked my way through the snow, sinking several feet in with each step. The top of a doorframe was visible. The wind whipped, making me shiver and wish I wasn't without gloves and a hat. The drift blocking the door was probably four or five feet wide. If the door swung outward, there was no way it was going to open. I sighed and began to dig, thinking I'd try for a minute or two before heading back to the garage to warm my frozen fingers.

A press of moisture began to fill the air again. I cringed against the weight of water filling the clouds quickly forming above. The feeling of something wrong kept digging down inside of me. Had Jamie told Sei about the storm? Even if he had, there were no working phones, so it wasn't like he could call the Dominion for help. I was a level-five water witch. Did they have someone more powerful they could send to put a lid on the magic? The problem was it really wasn't a water issue. Maybe if I was strong enough I could pull the water back down, but it was the air that bound it up, froze it and sent it spiraling downward. Did we even know of any air witches that powerful? Last I could recall the air Pillar was in California somewhere, or maybe it was Chicago. I groaned and continued to dig.

Pressure built in my head, making me shut my eyes for a moment to block out the light. Finally, I sucked in a deep breath and climbed up the pile, trying to push everything away from the door so I could open it. The cold stung and froze my fingers when I slipped and plunged into the snow. My feet stopped somewhat farther off the ground than I had expected. Was there an ice shelf or something? I dug through the drifting white mass thinking I could break through it and finally free the door until I found the red plaid of a flannel shirt. Everything beneath it was hard, cold, and unmoving.

The blue tinge of flesh was not something I'd ever imagined I'd encounter outside of a bad horror flick. Or maybe a crime show. Was it some kind of prank? I studied the edge of a hand. It couldn't be real, right? But the flannel led to a jacket, which lead to an arm. My heart pounded like a freight train. Dead bodies only happened in the movies. I was so not ready to be the next Sherlock Holmes.

I swept a patch of fluffy snow away and was looking down into the face of a very dead man. His eyes were open, face discolored from frostbite and death. Ice sheeted over the edge of his chin and around his ears, holding him to the ground. I swallowed hard, sucking in a deep lungful of subzero air, and stumbled backward away from the corpse, landing in a pile of fluffy bone-chilling snow.

I fumbled for a minute, trying to find my footing while not touching the dead guy. My heart hammered as I used the building to prop myself up and find my way back to the garage. I slipped and gasped for air like the fish out of water that I was. The cold stung deep, numbing my limbs and burning my lungs. Stars sparkled along the edge of my sight. I was dizzy as I reached the door to the garage and slammed it open. I slid and half fell to a stop in front of Jamie.

"Guy in the snow. Frozen!" I wheezed, lungs cinching tight.

Both Hans and Jamie blinked at me. *Fuck!* Was I not speaking English or something? My chest tightened, and I tried to calm myself so I could catch a breath. I waved my arms at them and motioned in the direction of the lodge. "Side door. Dead guy!"

The weight of the magic closed in on me, wrapping my vision in swirling sparklers and dark pops of color. I swayed, trying to keep my feet as the lack of oxygen made my head spin. I must have closed my eyes, because when I opened them again, Jamie was there, arm around me, holding me up.

"I'll go check the kitchen door. Get him inside. There's another storm blowing in," Hans said to Jamie when the garage groaned under the whipping wind. He headed out the door.

"C-coat?" I asked Jamie, offering it back.

He shook his head. He put his head to my chest, listening to my lungs wheeze and rattle. "You weren't sick. So this isn't a cold." He listened for another moment, cringing at the obvious wheeze in my lungs. "You have asthma?"

I nodded, though it'd been years since I'd had an attack this bad.

Jamie cursed. "Where's your inhaler?"

"Room," I rasped.

He scooped me up and raced through the cold to the main door. He tugged at it, but it didn't budge. I didn't point out that was why I'd try to go to the side door. "You've got to be kidding me." He set me down and put his hands on the wood. I could see the glowing green of his magic funneling into the wood. It curved and grew like a vine, twirling up into the mechanisms and around the handles. The door began to warp beneath his hand until a loud "pop" sounded and the lock fell out. Jamie kicked the door open, picked me up, and raced up the stairs. "Which one?"

I pointed to the one at the end of the hall to the left. Dark dots began to flood over my sight as I struggled for air. *Calm*, I reminded myself. *Calm is better than panic.* Tiny breaths were still breaths. Even if it was so little that my lungs burned with need.

Jamie fumbled around in my pockets, yanking out the key and opening the door. He set me on the bed and looked around the room. I leaned across the bed and pulled my inhaler out of the bedside drawer, taking several long puffs before some of the tightness eased. After that horrible intake of cold I could probably use a nebulizer, but I hadn't brought one with me. I sighed as the sweet heaven of air began to fill my lungs.

Jamie finally took a long, deep breath himself and fell to his knees beside the bed. I lay on my side, staring at him while I forced my body to draw even breaths.

"I'm a whole world of angry with you right now." He didn't look angry. His reddened face and wide eyes said scared, maybe concerned, but not angry.

"Why?" I whispered, happy the black dots had gone away.

"You never told me you have asthma. How many times have we done something that could have set off an attack? If I'd known, I could have been prepared. I'm studying to be a nurse, you know."

I laughed lightly. "I grew up with asthma. I know how hard I can push myself. I run and swim, remember? Lots of awards. Been taking care of myself a long time. Not your responsibility."

"But friends take care of friends. And we're that, aren't we?"

I blinked at him, frowning.

"Unless you don't see me as a friend."

"I do," I promised. "Just didn't want to be a burden."

He threw his hands up in exasperation. "You're just like Sei. Hiding the important stuff. He won't take his anxiety pills without me reminding him, but he needs them. Without them, he's a quivering mass of jelly."

"That he is." I sucked in heavy lungfuls of air and watched Jamie pace the room like a caged tiger.

"Okay, Yoda. Any other secrets you're hiding from me?" He looked me over, like he was expecting me to pull off a limb and say, *Ha! Got you, it's fake.* But I shook my head. He sighed and began to pick up things and put them away. Everything had a place, which was a motto that came from spending lots of time with Sei's OCD. "Better now?"

"Yes. Breathing is so underrated. But there's still a dead guy by that side door. Frozen, I think. He was hard as ice. Eyes wide open." I swore, remembering his face. It was probably going to haunt me for a while. "I hope to never see that again." I closed my eyes while Jamie still moved around the room.

"Why don't you tell me these things? Don't you trust me?"

I popped open an eye to stare at him. "I do trust you."

He folded his arms across his chest. "Like the nightmares."

"Just stuff I gotta get over," I told him. "Bad stuff happens to everyone. You gotta learn to deal with it. What other option did I have? That's not me."

"You could at least let the rest of us help sometime," he protested.

"Like you do?" I threw back at him.

He sighed. "I'll work on that too."

I grinned and relaxed into the mattress, closing my eyes. Sleep must have taken me fast because everything disappeared for a while. I never felt Jamie grab his coat off, pull the blankets around me, and leave. But maybe I dreamed of his lips skimming my cheek with a good-bye kiss.

Chapter Eight

Jamie

Kelly infuriated me almost as much as Sei did. I'd driven him around for weeks. Had hundreds of meals with him, walked him to class, cheered him on at practices and swimming competitions, and spent a lot of time watching movies beside him on the couch, only to find out he'd been hiding a serious illness from me. How many times had we gone running or swimming, or even now on the ski trip, and he could have had an attack? I should have been prepared. Could have gotten spare inhalers. Something. I hated that helpless feeling.

I didn't even realize I'd stomped to Gabe and Sei's room and pounded on the door until it opened to a disheveled, alarmed-looking Sei. Gabe relaxed on the bed, shirt half-unbuttoned, dangerous smile on his face and gold hair glowing in lamplight.

"Everything okay?" Gabe asked quietly as Sei stepped aside to let me in.

Crap, I'd interrupted them. "Never mind. I'll come back later." Heat burned my face. I *knew* what they did. Saw them kissing on occasion and walked into Gabe's place to unload groceries to hear them having sex. That had been awkward. This was...

"In," Sei growled at me. I stepped inside and let him close the door behind me.

"Nothing we can't continue later." Gabe adjusted his shirt, rose from the bed to kiss Sei on the forehead, and motioned me to the chair beside the table. I dropped into it feeling oddly betrayed. Was it because Kelly had obviously not trusted me enough to tell me about his asthma? Or was it more? The day had been going so well.

"What's wrong?" Sei asked, wringing his hands in that worried fashion he'd only started a few months ago. "Something's wrong. Jamie doesn't ever look like that," he said to Gabe.

How did I look? I tried to steel my emotions to keep Sei from becoming more concerned. He had his own problems to deal with. Gabe's eyes met mine and there was a question in his, but now was not the time. "Kelly found a body outside. It might be the missing maintenance guy."

"A body?" Sei collapsed on the bed. Gabe pulled him into his lap, wrapped his arms around him, and stroked his hair.

I filled them in on everything that happened since they'd left Kelly and me at the cabin yesterday. "He probably got lost in the storm and couldn't get inside in time. I'm going to go and try to examine him." It made sense that I should look over him. I was an RN after all.

"That doesn't make you responsible for that man's death. Let the authorities deal with it," Gabe instructed. I really hated when he told me what to do. But arguing with him often became explosive as we both had hot tempers when pushed hard enough.

"What if he was sick?"

"I think you're looking for trouble that isn't there. He was outside in a snowstorm and froze to death. It happens. Even in the middle of downtown."

"He'd been a maintenance man here for a while. He's unlikely to have just gone out wandering in the snow," I pointed out, mostly to be contrary. I sort of wanted a fight, even if it wasn't a good idea to fight with the vampire. Better Gabe to take my anger out on than Kelly.

"People make stupid mistakes all the time. Not everyone survives them." Gabe's look was warning enough. I sighed. Sure I'd told Sei most of my issues, but I hadn't shared the worst of it. Now was not the time.

"As soon as this storm ends, I think we all need to get out of here," I told them both to change the subject.

"Water and air are at play," Gabe said. Both Sei and I looked at him. He shrugged. "There was nothing on the radar before the storm yesterday. I'd been keeping an eye on it on my phone. The storm came out of nowhere. It showed up on the radar just seconds before the link went out."

Kelly had said the storm had been unnatural. He felt it growing like a living thing. I'd sort of thought he was being poetic. But maybe it wasn't all just pretty words. "You don't think that Kelly might be..."

"No," Sei said. "I trust Kelly."

But if he were bitten like Sei had been a few months ago, he could be doing it against his will. That could be why he had been trembling so badly. If someone was pulling power from him to fuel the storm, it would wear him out fast. Maybe even burn him out. I frowned at the idea. What if it wasn't a bite, but a spell? Could someone do a spell that strong from a distance? There was one very powerful air witch I knew of, and he wasn't human anymore.

Gabe got up from the bed. He set Sei down, but hugged him tight. He must have had the same thought I did since he said,

"Let's go check on the body. I will be able to tell if a vampire is involved in his death." Gabe and I would work it out. Create a plan. We'd evacuate Sei and Kelly if we needed to. What happened with Andrew Roman and Matthew a few weeks ago wasn't going to ever happen again. Not while I had any fight left in my body.

"Sei, will you stay with Kelly?" Gabe asked him.

Sei nodded. "Yeah. I take care of him all the time. I even brought his spare inhaler just in case." Sei pulled it out of his bag and held it up. Shit, so Sei had known too. I frowned at my little brother.

"Can you guys tell me next time one of you has a major medical condition, please?" I begged him. "Neither of you are hiding a severe allergy or anything, right? Like, say, sunlight?" I glanced at Gabe.

Sei grinned. He gripped Gabe's hand, and Gabe rubbed the back of Sei's thumb gently. We both led him to Kelly's room and let him in. Kelly was curled up on the bed wrapped in the blankets, a sock-covered foot sticking out from one corner.

"Be back in a while, beautiful," Gabe whispered to Sei, lips finding his in a soft kiss. I looked away and let them have their moment before assuring myself that Sei was safe inside my room. Once the door was closed and we were headed outside—the sun had finally set—Gabe asked, "So what else is wrong?"

"All the sleds were sabotaged." Though the words nearly killed me to say, he had to know. "Water in the lines."

Kelly

I DREAMED of a cabin deep in the woods. It was outlined in the dark by moonlight glistening off the snow. There were no lights on inside but I could feel that it wasn't empty. No fire was lit and yet I moved toward it as though compelled. In the distance an owl hooted and the sound brought a chill to my bones. I was tired, legs heavy and slow, dragging through the thick snow.

Books and instructions could only teach so much. And while words and ideas ran through my head, most of them didn't make sense. I stumbled, landing hard in the snow. The icy bite stung my palms and sank through my battered jeans. For a moment the white beneath me was all I could focus on. My breaths flowed forth in a pale haze, a sign of how dangerously cold the temperature drop was becoming. And I was somehow without a coat. In my mind's eye, I saw images of a family that wasn't mine, living in a cramped apartment, a man with dark hair and green eyes who fucked me fiercely, and then a flare of heat and dancing flames before the cabin returned to focus. In the distance was a tower, and my arms ached at the idea of returning to it. I glanced down at my worn long-sleeved T-shirt and found it stained with blood from scabs open beneath.

Come. The compulsion forced me to my feet and back toward the cabin, heart pounding, tears dripping and freezing on my cheeks. It was only beginning. I knew this and feared it. I prayed for a quick end, but when I reached for the door of the cabin, I only saw glowing red eyes and rage.

I startled awake to the scent of honey clover and the sound of someone humming. Sei had curled himself around me, twisting at the hip to leave his right hand free. He balanced his notebook against my side and was drawing something on the pages he was supposed to use to track his medication.

"What are you drawing?"

"Gabe's tattoo. He won't tell me what it means. Gets that guarded look on his face when I ask. So I'm going to look it up on the Internet. I think it might be for an old lover or something."

"Gabe has a tattoo?"

Sei's smile grew dangerous, naturally seductive. He nervously played with his short hair with one hand. He always complained he looked too much like a girl, but with the short hair, I just didn't see it. With long hair he was just a really pretty man. I liked him either way.

"It's really low on his back."

"Like butt-crack low? Tramp stamp?"

"Not quite, but close." He glanced at me. "Have you been looking at his butt?"

I smiled at his jealous tone. "Never. But it sounds pretty hot. Does Jamie have any tattoos?" I thought of Con's and how much that had turned me on when I was younger. He'd seemed so wild and dangerous. I knew the difference now. Con was about as dangerous as a puppy learning to walk. His only real danger was how he'd use you and spit you out. I frowned at the thought. Did I have a right to judge him anymore? He was an ex, but maybe he had changed. Never mind the confrontation in the hallway when I'd first come in. He said he was out, so maybe he was looking for someone permanent. Either way, it wouldn't be me.

Everything about Jamie said family, home, safe. I don't know why I compared the two. It wasn't like I would ever have a chance with Jamie. He was the sort of guy that should be out dating celebrities just to be on camera more. I didn't think he'd be the type to have a tattoo, but what did I know. He could have been covered in them, but I'd been too out of it to notice last night when I'd been plastered to his hot body.

"I don't think so. But if he had someone's name across his ass cheeks, I don't think he'd tell me."

"Would be a shame to change such nice cheeks." I flushed, realizing I'd said that out loud. "Shit, sorry. Shouldn't have said that. I so do not need to be cruising your brother."

Sei grinned and laid his head on my pillow. "It's okay. Why not look? If he weren't such a crazy muscleman, he'd be super hot." He frowned. "Is it bad to think my brother is hot?"

"Not when it's true. You're not doing him. So all is well. Plus I like muscles. He's not that bad. Buff but not scary. He's got that friend that is scary huge. What's his name? Michael, I think."

"The one with the tiny head?"

I nodded. "Yes. I'm always afraid when he flexes his arms that his head is going to pop right off."

Sei laughed. "He's nice, though. Works hard. I've seen him spend hours in the gym pumping iron while I run. I don't know how he does it."

"I'm sure there's someone out there that loves him for it."

"I like natural guys better. A little bit of muscle tone is okay." He tapped his pen on the paper and thought for a minute. "I like flat tummies more than muscles. The chiseled thing is really intimidating." He lifted up his shirt to look at his flat and very unlined stomach. "I'll never have a six-pack. So I like being with a guy who isn't perfect-looking."

It was my turn to laugh, because really, we were talking about Gabe. "Gabe's not perfect-looking?" I teased him.

"Not according the magazines and stuff. He's good for me, though. The media is all like 'want to get laid? You have to look like this.' I'd rather do Gabe. Or him do me. Maybe I should get a tattoo."

His logic always bounced around like a ping-pong ball, and sometimes I was slow on catching up. But... okay... Gabe had a tattoo.

"How does a tattoo even stay on a vampire? Don't they heal everything?"

"Maybe it was from before he became a vampire? His chest scar is like that. The one where he got stabbed..." Sei stared off into the distance, fingers tracing down his chest like he could feel Gabe's scar beneath his fingers. "Did they have tattoos back then?"

"That would mean that if it's a name for a lover, it's a really old and probably dead lover," I pointed out.

Sei blinked. "Titus."

"Huh?"

"His old lover was a man named Titus. Andrew Roman's wife killed Titus and changed Gabe into a vampire. Then Gabe killed her. Maybe it's Titus's name." He went back to sketching things in his notebook. "Maybe the letters are in Latin. I'll have to look that up when we get Internet access again."

"Would that bother you? If it was Titus's name?"

"I dunno. Maybe. It's not like he could have gotten it removed. But it's hard to compete with a dead man."

"Pretty sure competing isn't necessary. Since he's been gone a billion years. And

Gabe is crazy about you." I hugged my best friend. "Every crazy fucked-up bit of you. He even loves that you have to alphabetize the spices."

"By name and date. So I can throw out the bad ones," Sei informed me and went back to doodling.

I shook my head at him. If there was one thing I didn't do, it was mess with Gabe's kitchen. The one in our apartment was never as stocked or organized as Gabe's. We always had basics, but any intense cooking Sei did was in Gabe's place, usually with Gabe nearby. When Jamie came over to cook something, he brought his own stuff. But in reality most of his cooking was done at Gabe's place too. "Where did the super duo head off to?" The clock's blue numbers said it was after seven. At least I'd gotten a nice nap.

"They were trying to figure out what to do with the body."

"Crap! I totally forgot about that. It was pretty gross. He was like staring at me with these ugly dead eyes." I shivered at the memory. "Not as cool as TV makes it out to be."

"It was the maintenance guy. Jamie thinks he froze to death in the storm." Sei's bright blue eyes pinned me with a heavy and too-serious-for-him stare. "There was water in all the snowmobiles, so we can't leave. You don't know anything about that, do you?"

"Nope. Why would I get us stuck here?"

He shrugged. "Maybe you want us to have more vacation time or whatever. I dunno."

The past few weeks had made us all this way. Suspicious of everyone. Holding Jamie as he bled out had done it to me too. Being kidnapped, raped, and nearly beaten to death had done it to Sei. But there was no heat in his accusation. "I'd rather be at home where I can get to an indoor pool." I stretched. "I could so use a swim. My muscles ache from the trek back here. How are you doing after our skiing yesterday?"

Sei's face turned bright red and he nibbled on his lower lip.

"Gabe help you work all that out?" I nudged him, teasing. "I'm sure he gave you a workout."

His smile was small. "He doesn't have the skill that you do with deep tissue massage, but he knows how to make me jelly in other ways. It was good."

I laughed. "No tips needed, then." I'd learned massage from my older sister Keira. She worked as a massage therapist for recovering accident victims. She gave me a lot of great advice on how to help ease Sei's back pain after Brock Southerton had raped and thrown him against a wall while trying to steal his power. "How's your back?"

He didn't look at me, but I knew him better.

"Do you need me work out some kinks?" I prodded his lower back with gentle fingers. He melted beneath my grip.

"Everyone's suspicious that you might be fueling this storm," he pointed out as I rolled him under me so I could sit on his hips and work the knots out of his back. He had a couple real doozies too. I worked my fingers into the muscles, kneading at them until he finally gave in and began to relax. Sei's little moans beneath me were almost sexual, but I knew better.

"You wouldn't be all cozy with me if you really thought I had something to do with this."

He turned and pretended to nibble on my arm, like the critters in some of his favorite anime did. "I trust you. I told Jamie that." He paused as my hand caught another tight spot, wincing briefly, then closing his eyes as the pain ebbed.

Jamie doesn't trust me?

"Besides, I like you. You're my best friend other than Gabe. You don't look at me like you're waiting for me to explode."

"But you don't *like*, like me."

He shot me a wary look. "Do you want to have sex with me?" He wriggled his hips against my butt. But I wasn't hard. I realized at that moment why. There was someone else I wanted. Really, really wanted. *Fuck.* When had that happened?

"No. I'd rather have sex with Jamie." It was the first time I'd acknowledged the desire out loud. And apparently he didn't trust me, which stung. I thought I'd earned trust after holding him together while he was bleeding out and then rescuing his brother from the frozen north. But I guess you never knew a guy. I huffed in frustration, focusing hard on Sei's massage. "That's, like, the taboo of taboos. Wanting to have sex with my best friend's brother."

"Why?"

"'Cause if something goes sour on either side of the relationship, it's hard to keep seeing them around."

"Jamie needs someone permanent. He's a white-picket-fence kind of guy," Sei pointed out. "Not a trick."

I nodded. "Yep, and pretty sure he just sees me as a kid. Not boyfriend material. So no nookie either way."

Sei grinned at me. "You *are* a kid."

"Jerk," I teased him. "Why am I friends with you anyway? Just because you have a hot lover who gave me a well-paying job and a super-hot brother I wish would look at me like he wasn't measuring me for diapers?"

Sei laughed. "Diapers. He so does not look at you like that."

I shrugged. "He treats me like he treats you."

"Which is way annoying, but just how Jamie cares. Both you and Gabe point that out to me all the time. It's sort of fifties housewife-type stuff, but that's okay. He likes to cook, buy the groceries, clean, and organize our lives. Let Jamie be Jamie and see if you can work with it."

"So you're okay if we date?"

"Pretty sure that's all on you and Jamie."

"But you won't get mad at me if we don't work out? Like tell me you don't want to live with me anymore or be my friend?" Friends didn't used to be so hard to come by. Now I spent a lot of time analyzing just who was a friend and who was bullshitting me. Being an out male witch was harder in a lot of ways than being out as gay.

He gave me a dirty look through narrowed eyes over his shoulder.

"I'm just saying. It happens. Something goes wrong and you lose more than the kids in the divorce."

"But you'll stay friends with me, right?" He turned enough that I had to pause in kneading his rhomboids.

"You'd have to find wild dogs to drag me away. Or maybe a slew of naked football players."

"Fantasy football?" The hopeful tone of his voice made me laugh. Maybe he could pick a winning team by attraction alone.

"If we get out of here, I'll show you how it works."

He sighed and went back to drawing. I worked the kinks out of his shoulders, then laid back down beside him. He fit himself snuggly against me. "I'd like Jamie to have someone. You'd be good for him. That girl has been all over Jamie. I don't know if he does boys. But he could pick a better girl. That one's so fake she's plastic."

"Which girl?" Did Jamie have a girlfriend I didn't know about?

"Cat. The one with the tall, brooding gay guy, Con. He's hot with all those tattoos. But he's got something dark in him that reminds me of Matthew." Sei's eyes darted away, as if the memory caught him unaware. I didn't want to know what horrible memory brought that haunted look to his face. "He's the sort of guy who uses people and throws them away," he said after a minute.

"Constantine told you he's gay?"

Sei gave me his famous "duh" stare. "He came on to me the moment Gabe went to bed this morning."

And here Con had been talking about how he'd changed. "Really? Somehow that doesn't surprise me."

"Constantine Opal. Last name Opal, like the gem. They're Dominion. Not first wave like me, but still high enough to matter. They have a couple of family members in the regional office."

"They? Is Cat related to him?"

"Brother and sister. Sort of look alike, don't you think? I guess they would look more alike if he wasn't all badass tattoo guy and she so prim and proper." He shook his head. "Dominion girls..."

Conviction

I nodded my agreement, though I'd known a handful of Dominion girls who weren't the prolific bitches that Sei seemed to run into. But maybe that was a first-wave thing too. Everyone Sei knew was the daughter of someone who was *someone* in the Dominion. Most girls I knew were just like me, part of middle-class working families with no political connections. Though my baby sister Reanne could be a real bitch without trying, I was pretty sure that was just a jealous sister thing since I had more power than she did.

"Did they recognize you?" I asked.

Sei snorted. "Of course. Cat was all sweet and simpering with fake sugar telling me how great it was that I was Pillar. Had platitudes about how men should have more rights within the Dominion. I could see it pissed her off. She treats her brother like he's only around to do her bidding. Met a ton just like her."

Hmm. What was Con doing up here on vacation with his sister? He'd never spoken of having a sister, though to be honest, we hadn't talked about anything not related to sex or sports. Teenage boys and hormones. I was happy I'd mostly outgrown that stage. "Seems odd to vacation with your sister."

He glanced my way. "Jamie's my brother. We're on vacation."

"Good point." I laughed. I didn't tell him that Con didn't seem like the kind of guy to vacation with family now that he was a grown man. Jamie rarely let Sei out of his sight, and at least now I knew why. All back to an eighteen-year-old boy watching his brother being dragged away by political assassins. "So you don't remember Jamie at all from when you were a kid?" Did Sei have nightmares of a bear standing over him, dripping with blood?

"Nope. He said you needed to tell me something. Details or something about magic. The storm."

"Oh yeah. About the storm. It wasn't normal. I felt a lot of malice in it. Panic too. It's starting again, the pressure building. Though deep inside the lodge it doesn't feel as bad as it did at the cabin." Just a distant nudge of energy tugging at me.

"But you're the water witch. Why tell me?"

"I don't know. Something in my head says you need to know. Do you ever feel stuff like that? An element with pure malice in it?" Or almost-voices projecting emotions from elements that couldn't possibly identify with humans? I sucked in a deep breath to steady my thoughts. Was the malice really there? The panic? Or just my own head making everything more substantial than it needed to be? He'd been studying magic longer than I had. Set a new bar for all male witches to reach. I hoped he had some answers. Unless, of course, I was going crazy.

"At the witch levels exam, Bernie made the river rise that way. By forcing her element to do something it didn't normally do." He turned away, keeping his eyes down. "There wasn't malice in it, but it wasn't natural. Anyone higher than a level one would have felt it. I can try to focus on the storm. Winter makes it harder because my power is more... sleepy, I guess? It's not as active. But I'll try."

Since both Sei and I were level-five witches, anything weird should set off internal alarms. "We saved the day, you and I." The test could have been fatal all because one girl had been bullied into showing off for girls who weren't really even her friends. Bernie and I talked pretty regularly since then. She no longer hung with the girls that Sei called the Queen Bees. But they'd also lost their ultimate queen as Rose Pewette, former earth Pillar, had been murdered by the man who tried to take Sei's power.

I rubbed his soft hair, massaging his scalp, and pulled him into my arms like I could save him from the memories, hugging him from behind. "I thought I could hold the water back, but I'm just human. There's no way to stop nature in all its glory. You'd think years of competitive swimming would have beaten some sense into me. All it takes is one mistake for water to become deadly."

"I never got to see you swim for competition. But you're an amazing runner. I loved watching you pace yourself and shoot ahead in the last few seconds."

"Smooth transition," I teased him. "The days of competitive sports are behind me." Ever since enrolling in the Magic Studies program at the U, I'd had nothing but trouble. I hadn't even officially started classes yet. But the world had become a very biased and hateful place. Guys I used to run with every day wanted nothing to do with me. People I'd never met shouted profanities at me or stuffed mean notes in my locker. Just because I'd been accepted into the program by the college didn't mean that the student body had accepted that the world was changing. Male witches were becoming part of the Dominion. Maybe someday the world at large would realize it. "It's easier to focus on my studies now. And Gabe says he always needs help at the bar. Having extra money doesn't hurt and the tips are nice. Even if I don't make near as much as you."

Sei's expression said he knew the truth about why I gave up sports but didn't call me on it. I smoothed the wrinkles out of my pants, got up from the bed, and offered him my hand. The tremble had started again along with the whipping wail of the wind. I think he did feel the power growing, but was used to having so much flowing around and through him it was hard to focus on just one thing. "We should get food." I glanced at his wrist, realizing he wasn't wearing his tracker. "You took off your bracelet?"

"Yeah, Gabe says we won't be going back to the cabin. The owner was going to retrieve the rest of our stuff as soon as he could."

It made sense since they wouldn't be going anywhere. I glanced down at mine and rubbed at it. Was it odd that it felt cold? Maybe that was just the plastic coating. I'd never been much for wearing jewelry. "Let's get you food. Maybe some soup." I pulled Sei toward the door.

"Jamie won't let me in the kitchen. It wasn't clean, so I started to clean it. But he wouldn't let me. The chef had a fit 'cause I said his kitchen was dirty. He probably won't cook for me." He shook his head like he'd been horrified. "But you should have seen it. There were piles of crumbs on the counter, dirty dishes, stains in the sink, and the grill..." He shuddered. "It was awful."

"Okay. Let's go down and sit by the fire. I'll bring you food." Maybe some tea or cocoa if I could find it.

Chapter Nine

Jamie

I DID my best to examine the body without touching it too much. I worried that if there was an investigation later, I'd be tied to it because they'd found a fiber or some other CSI crap from my search. I was in training to be a nurse, not an ME. There really was a difference. I could bandage a cut with my eyes closed, but didn't see dead people all that often. The cursory glance made me think his death wasn't an accident. He had a pretty big crack in the back of his skull. Maybe he'd fallen, hit his head, and frozen to death, but I suspected—after Gabe had told me the area he'd been found was soaked in blood—that it'd been a toss-up whether he'd bled to death first or the cold got him.

With him lying in the corner of the sled garage covered in a couple ski blankets, I wondered why someone would want to kill the maintenance man. Had he seen something he shouldn't have? Had he just been in the way? Or was it really an accident?

"The cold has pretty much killed the smell of anything on him other than death,"

Gabe whispered to me. "Sei might be able to smell someone else on him..."

"I'm not letting Sei anywhere near a dead body," I told him immediately.

"I agree." Gabe glanced around at the sleds. Most of them were taken apart by now from Hans's attempts to fix them. I suspected the man knew very little about the machines and shouldn't have been trying to fix anything. "It's not really safe for anyone to be out on the sleds anyway. Maybe I should go for help."

I shook my head, not wanting to imagine how Sei would react when he learned that Gabe had left the lodge without him to trek hundreds of miles through barren wilderness to try to get help. "Sei needs you." And Gabe looked like shit. Tired, like he hadn't been sleeping well enough. I knew he had enough blood because I'd brought several cases of QuickLife with us and handed it off to Hans to store for Gabe before we left for the cabin the first day.

He sighed. "He might be in danger."

"But safer with us." I shivered at the idea of someone taking over Sei again. Matthew and Andrew had been idiots to kidnap him. He was not only a level-five earth witch, he was Pillar. He could have brought the forest down around them. Of course

Matthew being a null had helped. I had a theory about death magnifying the powers of a born null that I'd sent off to my aunt in California. She'd said she'd have someone look into it. There was a lot of unknown, or at least unreleased, information about magic. Things that could be very dangerous. I'd also suggested that they train all witches in all elements so they wouldn't be so blind when it came to magic that was not specifically in their element, but had yet to hear a reply on that initiative. Kelly's instance of the magic in the air had me searching for it. Maybe if there were other ways to detect it...

"And if Kelly is involved?" Gabe insisted.

"It's not willingly," I defended.

"You think compulsion or a spell?" There wasn't really a question at this point that someone was using Kelly's power. There was too much water at play, and his feelings about the storm being unnatural made us both look at him with worry.

"Compulsion you could fix," I pointed out. "If you bit him."

"Not happening," Gabe cut me off.

"Even to stop the storm?"

"We don't know enough to go there. It could be a spell." Gabe glanced down at my bracelet. "I wonder how far those trackers really go?"

I frowned at the rubber watch-like tracker. "You think there's something up?"

He shrugged, brushed back his jacket sleeves to show me he wasn't wearing his, and glanced back to remind me we weren't alone. Hans paced near the door, fiddling with a small weather radio, trying to get reception. "We should go back in," he told us. "It's starting to come down again. I've got a couple of satellite phones in the lodge. We'll keep trying those."

"Better safe than sorry," Gabe said. I realized he was speaking more to me than to Hans. I nodded at them both and followed them out the door. I pretended to shove my hands in the giant front pocket of my coat, but fumbled to take off the wristband.

The wind blew hard at us until we reached the door. It was unlocked now. Hans again shook his head at the door. "Not sure how it got locked like that earlier. It's solid oak, made from a tree that fell twenty years ago." He frowned at the damaged lock. I'd popped the whole thing out of the door like a knob of wood sliding free. He'd jerry-rigged it back into place, but it would need either a new lock or a new door when the storm finally died down.

"Sorry about the door," I told him. I wondered at that moment, clutching the quickly chilling bracelet in my jacket pocket, if someone had borrowed my power. A glance at Gabe and we shared a look of understanding. There was something pretty dark at play here. I wondered just how much the owners of the lodge knew about it. With the howling wail of the wind outside, I figured we'd give it one more night before going to the extreme of sending Gabe for help and leaving Sei, Kelly, and I behind to possibly fight off a very powerful madman. I hoped the fear in my gut was unfounded, but the apprehension in Gabe's eyes echoed my unease. Something wasn't right, and we were stuck in the middle of it.

Kelly

GETTING SEI into a chair by the fire with food had been harder than I originally thought. Neither Jamie nor Gabe was in the lodge. Mrs. Gossner said they'd gone to the garage and were putting Ron, the dead maintenance guy, in there until help could come. The second storm was blowing in like another snow twister on a warpath.

The kitchen, while not as bad as most college dorm rooms, did show the signs of not being as well tended as it should have been. I asked the cook for several very specific things that wouldn't have to be cooked on the dirty grill. A clean knife and cutting board shouldn't have been too much to ask for, but the he gave me a disgruntled huff and walked off to find what I asked for.

Hans had already fixed the front door, shaking his head as to why it had been locked to begin with. Mrs. Gossner expressed apologies about it. The whole thing made me wonder just who wanted to ensure we wouldn't get back inside before the storm. I gripped Sei's hand and was determined to keep him close to me.

He had tried to follow me into the kitchen, twice. He didn't want others staring at him, and Cat had already asked him where Jamie was. Con glared from across the room like he already knew Sei intimately. Every time I got between them, his eyes lit up, and he smiled an invitation my way. I wasn't going there.

Sei vibrated like a cord about to snap. And with no other option, I became the buffer that separated him from the world. By the time the two older men returned to the lodge, Sei was in my lap reading a romance novel, sipping cocoa, nibbling on an egg, avocado, and tomato sandwich, and wrapped in a borrowed blanket. The wind slashed around the outside of the lodge, whipping up so much snow the windows appeared covered in fog. I shivered from the pressure and clung to Sei like he had clung to me so many times before. Nausea swirled in my gut, making it impossible for me to eat. And once again I couldn't get warm. Even sitting next to the fireplace, curled up beside Sei, I shivered.

"Everything okay?" Gabe asked as he leaned in close and kissed Sei lightly.

"We're good," I said.

Sei glanced back at me, then up at Gabe, his eyes narrowed with that observant nature of his. He didn't believe me for a second, but he also wasn't going to call me out on the lie. After all, what were best friends for? Sei stretched and whispered to me, "Come to me if you need to."

I nodded, hugged him, and let Gabe lead him toward the stairs. At least one of us would get lucky tonight.

Jamie dropped into the chair next to me. He looked tired, beyond tired.

"So was it the maintenance guy?"

"Yeah." He slid the rubber band out of his hair, which he must have put up again while he'd been working on the sleds, letting the blond length flow through his fingers. It reminded me of the dreams I'd been having. He looked really tired. "Appears to have frozen to death, but until we can get out of here, no one will know for sure."

"Do you think it might be something else?"

Jamie just shrugged. His lack of trust still stung.

"Sei already asked if I'd put water in the sleds to try to extend our vacation."

"Yet he was curled up in your lap."

"He has to suspect me. Sei is my best friend, but if I were going to extend our vacation anywhere, it would be a place filled with sunshine and warm blue ocean." I tugged the blanket up around my shoulders and flipped through Sei's abandoned romance. It was the only one he'd brought that wasn't on his reader. "Besides, you were with me the whole time. When exactly would I have done it?"

Jamie nodded, his body sagging deeper into the chair like he was just tired of it all.

"Have you slept more than a few hours? I know I was out before you last night, but you look beat."

He rubbed his eyes. "I'm okay."

I nodded like I believed him.

He stretched back in the chair and let out a huge sigh. "You'd tell me, right?"

"About?"

"If you were doing this. Or knew something about it?"

"I did insist we come back here to talk to Sei about the storm. I told you it doesn't feel natural. Not sure what more I can do. I haven't had much training as a witch. Just some basic stuff my mom showed me."

"You have sisters. Didn't they go to witch school?"

"Only rich kids go to witch school. And my sisters are all level two or lower." I winced at the lecture I got from Reanne when I dared to make the news about getting into the Magic Studies program and testing as a level five. She'd accused me of cheating. I'd told her I wouldn't even know how to cheat, which took a lot of wind out of her anger because I was pretty sure she didn't know either. "I'm reading a lot of Sei's old books and asking questions. But it's not the same as growing up with a witch's education."

Jamie seemed to think on it for a few minutes. Cat wandered into the room, saw Jamie, and made a beeline for him. She slid onto the armrest of the chair. Her hair was styled up with sparkling butterfly clips, making her look older. But the pale flowery dress was too shapeless and young if she was trying to go for sophisticated. She leaned over and I caught a whiff of very heavy rose perfume. Sei would have dissolved into a fit of sneezes if he'd been in my place, and she wasn't even leaning over me. I scooted back in my chair, hoping to clear my nose of some of the smell. Her skin had that perfect sheen only too much makeup could give a girl, and when she put her hand on Jamie's arm, I feared she'd turn his sleeve "perky peach." Plastic indeed.

"Have you eaten? I saved some soup for you," she said to Jamie, stroking down his arm lightly. "What a horrible day. I'm sure you could use some food and rest."

"You hungry?" Jamie asked me. I blinked at him, wondering if he was that clueless or purposely putting her off. Cat flailed with momentary panic at the thought of me joining them.

"Nah. I'm good." I waved the book at him. "Just going to sit here a little longer and read about some great warrior's throbbing rod. You go get some *soup*." I was pretty sure soup wasn't what Cat wanted to feed to him.

Jamie's lips twitched, hiding a smile. He got up and followed Cat out of the room. He even let her put her hand in the crook of his arm. I shook my head at the whole scene and wondered if I ever tried that hard. Jamie was hot and I kind of liked his dry sense of humor, but I wasn't about to throw myself in his lap with a big sign blinking over my head that said "Take me." Hell, that might not even work. The guy seemed oblivious to everyone's flirting. But that wasn't quite true either since I'd watched him at the bar deftly fend off wayward admirers. So maybe he just didn't get flirting from another guy.

I shrugged to myself, happy the thought had at least pushed some of the cold away. The late evening nap had stolen any desire to go back to sleep already. Maybe if I read for a little while, I could keep the growing, raging storm from overtaking my senses again. I opened the book. Sei did like his smut...

I actually lost some time reading Sei's novel. The struggles of the characters' world seemed a simple escape, and before long I was so lost in their story I was worried if they'd make it out alive. Fuck. My heart pounded when one character got shot and his lover rushed to save him only to black out. If it hadn't been so eerily familiar, it might not have had me gripping the side of the chair. Suddenly I knew why my best friend had a library full of this stuff. Maybe he'd let me borrow more. Fuck, these characters better make it out of this novel to have another one. Their sex scenes were hot.

The sound of laughter floated to me from the kitchen, interrupting a tense hospital scene. Once again I was struck by the lack of guests and emptiness of the lodge. I was alone by the fire and couldn't even recall Con coming in at any point. I glanced at my tracker watch, which said it was after ten. Okay, it was a little late, but still it wasn't like people had to get up to work in the morning.

I marked my page with a fresh tissue, rose, and headed for the kitchen. Jamie had one of the keys, but we hadn't spoken about the sleeping arrangements yet. I didn't want him to freak because I preferred to sleep naked. Sei didn't care, mostly because he was used to seeing my bare ass around. Jamie might not be so kind about curling up to a naked gay boy. Separate beds was one thing, having to share one would be too much for most guys.

Jamie and Cat sat at the counter looking like an old married couple. She leaned over him, flirting, touching, and making jokes that had him grinning ear to ear. Her rail-thin body and tiny breasts were nearly plastered to his side. I had to fight to keep from growling at her to stop touching him. *Damn.*

I had no reason to be jealous. He wasn't mine and had made no indication that he was even interested. But I'd never felt the green-eyed monster so strongly, not even when I thought I had a thing for Sei and found out he and Gabe were an item. My throat felt tight, and instead of speaking to them, I turned and headed to my room, taking the stairs two at a time.

Constantine leaned against my door.

"Go away," I told him.

"Do you really want to go to bed alone? Your beefcake friend has his own company." He gripped my shirt and yanked me close enough for me to breathe in his soapy scent. My heart pounded, and the heat of him made my cock swell. Stupid body. "We were so good together."

"Until you fucked me over."

Con sighed. "Remember that summer camping trip? It rained for four days, but we still snuck out of our parents' tents to jerk off together."

"That's just it, Con. It was always about the sex. I'm done with that. I didn't even know you had a sister. How much of a relationship is that?" Done with being used, I pushed him away and put my key in the lock. Con's hand fell over mine, not letting me open the door. He pressed his front into my back, his erection hard against my ass crack. He was no bodybuilder, but he had half a foot on me. Though, unlike Sei, martial arts gave me an added edge.

Sweeping a quick turn and twist of his wrist, I slammed Con into the wall beside the door, pinning his arm behind his back at an awkward angle. He yelped in surprise.

"I'm really not kidding."

"Fine. Whatever. Let me go."

I kicked my door open, shoved him away, then stepped into the room and shut it firmly. Watching from the peephole, I waited until Con wandered away, shaking his head and grumbling something I couldn't understand.

The night had already been a wash. And since I had the room to myself, I figured I'd enjoy it. I cranked up the heat, stripped out of everything, and sank into bed with the romance novel. Sadly, the bed didn't smell like Jamie, but I hugged a pillow to my chest and pretended it was him I cuddled as I read. For some reason the warrior kissing the girl in the novel made me remember one terrible day in school with Con.

CONVICTION

We spent the weekend together and had sex often enough that I didn't need much for prep anymore. We'd even bought a book that illustrated different positions for us to try. Con wasn't agile enough for a lot of them, and no matter how much I asked, he had yet to bottom.

I sighed and tucked my books away in my locker. Practice had been canceled today due to rain. Stupid Minnesota weather. Searching for Con had proved useless, as his car seemed to have vanished from its usual spot in the lot when I'd looked for it before I came in from lunch. Study hour would drag without him.

"Hey, Harding!" Derrick, a track teammate, waved from down the hall. "We're meeting at Peppicino's tomorrow. You game?"

"Sure. Are we running?"

"Normal loop, back for lunch. We'll start about nine, rain or shine."

"I'll be there," *I said, pausing to deliver the required hand-slap, low-five handshake.*

"Tell Con. He was too busy sticking his tongue down Ann Pugget's throat when I passed."

My body froze as my brain seemed to go white with shock. "You sure it was Con?"

"Yeah. His ugly tattooed puss is hard to miss. Is Ann your girl or something? 'Cause that's so not cool." *Derrick flipped his black hair back and glared at the hallway behind him.* "I can go with you—"

"No. It's nothing. He just didn't tell me he was seeing anyone. It was sort of a shock." *More than a shock. A betrayal. He'd had his cock up my ass just eight hours before, telling me he loved me.*

"Yeah. But Ann's got a rep for being an easy spreader. He's probably just looking for tail." *Derrick patted me on the back.* "See you tomorrow, K."

"Yeah. Thanks." *My legs felt like concrete when I headed down the hall toward Con's locker. The walls seemed to be closing in as I moved, my sight getting fuzzy.*

He stood at his locker, body close to Ann's, hand in hers, smiles on their faces. I had almost reached them when the world dropped out from under me. All I remember was the alarm on Ann's pretty face and Con's head turning my way.

When I awoke I was in the nurse's office, lying on an uncomfortable cot. Con sat beside the bed. His eyes were wide and worried, and his legs fidgeted in a random tapping.

"Hey," he said, noticing I was awake. "How are you feeling?"

"What happened?" My lungs hurt, and I struggled to pull in another breath.

He reached back, grabbed something on the desk, and a second later my inhaler was pressed to my lips. "Asthma attack. Bad one. Your mom's on the way."

I didn't remember having an attack, but the tightness of my lungs proved is words true enough. His fingers caressed my arm absently, and he finally tucked my inhaler in my pocket. The feel of him touching me so tenderly hurt. My eyes burned with tears I fought not to show.

"Everything okay, K?" he asked like he hadn't done anything wrong.

"You kissed Ann."

He shrugged. "Gotta keep up the show. You know my parents would freak. You're still my number one."

Footsteps crossed the room, and the curtain slid back. My mom smiled at me with concern. I'd never been so happy for the interruption. If she noticed the tension, she did well at ignoring it, even making Con go back to *class. But the day had already been ingrained in my head as the beginning of the end.*

I shoved the book onto the nightstand, clicked off the light, and hit the pillow. Seeing Con again was really messing with my head. I'd never be anyone's dirty little secret again.

Chapter Ten

Jamie

Cat's smile was easy and her eyes bright. She clung to my side like most Dominion girls did when they heard I was from the second wave and related by blood to someone in the first wave. Stupid aristocracy, at least I could make it work for me. Thankfully my sister Hanna never acted this way. Since she was now a high court Dominion judge, she had more right than most to act like the world owed her something. Only she never did. She put the law and people first, was even married to a non-Dominion girl, which sort of made her a persona non grata to most of her coworkers. Maybe it was just how they were raised. Hanna didn't crave power and money. She created those things for herself, and I was so proud of her.

"So how long are you and Constantine staying?" I asked, ignoring the way Cat's hand caressed my arm. She'd been staring at me for a while now, eyes all over me like I was some side of beef she was thinking of purchasing.

"Awhile, I guess." She didn't seem to like talking about her brother. Bringing up his name had made her flinch twice already. I poured her a glass of red wine, watching her sip at it. She'd already downed two glasses. Hans apparently had no issue with any of his guests taking what they wanted from the liquor cabinet, a fact for which I was grateful.

"It's good to see you're so close. I don't know what I would do without my little brother." My words made her cringe, but she covered it well. "Then there's my sister Hanna. She's pregnant, so there will be a baby coming soon. We have an appointment next week to look at the ultrasound."

Cat flipped her hair back and put on an inquiring smile. "Babies are wonderful. Does she know if it's a girl yet?"

Because all that mattered was that the baby was a girl. "We'll know soon." The baby would be born whether it was a girl or a boy. "So you and Con are related to the Gossners?"

"Yeah, Hans is my mom's brother. But Louise wasn't Dominion."

I smiled at her like she was the most fascinating person on earth and leaned against the counter beside her. "Must have been hard on your family. Expecting him to marry Dominion."

"It was a huge scandal. People still talk about it."

I'd never heard anything about it, so they couldn't have been that high up in the Dominion. I heard a lot of gossip from Hanna about the Dominion aristocracies. Admittedly more about earth than any other element, but if something big happened—like Tanaka giving birth to a baby boy instead of aborting him the second she knew he was male—was big news. A first-wave family member not marrying someone else from the first wave would have been pretty big news. "What element are you?"

"Air. My great-grandmother was one of the most amazing storm makers of the twentieth century." She leaned in close, resting her head on her hand and staring at me dreamily. She smelled a bit like freshly aired laundry and flowers. It wasn't unpleasant, but it was a little overpowering. "Earth and air are a great combination."

Storm makers. Well, wasn't that interesting? "So what level are you?"

"I tested at a three. But that was years ago."

"You don't work for the Dominion?"

She looked away. Shame. No, she didn't work for the Dominion. Which meant if she was a three, she didn't have a lot of control of her power. But level threes of any element were fairly common in the bowels of the Dominion. Paper pushers and the like. If she hadn't even made it to an entry-level position, then maybe her family was more out of favor than she let on. "I'm thinking of taking over my uncle's business."

"The lodge, you mean?"

She nodded and smiled at me. "It's so peaceful up here. Away from the city and all the people. You seem like the sort of guy who likes nature." She traced my bicep. "A strong man to cut and carry wood. The lodge makes good money. Lots of tourists in the summer and quiet in the winter."

Except for the raging storm outside that would have been more commonplace in Antarctica than northern Minnesota. "Have you ever made it rain?" I brought her attention back to her power again.

She shrugged like it wasn't a big deal. "Any air witch of reasonable power can make it rain. It's just a gathering of the mist into the clouds. As long as there's enough moisture, it's easy."

I grinned like I was an idiot when it came to magic. "So you don't actually control the water portion of rain. Just the air?"

"Yes. Wind can heat it into a mist or cool it to snow."

I nodded. Very few were powerful enough to cool it to snow. And a level three wouldn't have that kind of power. "Have you ever made it snow?"

She frowned at me. "No."

"How about your brother. Can he make it snow?"

"He's male. He can't even make the wind blow." There was no mistaking the venom in her voice this time.

"My brother's a pretty powerful earth witch," I pointed out, smiling like it was an everyday occurrence for a male to be Pillar.

She frowned at me. "I've heard that was Tanaka's doing. That he's really not that powerful. She's just trying to get back at all the people who've made fun of her all these years for only having a boy. Faked his results and spun the media."

"I've seen his power," I told her. "He could make the Earth split in half if he wanted to."

Her frown deepened, a little bit of fear entered her eyes, and I was okay with that. Sei should scare people, especially anyone who didn't feel like he was good enough to be Pillar.

"I've met a lot of witches," I said, slightly amused. "Never met a stronger witch than Sei. Hanna's pretty powerful, and having his baby. I can only imagine how amazing their baby will be."

She sucked in a deep breath and took a step back. "I'm sure she'll be perfect," Cat said with a forced smile. I watched her fiddle with her necklace nervously and glance toward the window when the wind rattled the pane. Mhmm. Suddenly Kelly's insistence of the storm being not natural didn't sound so farfetched.

Kelly

PANIC RIPPED me out of sleep when the bed moved beside me. Fear that Con might have gotten into the room kicked my fight instinct into high gear. I brought up a quick knee in the dark, aiming to hurt, but got a grunt when it hit a thick and solid thigh.

"You didn't kick like that last night," Jamie complained.

I opened an eye and stared through the minimal light at him. He stared back, wearing nothing but boxers and kneeling on the edge of the bed. He looked exhausted, dark circles around his eyes and a tired set to his shoulders. He frowned at me. "You going to share the bed or lay in the middle all night?"

I rolled over, kicked off the blankets, and snuggled into my pillow, giving him a view of my bare ass.

He sighed but lifted the blankets and buried himself beneath them on his side of the bed. "You were right about the storm. I'm pretty sure at this point it's not natural."

"How much snow is there?"

"Seven feet without the drifts. Ten where the wind is blowing it. They may need to fly us out of here. I'm surprised the power is still working, but I know Hans has a lot of backup generators and fuel.

"The other thing I'm finding a little suspicious is that there are no other guests here but us and the Opal siblings, who just happen to be related to the Gossners," Jamie pointed out.

I nodded. "Yeah and Cat's power is air." I turned back to face him, feeling more than a little raw with all my old memories of Con running through my head. "Do you really think it's me?"

"It wouldn't be you alone. And maybe you don't even want to do it. But maybe Roman bit you. They never found his remains. Or there could be a spell. I don't have much witch training either. Just what I read in books. Gabe said he'd talk to Sei about that option, but I don't think the Dominion teaches stuff like this. So even Sei may not know."

"You can search me for bites if you want."

He shook his head, looking indifferent. I didn't want him to be indifferent. I wanted him to care. There had to be more to this man than just a guy who obsessed over his little brother. Why wouldn't he let me in? And how could we get back what had been stolen from us? "Roman would know to heal them. And you might not be aware that you're helping him."

"So what do you want me to do? How can I prove I'm not doing this?"

"I wish I knew. I wouldn't blame you for that anyway. Matthew made Sei stab Gabe. Vampire power is crazy strong. If you are helping him somehow, we'll have to find a way to unlink your powers and stop the storm."

"But only Matthew's death stopped his hold over Sei, and Andrew Roman is a lot more powerful than Matthew was," I pointed out.

"If it's him at all." He sighed, settling deeper into the pillow. "All we have is speculation at this point."

"Fuck." I groaned. None of this was fair. Could someone use my power without me knowing it? The truth was probably yes, since I knew so little about magic—a failing of the Dominion. I laid my head on Jamie's shoulder and set my hand on his bare stomach. He didn't flinch or pull away. In fact he seemed to relax into my touch.

I leaned in close, loving those big chocolate eyes of his as they widened, and kissed him. The press of my lips against his was little more than a chaste kiss until he parted his lips and opened for me, letting my tongue explore the taste of him. The mint of toothpaste and hint of him made me hard. He made no move to kiss me or push me away, so I stopped.

"Am I even on the same planet as you?" I had to ask. "You can't be this oblivious. A kiss is a kiss. You have to know I'm interested."

"I'm sorry, Kelly."

Sure. Everyone was sorry. Poor Kelly. "Whatever." I went back to my side of the bed and huddled around my pillow, doing my best to ignore him. My cock was hard and didn't want to go back to sleep. My brain kept cycling through scenarios as I tossed and turned.

Jamie slept like a bear in hibernation beside me, unbothered by all my floundering. I wondered if it was the first time since we'd arrived that he'd really slept. I felt bad for dragging them all on this vacation, even if I hadn't been the one doing the planning.

I sighed and stared at the ceiling for a while, remembering the taste of Jamie's lips. Was there a way to get him to see me as more than just his little brother's best friend? I'd be twenty-one in less than four months. Twenty-one wasn't a kid to anyone. Not really. Old enough to vote, die in a war, or buy my own house; it had to be old enough to not be a kid to Jamie. I just had to make him understand.

I turned over and hit my pillow in frustration. Jamie didn't stir, but I did spend some time admiring him. Even in the dark with almost no moonlight, I could see the outline of his thick, muscled shoulders all the way down to his toned thighs. I ached to trace the long trail of muscle, taste his skin, maybe even kiss the protests out of him. Fuck. I was so gone for him.

Just after 2:00 a.m., I decided I'd had enough, got up, threw on some sweats and a tee, and made my way downstairs. The lobby and lounge area was dark and empty. Light in the kitchen drew me like a beacon. I prayed it wasn't Con and that the lodge had some sort of ice cream tucked away even in the dead of winter. I needed a sugar fix like Sei needed a piece of dark chocolate after a therapy session.

Gabe sat at the large kitchen counter, fussing with the CB radio.

"Still not getting a signal?" I asked.

"No one's replied yet."

"Sei sleeping?"

"Yes. Sleepytime Tea puts him out in less than a half an hour. I'm hoping he sleeps most of the night. The winter does funny things to his power so he's been pretty low on energy anyway. I had thought if this vacation worked, I'd talk him into another one, only someplace sunny." He frowned at the radio. "Pretty sure he won't want to leave home again any time soon." He smiled faintly. "My apartment has become his safe place."

"That's good, though. When he's close to you, he's good. Happy. Stable. Mostly." I thought about it for a minute. There was nothing really wrong with Sei. Nothing that could be fixed with a magic pill and a good night's sleep at least. His anxiety was a lifelong condition, and the abuse he'd suffered made it worse. Only support from someone who loved him could help. And friends. I hoped I was helping him some. "He's healing. You're helping him heal."

Gabe threw me a happy smile. It was odd that he looked tired too. Had ever since we'd pulled him out of the ground once Sei had led us to his body. I know he slept more during the day, even cut back his hours at the bar so he could spend time with Sei or rest. But none of it seemed to be helping. Maybe he needed the vacation more than Sei did. After all, how many people pretty much died and were dragged back to life? I couldn't imagine it was an easy process.

"You okay?" I asked him.

He nodded. "Just worried about Sei. Always worried about Sei."

"Bet you had no idea the trouble you were getting into when you met him." I grinned at him.

"Not by half." He sighed.

I dug into the freezer and found a giant bucket of ice cream, then scooped some into a bowl. Sucking on the spoon, I put the pail away and sat down across from Gabe to devour my treat. "He's good. I promise. No nightmares. Sleeps better than I do. His back is getting better. Therapy seems to be helping with the shakes." There was a bit of heaven in every bowl of mint chocolate chip ice cream. I wondered if I could sneak this up to Sei and polish it off with him. Maybe if I hid it in the back of the freezer, we could share it tomorrow.

"You're as bad as Sei with the sweets."

Actually, the habit had grown since I'd moved in with Sei. Now I just worked out more to cover for all his amazing cooking. "You must have lots of sex to keep him so skinny."

Gabe smiled, looking wistful. "Never enough for Sei, though his libido is not as supercharged as it was four years ago. Back then he'd show up at my door and jump me. Now he does sweet shy things like start a bath for me or rub my shoulders when he wants sex. I tell him it's romance; he snorts and says it's foreplay." He shook his head and I laughed. That sounded like Sei, all right. "He's actually still five pounds under his normal weight. I was hoping the trip would help with that, but he's not been eating much here."

The kitchen was clean. I wondered if Jamie had cleaned it, as even the grill looked spotless. If Sei woke early enough, he could probably cook in here without having a heart attack. "Cuisine hasn't exactly been five star," I told Gabe. "But the ice cream is excellent." I shoved another giant spoonful into my mouth.

He ran his hands through his blond hair, making it stick up in a disarray of messy curls, then played with the radio dials again. He seemed to think for a while. "I'm more tired than I should be. That's why we're here. I probably should have researched this trip more, gotten references, had a backup plan. I'm always putting him in danger."

"It's not your fault." Why people seemed to be drawn to hurt Sei, I didn't know, but it wasn't right for Gabe to blame himself. "If you want to blame anyone, blame me. I suggested the trip." I swirled the ice cream in my bowl until it looked more like soup. "But I'm not doing this storm thing. Just so you know. At least not willingly. Jamie suggested there might be some sort of spell pulling energy from me." I had been more tired than usual since we arrived at the lodge that first day, but did that really mean I was involved in this storm somehow?

"I didn't think you were."

"But it's not normal. I feel the water. It's like it's being tossed around carelessly. I'm just not strong enough to stop it. Or maybe not that I'm not strong enough, but more that I don't know where to start?" It really bothered me that I didn't have the training to even know where the storm was coming from. Was there a way to focus the snow to find the center of the power? I'd never used it to find someone I didn't know. Usually I had to focus on the person in order to direct the snow to tell me what it saw. Otherwise opening myself to the expanse of a snowstorm would drain the last of my energy fast. When I'd waited in my car searching for Sei a few weeks ago, I'd never remembered flinging my power wide for so long before. I'd eaten a dozen protein bars to try to keep up my energy, but in the end I'd slept almost twenty-four hours once Sei was rescued, lost ten pounds from the exertion, and took more than a week just to feel like I wasn't walking in a dazed exhaustion. And the search area was only a few miles wide. This was hundreds of miles of endless forest to search with no known focal point. I sighed, frustrated with not knowing what to do.

"Sei and I talked about it before he went to bed. Air is at play, which probably means Roman again." He sounded matter-of-fact. "But Roman shouldn't have this kind of power. If he were to test, he'd be around Jamie's level of power, not yours or Sei's. I'm not even sure his power is natural. Perhaps inherited like Jamie's."

"Does that really matter? Him not being born with the power?"

Gabe nodded. He paused, closed his eyes, and took a heavy breath, which was unusual since he was a vampire. He rubbed the bridge of his nose, exhaustion obviously getting to him too. So much for our vacation. "People who inherit power have a harder time controlling it. It's like giving a toddler a gun. He may have the strength to fire it, but there is no skill. I've heard training can help, but there's always a difference between a natural-born witch and a power-enhanced one."

"Do they teach that in the Dominion Magic Studies training?" I had to ask.

"Not that I know of. I've seen that myself a few times. I think if you stood Jamie and Sei beside each other and asked them to do the same low-level spell, you'd see a big difference, not so much from the level of their power, but from control. Sei's had his whole life to rein in the power and let it go at a trickle. Jamie wasn't meant for that sort of ability. It's what makes his shifts harder, less natural. Even on the new moon."

"What if Roman has others helping him? Like other air witches. Could he borrow this kind of power from them? Use it to fuel the storm?"

"Not the same. Now that Sei is my focus, I understand his much better. Most witches draw the power into themselves and can only expend so much. They can create a pool of stored energy to use for spells, but it's limited. Several witches in a coven can even create a community pool of energy. But even then they can only hold so much. For Sei, it's like he's standing in the middle of a ley line all the time or is a lightning rod that's constantly pulling in storms. He has a never-ending supply of power. Most witches are selfish and can't control the power they do have, so lending it to someone else would be unheard of. Sei, of course, can do it without a passing thought. Maybe that's a Pillar thing? I've never known any other Pillars personally. The way he controls his power is like the subtle strength of a flower opening its petals to let in the sunlight."

I stared at him for a while, knowing why Sei had such a thing for the guy. Sure Gabe was hot, but he was also smart, and always thinking.

"What?"

"You're kind of poetic." And sappy.

He rolled his eyes at me.

"So you think Roman's still alive." There had been a massive explosion that had taken out a barn and likely its occupants, which had been Andrew Roman, Matthew Pierson, and maybe, Sam Mueller, all men who wanted to harm Sei at one time. Sam had been under vampire influence, but the other two were pure evil in my opinion.

"The police found Roman's badge at the house, but no sign of his remains."

"And Sam survived."

"Poor kid is still trying to figure himself out. Sei hasn't heard anything in a few weeks. I have a private investigator out looking for him, but he's gone to ground." He flinched at the term, I didn't understand why, but it was a reaction I couldn't miss. "Hiding. Probably afraid of legal action."

"Will you press charges against him when you find him?" I asked.

"No. But he needs help. Emotional help. He's been through a lot of the same things Sei has."

"At least Sei has you," I pointed out. As far as I knew, Sam was just another kid Matthew had abused and warped with his madness. Now he was alone, trying to figure himself out. I couldn't imagine being in his shoes. The wind howled, and the lodge creaked. It felt closer now, almost tugging at me. I silently tried to reach back, trace the storm to its origin, but all I got was a wall of ice blowing in the wind. I shivered. "It's building again."

"The storm?"

"Yeah."

"You should go back to bed. Get some rest. Not sleeping will make it feel worse. I'll keep trying to reach civilization. If anything, I can go out in the storm and walk somewhere. I won't freeze to death, and I can bury myself in the snow in the daytime. It'll be uncomfortable, but I can manage. We'll be fine."

I put my hands over my heart and batted my eyelashes. "My hero."

He laughed. "Go to bed, Harding."

But I didn't like the idea of Gabe going out there alone. Were there any another options? I'd been skiing, snowshoeing, and snowmobiling my whole life and never been stuck like this before. It had me thinking about the snowmobiles. All the ones here were damaged by water, but you had to be pretty close to do that sort of damage, pull the water out of the air to flood a tank or something. Though the Ski-Doo at the cabin was buried with snow, how likely would it be that whoever was sabotaging our stuff would know it was there and travel far enough to do it?

"Something still on your mind?" Gabe asked when I didn't head toward the bedrooms.

"I was just thinking about the snowmobiles. If you do end up walking, remember there's a sled at the cabin still. That one might not be filled with water. Just buried in snow."

He stared at me for a minute. "Okay. That might be an option."

I turned to head back to the room, but paused. "I would never hurt Sei. You know that, right?"

"Sei trusts you. Just remember how often that trust has been violated. The next one who comes against him, I will destroy." Gabe's voice was cold and for the first time I caught a glimpse of the vampire he truly was. I took a step back. Knowing in the back of my mind that he could be ruthless was one thing. Seeing it was another. But I knew he only had Sei's best interest at heart.

"Understood and agreed." Despite being tempted to ask if I could curl up with Sei just to try to get some sleep, I didn't. I made my way back to my room and contemplated the blowing snow. The icy crystals couldn't give me anything more than vague impressions. Trying to feel for more sucked more energy out of me. Maybe I'd sleep now. Even if it was nightmare-filled sleep, some had to be better than none, right?

Chapter Eleven

Jamie

I WOKE up to find Kelly gone. The first instinct of panic made me roll over to see if he was just in the bathroom, but the door was open and the light off. It was almost 3:00 a.m. Where could he be? Maybe Sei's room?

Throwing on a T-shirt and grabbing a key, I tiptoed down the hall to Gabe and Sei's room, using the spare Gabe had given me to open the door. Sei slept curled around Gabe's pillow, but otherwise alone. I watched him sleep for a few minutes, marveling at how young and vulnerable he looked. It made me tense to think he was alone, but I knew Gabe was never far. And since Sei was Gabe's focus now, they were forever bound. Still, I couldn't help but worry.

How many times had Sei been hurt by others? Used like he was nothing more than a puppy someone could throw away when they were done? Abused by the people who claimed to love him. First Tanaka, who always treated him with an iron fist, shaping his life for him while condemning him at every turn. Then Matthew, who convinced my brother he was nothing more than a hole to fuck, making him fear commitment, love, and emotion of all kind. And then Brock, who had been the first real friend that Sei had made in his college years.

Now there was Kelly—who spent endless hours with Sei—had convinced us all to trust him, let him into our lives. He knew all of Gabe's secrets and had a key to the underground apartment, which put Gabe in danger. Kelly slept just feet from Sei. Had access to their food and water and could stage an accident at any time. He'd wormed his way so deeply into our lives that even I'd begun to wonder how I'd existed before him. I couldn't help but wonder if he was a plant.

He'd been part of the Ascendance—a group of male witches trying to gain equality in less than moral ways. He'd also been a friend of Brock's. Did that mean he knew? The police said Kelly had been on Brock's hit list, only he hadn't made it to him. What if it was staged? My gut hurt at the idea. I *liked* Kelly. More than liked him. Cared about him, worried about him, wanted to see him happy. I really didn't want him to be another bad guy in Sei's life.

But the snow and the storms would need a strong water witch to create them. How easy it would have been for him to put water in the lines of the sleds. He was a level-five witch. He could probably drown a man where he stood without breaking a sweat.

Sure, he didn't have much training, but that made a witch more dangerous, didn't it? And who knew what the Ascendance was teaching the male witches it recruited. I'd never attempted to join, fearing it would alienate me from Sei further, but now I wondered if that was a mistake.

Could Kelly be part of it all? Maybe he'd been bitten by Roman months ago. Forced to befriend Sei and dig so deeply into our lives that we wouldn't suspect him. There could be more than one reason he wasn't in bed at this hour. Was everyone but Gabe and I out to hurt Sei? As much as it hurt to imagine Kelly was involved, I couldn't think of another way this was all happening.

Sei had to be shown the truth. We couldn't trust strangers anymore. Kelly wasn't family. Him not being in bed when everyone else was meant he had to be off doing something to hurt us all. My gut churned with unease, my brain telling me that Kelly couldn't be involved. He'd had thousands of opportunities to hurt Sei and never once been anything but a friend. *Fuck.*

I shut the door and headed back to my room. It had to be him. Someone might have been pulling power from him, but he'd feel that too, right? He'd have to know something was up. The storm's not natural, he told me. No, it wasn't natural.

Someone wanted to hurt Sei again, and they were using Kelly to do it. Anger welled up in my chest until it was hard to breathe. We were finding a new normal. Sure it wasn't perfect or all rainbows, but we were starting to find a normal life without all the crazies. Was that too much to ask for? Kelly and Sei were friends. Sei needed friends badly, guys his own age who didn't look at him for sex or to use his power. Dammit, I wanted Kelly to be a good guy.

The storm outside raged as bad as it had last night. Wind howling like a banshee and cold saturating everything. Magic penetrated the air, filling it with malice and pain. Why hadn't I felt it before? Now that I recognized it, I could feel it send an ache down into my bones. My abandoned tracker bracelet lay on the nightstand. Was that it? Had it been blocking everything before, making it impossible for an inherited witch like myself to detect the magic? It was unmistakable now. Air, for sure. I wondered where Cat and her brother were.

Where was Kelly? I hated this deep suspicion. I wanted to trust him, wanted him to be family. Why couldn't he just talk to me? If someone was making him do this, I could help. Somehow we'd get him free. The idea that he may be hiding it from me out of fear or something as equally stupid just pissed me off. If anything happened to Sei because of all this, he'd really get to see the bear I was.

The thought stilled me. A deep well of pain burst upward, shattering years of walls and barriers, and cascading through me. I remembered vividly that day that I'd stood over Sei, covered in blood and gore, howling my victory as an animal I'd never changed into before. My world had shifted that day. My heart broken, soul damaged, and happiness ripped away. I'd never cursed my father until that day. His *gift* had been a nightmare. I wasn't meant to be powerful enough to change, to kill. Even if it was to protect my tiny little brother from right-wing crazies. I struggled to breathe for a moment through the pain and anger, trying to find a focus for all the self-hate that had added to my long list of life issues. The eating disorders, the depression and codependence, that I thought I'd finally overcome. Yet they were all still there. Pulsing with renewed life, making my gut churn. The door opened and I suddenly had someone other than myself to aim my rage.

Kelly

I OPENED the door to my shared room and tried to crawl back into bed. Jamie sat up and stared at me. His expression was unreadable. Dark, but mostly empty. I wondered for a moment if he was really awake.

"What?"

"Where did you go?"

"To the kitchen to get a snack."

"It's after 3:00 a.m."

I could tell time, but I tried to keep my snarky comments to myself. "And there's mint chocolate chip in the freezer. Ask Gabe if you don't believe me. He's monkeying with the CB in the kitchen."

"You sure you weren't out tampering with generators or poisoning our food supply?" His tone was colder than the storm blowing outside.

Ow. Where was this coming from? "What the fuck?"

"Stay away from my brother."

My heart skipped a beat. Here it was, his final moment of telling me he didn't trust me. Could I handle it? My soul ached with the idea that any dream of us being together was shattered in that moment. Sure it had only been a dream, but I'd begun to want it. Stupid. Why was I always attracted to men who saw me as nothing more than a burden?

"In case you've forgotten, he's my roommate now. When we get out of this place, his bedroom is less than fifteen feet from mine." I yanked the blankets away from Jamie, threw myself on the bed, and stuffed the covers around me like a shield.

"That just burns you, doesn't it? That he's so close but not interested."

"What the hell has gotten into you tonight?"

"It's after three in the morning, and you're sneaking around. We're trapped in a hotel under more than ten feet of snow, and you have to ask what's wrong with me?"

"I'd say cabin fever. But whatever. I'm going to sleep." I put a pillow over my head and burrowed myself farther into the blankets to try to ignore any more harsh words. He tossed and turned for a while. Hit his pillow and huffed in anger. I wondered at what had really caused his odd mood. I longed to ask Sei if he knew a way to work my way back into Jamie's good graces. He couldn't really be pissed about me not being in the room. One short conversation with Gabe and he could confirm I wasn't off trying to kill us all. So it had to be something else. Misdirected anger. Frustration with himself perhaps for not being able to remove us from what seemed to be a dangerous situation.

After a while he seemed to settle down, and his breathing became even with sleep. His back was turned toward me and displayed strong, tensely wound shoulders that I longed to massage until they relaxed.

Time passed agonizingly slowly. I focused on the storm to get my mind of Jamie. I thought of a million possibilities about how the storm had formed and how to get us out of here alive. Most of the escape plans hinged on finding that last sled undamaged.

We had filled both tanks from fuel cans when we got to the cabins to be sure they wouldn't freeze overnight. In fact, we had two full gas cans that we could strap to one of the sleds if needed. Not safe, but a way to keep from running out. The one Gabe drove back with Sei would have been running low. He'd also parked it in the garage when he returned, so it had been easy prey for whoever was doing the sabotage.

If I got the sled left at the cabin and got to one of the ranger stations, I could get help. Rescue helicopter or whatever. Maybe then everyone would stop looking at me like they were expecting me to be a villain too. Well not everyone. Just Jamie I guess. While Gabe's threat had been filled with vampire venom, it had also been without any real conviction. He didn't believe I was controlling the storm, and I knew Sei didn't either.

The more I thought about it, the more I needed to get to the sled at the cabin.

It was probably close to five in the morning before I got up, tired of trying to sleep, and dressed. I watched Jamie's sleeping form for any sign that he was awake, but his deep, even breaths reassured me that he slept on. After snapping into my snowsuit, I checked the charge on my cell and made my way downstairs. If Gabe was still haunting the kitchen, it'd be a bust, since I'd need food.

When I found the kitchen empty, I felt like I hit the home run with bases loaded in overtime. I stuffed a bag full of nonperishables, strapped it on my back, and took a pair of snowshoes from the rack beside the door.

My cell had a reasonable GPS, even if the signal barely worked, and I knew where to go. The cabins were about four miles to the southwest of the lodge. Easy to reach by ATV in the summer or sled in the winter. Not so much on foot. The whipping wind made me hesitate. But I pulled my goggles down, scarf up, and grabbed an extra pair of gloves. It was going to be a long, cold walk.

I started strong, getting far enough away from the lodge to not even see the lights in the distance just as the sun began to trickle over the horizon. The farther I got from the lodge, the colder I felt. Snow pressed at me, shouting in my head that it wanted to be free from the restless wind. And though I didn't want to expend the extra energy, just to keep moving I had to use a trick my mom had taught me as a kid while swimming: I created a field of calm energy that surrounded me in a sort of bubble. Snow that entered the bubble fell to the ground, free from the wind until I moved away. It was a trick to ease strong currents if I were being pushed around in the water, and it worked well enough on the snow.

It kept the wind from beating at me. But unlike Sei, I couldn't pull energy from the ground. Without running water I was pretty much drawing on a battery that would eventually run dry. Still, I kept moving, pressed strength into the barrier, and fought my way through the heavy snow, which grew denser by the minute.

The sun was high in the sky by the time I reached the cabins. Knowing they'd only been a few miles away from the lodge had kept me walking, even when I was so tired it was hard to stand. The tops of the cabins were hardly distinguishable from the rest of the landscape. Only the chimneys stood out.

I examined the chimney of Sei and Gabe's cabin, found it full of snow, and checked the one I'd shared with Jamie. It was fairly clear. I barely recalled closing the flue before leaving. I dug to find the door, needing warmth, food, water, and sleep. A few hours wouldn't hurt anything.

After finding my way inside, I dragged the frozen logs out of the fireplace and put fresh ones in before lighting a fire. Once I had it raging, I pumped up some fresh water, thrilled that the lodge had seen fit to bury the pumps far enough down that they didn't freeze. I ate a cold turkey sandwich and left my snow things by the fire to dry.

The heat from the jumping flames was almost hypnotizing. When I got up, I'd find the snowmobile and try to figure a way to get back to the lodge with it. I could take one other person with me. Gabe maybe, but no, that would leave Sei at the lodge unprotected. And Jamie who was pissed at me for some unknown reason. Maybe I'd just make my way to the ranger station fifteen miles south and get help. Either way, it could wait until I got some rest. I curled up on the heavy woven rug beside the fire, blankets wrapped around me, and fell asleep.

Chapter Twelve

Jamie

Gabe's knock brought me out of sleep just before dawn. I expected to wake and find Kelly snug beside me again, but he was gone. The room looked oddly bare as I got up and let Gabe in. I felt awful for the things I'd said to Kelly. Had I really lost so much of my faith in myself that I suspected everyone? Now that the anger was gone, I could see it clearly for what it was: self-loathing that needed a focus. If I'd had a phone, I would have called my therapist and spoken to her until my brain unwound from all the misplaced aggression. Mental issues were lifelong, I reminded myself. No magic pill. Sometimes I just couldn't see beyond the pain to keep moving forward. Maybe if I'd been smart, I would have reached out to Kelly, or even Sei, and said my heart was heavy. It might have helped, though I suspected I'd already damaged my relationship with Kelly beyond repair.

"I was going to tell you to keep an eye on him, but it looks like he's already gone," Gabe said.

And the emptiness of the room suddenly made sense. All Kelly's snow gear was gone, and his backpack no longer sat by the door. "You've got to be kidding me. Where the hell is he going?"

Gabe's look meant he knew more than he was saying. "He told me that your sled is still out by the cabin, buried, but likely not damaged like the others."

"You know Andrew Roman or some other asshole is involved."

He still said nothing.

I knocked the stack of magazines off the nightstand in frustration. First I fuck up, and then Gabe lets Kelly go off on his own. So the kid could go out in a blizzard to get a single sled? And what would we do with it then? Send someone for help and pray they didn't run into Andrew Roman or whichever madman had decided to play God? If he survived the trek at all. Damn it.

I began to pull on all my gear. The anger was back and it was hot, burning me from the core of my soul.

"You going after him? Maybe you should take a few minutes to breathe first."

"And let someone hurt him?" I threw back.

"I'm pretty sure someone already did. For what other reason would he leave when he suggested that I be the one to get the sled last night?" His questioning look was pointed.

My angry words from last night came back in a rush. I'd told him to stay away from Sei. Practically accused him of trying to kill us all. *Fuck.*

"I can head for the cabin after dark," Gabe offered.

I shook my head. "You need to stay with Sei. I'll go." Like I had a choice. I had to apologize. Hopefully Kelly wouldn't die before I found him. If my heart beat any harder, I'd think I was having palpitations just from the thought of him being out there alone, pushed to do something stupid because of my irrational anger.

Gabe put his hand on my arm. "You can't keep running from your feelings for him, Jamie."

"I don't know what you mean."

His look was unkind. "You can't protect Kelly from himself. The more you try to protect him, the more he'll turn away from you. If you learn anything from me, look beyond what you want to what he needs. Sei loves you, but he doesn't need you anymore. He has me. Maybe that's why you're so set on not opening up to anyone else. Kelly, however, deserves the whole deal." He left with that, closing the door behind him in that quiet, ghost-like way that reminded me he was a vampire. He didn't understand. I had to take care of Kelly, just like he had to take care of Sei, and Sei *did* still need me. Didn't he?

Kelly

THE CARVINGS on the floor swirled in my head. Something wasn't quite right. Maybe one of us wasn't strong enough. Or the connection had been severed. The edges of the spell faded, blood turning from red to brown. I'd have to cut myself again to recharge that part, use more of myself. If I even could. The books only said so much. *He* was no help, too far gone with rage and pain, healed physically but completely gone of the mind.

I sighed and brought the knife to my wrist. If only I could cut deep, dig in along the pale blue line running down the length of my arm. *He'd* feel it. Come and heal me before I could bleed out. Had before. It was all his, he claimed—my blood. But I was so tired. Maybe if I did both?

CONVICTION

How long would it take, I wondered, swallowed hard, and dug the knife into the first wrist.

The banging on the door woke me out of a deep sleep and dreams of bleeding wrists.

The banging came again. Rolling over, I glared at the heavy wooden lock on the door before finally giving up my warm cocoon and making my way to see who the crazy person on the other side would be. For a moment, I worried that it might be whoever was making the storm so bad. But since they hadn't approached any of us so far, I figured it was unlikely they wanted a face-to-face confrontation.

I swung the door open and was surprised to find Jamie standing there, head to toe in snow gear. Stepping back, I let him inside, then watched him snap off his snowshoes and close the door.

The snow still fell, but not as fast or large as it had been. Maybe some of the worst of the storm had let up. I rubbed my wrist at the bracelet in irritation. Damn thing was cold. If I ever got out of here, I'd never use one of those fitness bracelets. It was annoying, and the skin around the band was inflamed. Maybe I was allergic to it. Jamie stepped in close, ripped the bracelet off and threw it into the fire.

I blinked at him in confusion. He said nothing as he began to strip out of his snow gear. Jamie's hair was wet with what looked like sweat. I checked the clock on my phone. He must have made good time because I'd only slept two hours.

"What the hell are you doing here?" I asked him.

"Saving your sorry ass from freezing to death. Are you crazy? Didn't you notice the blizzard going on out there?" He sounded so angry. Was he still mad at me? Did he still think I was the one out to get them all?

"In case you didn't notice, I'm fine." I threw another log on the fire and got more water, which felt icy smooth when it went down. Wow, I was thirsty. I gulped down a half gallon, letting the pull from the well recharge me a little. I focused on the well and pump, filling up a bucket, I basked in the energy of the water, realizing I must have used up too much power on the way here.

"Why did you come here? It's not safe. We need to go back to the lodge."

"I'm fine here for a day or so. I'm going to unbury the sled we left the other day and get to the ranger station to call for help." I went to the corner chest which had a map to all the ranger stations within a four-hundred-mile radius. There was one not that far to the south. Maybe that one wouldn't have as much snow to slog through.

Jamie swore like a sailor. He threw his snowsuit aside and stripped out of his sweaty shirt and pants, tossing things around the room like a child in the midst of a temper tantrum. I think my jaw dropped from the shock. Cool, calm, easygoing Jamie Browan was having a hissy fit. He stopped at his boxers, leaving me more than a little disappointed. He must have pushed really hard to get here fast since he was covered in sweat.

"Why are you freaking out? You didn't have to follow me. I know you think I'm the bad guy, but I'm not, and I'm going to prove it to you all by getting help."

"I don't think you're the bad guy. Dammit, Kelly. Gabe said he thought you were going to do something rash. And when I got up and you were gone... I just never thought you'd do something so stupid."

I sighed, not wanting to listen to his insults. "I know what I'm doing. I've been doing the outdoor thing for years. I camped out in snow forts as a kid and took survival classes. I got here in one piece, all my fingers and toes intact. I could even build a snow cave to protect me if needed. I'm not new at this. I'm not your little brother, stop trying to treat me like him." I began to pull my snow things back on, intending to go find the Ski-Doo. Digging in the snow had to be better than all the unspoken accusations.

"Where are you going?"

"To find the snowmobile."

"It's dark out. We'll look for it tomorrow." He turned away from me, his back looking like a sculpted masterpiece of man art.

It would clear my head to keep moving. I finished pulling on my snow things.

"I won't be out there long. I promise."

He sighed and sat down heavily on the bed. "If you're not back in ten minutes I'm coming out to get you. And I'm really not looking forward to putting the suit back on."

His words made me smile and think of inappropriate things. But I shoved the goggles down and headed out into the snow, flashlight in hand. The wind barely blew, and the snow fell calm and slow around me. I wouldn't have had the energy to stop it from smacking me around anyway. It would take me a while to recharge. Less time if I could spend an hour swimming or even in a bath. Fuck, I was tired.

Conviction

The other cabin sat still and dark, buried beneath the mounds of snow. I tried to recall where we'd pulled the sled to a couple of days ago when we'd arrived. It had been opposite my cabin, so the far side. I wandered around, clomping through white hills until I got to the spot I thought it would be, and began to dig.

I knew I'd passed the ten-minute mark when Jamie came out, dressed again, but only wearing his coat, hat, and gloves instead of the snowsuit. He watched me for a while, even pushed me aside to dig a bit.

On my third turn throwing snow up out of the hole like a dog burying a bone, I hit pay dirt. The dark mass of the sled's handle was the first thing I found. My shout of joy brought Jamie back to the edge of our treasure spot. He began carving a ramp from the white heap. I kept peeling the snow away as much as I could until I cleared enough of it to check the fuel line.

"It's not frozen!" I cried. Since it'd been buried in snow that was a surprise, but it also meant that whatever happened to the sleds at the lodge had been deliberate, not just some fluke of too much condensation in the lines.

"Try to start it," Jamie said.

Clutching the keys with trembling fingers, I turned them and nearly flew off the seat when the machine roared to life. I just wanted to get on the road to the ranger's station.

"Shut it down. We'll head out tomorrow."

I began to protest, but he held up a hand.

"It's too dangerous to drive in the dark. We'd have to go really slow." He peered at me, hands twitching like he was trying to keep from yanking me out of the hole.

"Shouldn't we pull the sled up? We may get more snow overnight."

"What if someone is watching us? It's better if no one sees it."

I sighed and climbed out of the hole, kicking some snow back down just to cover it in case anyone was near and nosy.

Jamie was already back at the cabin door. He disappeared inside while I made my way across the heavy snow pack. Inside the cabin, the heat hit me. I stripped out of my snow things, leaving them to dry by the door. Jamie stood in his boxers again, sweating like some golden god of debauchery.

I took a long gulp of the water and let myself commune with the broken ripples in the bucket for a minute, wondering if I should just pump the water up and pour it back down to feed hungrily on the energy. My magic was still low. Though I supposed if I lived near the ocean, I'd be always "plugged in" like Sei was.

"It's like a sauna in here. I saw the smoke from a mile or so away. I hope no one else notices it." Jamie took the bucket of water from me and dumped it over his head. The water splashed around him in a puddle but didn't get anything other than the grungy floor wet. He sighed in relief as the water cascaded over him, cooling his overheated body.

I blinked at him, somewhat shocked. The water slid over those strong shoulders, leading to a stream that wove down his chiseled chest and washboard abs, dripping from his bulging arms and running over his belly button to soak into those already too-thin boxers.

Until that moment, I hadn't realized how connected I was to the water. But I was rooted in that spot, watching him, my senses alive and alert. It felt like I was running my hands over all that beautiful flesh.

The hint of hair regrowing around his nipples caught the water and beaded lightly. I wondered how often he waxed and if I could get him to stop. His pecs glistened with water droplets in the firelight. My mouth went dry at the thought of tasting all that golden skin. Would his cock be that beautiful bronze as well? How much of it would I be able to take?

He caught me staring and put the bucket down. "Were you going for tropical?"

"Tropical, yeah." Like pool boys in skimpy Speedos or margaritas on a nude beach. I was so fucking hard it hurt.

His hair dripped, sending wet trails down the rough planes, outlining muscles that I longed to touch. The boxers sagged from the weight of the water soaking them, and vaguely, I hoped he hadn't brought a spare. "Gabe is still trying to reach the ranger station by radio. We'll head back to the lodge and wait."

That knocked me out of my stupor. "No."

"What do you mean, no?"

"I'm not waiting for someone to save me. I'm going to get help."

"That's a suicide mission."

"And waiting isn't? How long before the generators go out? Or the snow is too high to dig out the wood? Or food runs out? Do we wait until whoever killed Ron comes and gets us?" I shook my head. "I don't need a hero. My back is strong enough to lift my own goddamned burden."

"You don't even know that this isn't just a bad storm," but I heard the lie in his voice. He knew too. There was nothing normal about this storm. Denying it wouldn't make it go away.

"I feel it. I know you do too." He opened his mouth to interrupt me, and I held up a hand. "You can feel when the earth does something unusual, right?"

"Sometimes," he admitted.

"Well, I know that water is being made to do something unnatural. Like the levels exam when the river nearly flooded and killed us all." I looked him in the eye and dared him to protest again.

He sank down onto the bed and put his head in his hands, pulling at his hair. "I'm sorry for what I said last night. I was tired and confused and angry mostly at myself. I just don't want you to get hurt. I feel like it's my job to protect you and Sei." He held up his hand this time before I could protest that I didn't need his help. "Not because I think you're weaker than me, but because I'm older. I've been through more. And dammit, my gut just tells me to take care of you. It's how I operate."

The admission made my heart swell. About time the bastard admitted I was more than just his little brother's friend. "I don't want to get hurt either. But I'd rather be hurt than let Sei, Gabe, or you get hurt. I have to protect my family."

Jamie peered up through his fingers, staring at me with a face full of naked emotion. It hit me like a dump truck hauling concrete. He looked scared, terrified almost, and I didn't know how to react. I crossed the room to sit beside him on the bed and wrapped my arms around him. He sighed, some of the tension leaving his face before resting his head on my shoulder.

"You really think we're family?" he asked quietly.

"I'm closer to you guys than most of my siblings. So, yes. You don't judge me for being me, gay, a witch, a runner, whatever. You smile and worry and that's nice. I don't want to be a burden, but I do want to be liked. And the little things you do are appreciated even if it's just cleaning or cooking or taking us to the gym. That's what friends do for each other."

He nodded and was quiet for another minute. Whatever his thoughts were, he wasn't sharing, but the must have been loud in his head. "I'd rather we just go back to the lodge tomorrow. Gabe can leave at dark to try to find help." His breath was hot against my shoulder, and my cock filled, arching up as if saying "Me next!"

"And if something happens to Gabe, think of what will happen to Sei." I pulled away from Jamie before he could feel the stiffy that wanted to press against all that bronzed skin. Resting my head against the wall beside the door, I tried to suck in a deep breath and calm my body. Jamie needed a friend as much as Sei did. I could be the friend he needed. Maybe.

Jamie's arms came up and wrapped around me from behind. Not restraining, just a light hug, fingers moving in soft caresses. "Can we talk about it in the morning when we've both gotten some sleep?"

"Jamie—"

He rubbed my chest through the thin material of the T-shirt, lingering on my nipples until they hardened to tight little buds. *Damn.* But when his hand wandered farther south, I caught his wrist.

"No."

"You want me. You've never made a secret of that," he pointed out. "You think I'm oblivious, but I'm not."

"You're only trying to distract me."

"You're right. But it's late. You're exhausted and depleted of the magic energy you need to help anyone. The storm is building again outside, which is making you shake like Sei does. What else are we going to do for the next fourteen hours? I'm tired too, but I want you." His voice was soft in my ear, almost uncertain. Wetness dampened my boxers, and I knew I was leaking precum already. "I've wanted you for a while. Tried to ignore it. Told myself it's bad to want you."

"Why? Because you don't trust me?"

"Because you're my brother's best friend. I don't want to mess that up. Plus you're so young. You have your whole life ahead of you." He sighed heavily. "I don't want to ruin what we have. Or did have before I fucked it up last night with my self-loathing."

"You're straight," I pointed out. All good Dominion boys were straight. They married Dominion girls and had Dominion babies. That's why Sei and I got so much crap, because we weren't good Dominion boys.

"Says who? Have I ever brought a girl around? Or anyone really?"

No. But I'd thought that was just because he didn't want anyone close to Sei.

"If there was someone I loved, don't you think I'd have incorporated them into Sei's life by now? Especially a woman. He has such a tainted view of women thanks to his mother. I've been hoping Hanna could help with that, but Allie is jealous and keeping her away." He sighed. "Can't I just do what I want for once? Without worrying about Sei, Hanna, the Dominion, or any of the million other reasons I have to fit into some mold?"

My heart pounded. Did I really have a chance? Sure, I'd never seen him date, but that didn't mean he never had sex with anyone. If he wanted me, then I was all for it. Even if it was just for the night. "Okay."

My okay must have been answer enough because he flipped me around, shoved me against the door, and dropped to his knees before me. I had a few seconds to say no, push him away, or cry foul, but I didn't. I wanted him however he would let me have him. He unbuttoned my pants, pulled them down, and pressed his face to the erection that he'd freed. His breath and skin were a warm and soothing caress around my sex.

His hand wrapped around me, the feeling almost painful, but so impossibly sweet. His warmth combined with the light scratch of stubble on his jaw made my head spin. That hard grip of his moved in a slow, circular motion, thumb teasing the long vein that ran down the center of my cock before flicking the head and coming back down.

I fell against the wall, letting the sensation take some of the pressure off my mind and build it in the growing tingle within my balls. I would have been happy with just a hand job. But when his tongue flicked out to deliver a round lick to the mushroom-shaped head of my cock, I thought I'd explode right then and there.

A second later his hot mouth engulfed my tip, teasing, sucking, nibbling like it was some sort of delicate pastry. I couldn't keep myself from grabbing that pretty blond head of his, winding my hands in his wet hair, and thrusting my hips forward.

He met my thrust, let my cock slide into his mouth, and even bump the back of his throat. One hand gripped at the base, strong, smooth strokes following each shove into that pretty face. He sucked me, cheeks hollow, looking so much like a porn movie dream I felt my balls draw up. I freed one hand from his hair and gave them a quick, painful squeeze to keep from embarrassing myself like some teenage horndog by coming too quickly.

"Jamie..."

"Hmm?" he mumbled around me, sending vibrations right to my spine.

"Obviously not new to this."

He smiled around my cock, eyes half-lidded, and chuckled lightly.

I writhed against him and fought not to let it all go so soon. When he rolled my balls in his hands and reached below to tickle my perineum, I knew I was going to lose the battle. He gave me one final lick before his brawny grip quickened me to that shooting edge.

"Gonna—" I barely said before the feeling poured forward. My come landed on his chest, painting his succulent bronze pecs with white ribbons. I sank against the wall, then fell into his lap. His hard-on pressed against my thigh. "In a second, I can—"

"Don't worry about it." Jamie crushed me to him, smearing my T-shirt with all that spent passion and breathing into my hair. "Let's get some rest so we can make the most of tomorrow. You look tired."

I was tired. Beyond tired. Laying my head on his shoulder felt like the most natural thing in the world. I barely felt him pick me up and take us to the bed. The secluded cabin didn't feel like such a bad place for once. Whether it was the sex or the company, I didn't know.

"Really, I can do it for you. At least get you off, it's only fair," I told Jamie, reaching down to rub that amazing length of his. Though I still hadn't seen it, I was sure it was a sight to behold, and I would be honored to worship his monster cock.

"Another time, maybe." He pulled my hand away, gripped it in his, and shrugged the blankets up around us. "Sleep. We have to save the world tomorrow, remember?"

"Not the world. Just our little family." The heat of him settled me into that sleepy calm that often came from cold weather and warm fires. Tomorrow I'd give him a little release. And sleep took me back.

Chapter Thirteen

THE BED I slept on was small, stunk of mold, and could have been a block of ice for all the warmth and comfort it offered. Groggily, I opened my eyes to the unnaturally darkened room. The windows were covered, and I could barely muster energy to do much more than breathe. My arms throbbed, but my breath was shallow.

In the corner I saw *him*. The distant drip, drip of melting snow on the roof seemed to fall in time to my sluggish heart. There was a hint of copper in my mouth beneath the bile and spit—blood. I sighed and let my eyes close again. He wasn't pulling at me now. The day made him weak, so in turn he'd made me too hurt to further injure myself. If he'd just left me in the tower, I'd have frozen to death already. Or bled out. Either would have been fine.

The dark discomfort faded and I hoped at least sleep would take me back to dream of a better place. Maybe people who cared. In the distance was a strained bond that showed me what it meant to have family, people who loved and cared. I'd thought I'd known what that meant. I'd been so wrong. Maybe if I'd gone for help. Or had let *him* be consumed by the flames.

But I had no energy for maybes.

Jamie shook me awake. I blinked bleary eyes at him, unsure for a moment where I was, why the cabin around me was different, and why my arms didn't ache. He told me the sun was rising and we had to get moving. I was still groggy and emotionally tired from the day before. When I got home I was going to spend hours at whatever indoor pool I could find, soaking up the energy and heat, and letting the water soothe away all the tension.

"You should eat," Jamie said.

I got up to relieve myself, glad it was an indoor toilet.

When I exited the bathroom, there was a fresh bucket of water and a plate full of bread and meat. I washed up and sank into my breakfast, somewhat annoyed. Were we going to talk about last night? He didn't seem interested in having my hands back on him, nor continuing what we'd begun. I sighed internally, irritated that in the light of day he had no interest in me.

Either way, the ranger station was my destination. If I had to steal the sled and leave him here, I would. I yanked out my map and studied it again. The station wouldn't be more than an hour on the sled. Getting back to the lodge from there depended on whether there was gas in storage or not.

I took a deep breath and figured I'd put it all out there. "I'm going to the ranger station, with or without you."

Jamie stared at me for a minute, expression blank. "You think you could take me down?"

He had size, but I could take him. One good hit to a joint and he'd be down for the count, though I'd rather not attack him if I didn't have to because then I'd feel obligated to help him get back. And I couldn't imagine he'd be light enough for me to fireman carry. "Yeah. If we get out of here, you're all going to be doing self-defense classes. Especially Sei. Even if I have to teach him myself."

"Fine," he said after a moment of contemplation. "We'll go to the station. Maybe they'll have another sled we can borrow to get Sei and Gabe out of that lodge." The wind whipped by the cabin again, making the walls creak and groan. He shivered while pulling on all his clothes.

"You feel it too?" The storm had become a living, breathing menace now, some sort of growing parasite that fed off the rage it poured into the blizzard. The water wasn't as strong, but the wind howled and wailed enough to make up for it.

"Don't focus on it."

Right, 'cause that was easy or something. I stuffed everything away and climbed into my snowsuit. "Are we going to talk about last night?"

"What about it?"

I sighed. Had I really expected anything else? Everyone treated me like the throwaway lover, even my best friend's big brother. He'd admitted it was just a distraction. Got me off so I would just lie down and sleep instead of climbing on the sled to go for help in the dark of night. Was it wrong to want more? "Never mind."

We made our way outside to the buried snowmobile. It took a little work to get it up out of the hole we'd dug, but once it was up and running, I felt like we had a chance again. The wind picked up while I revved the engine.

I insisted on driving. Jamie finally relented, slung all of our supplies on his back, and slid up behind me. With the snowsuits between us, I couldn't feel much of him until he wrapped his arms around my waist.

"Whenever you're ready," Jamie shouted through the helmets.

CONVICTION

Easing the sled around to the south, I pointed it in the direction of the ranger station. The trek would be slow. Not as slow as if we walked, but not much faster either. With the snow as high as it was, we could hit a treetop or something and be thrown. Not even the helmets could save us if we went through a tree, though I was happy to find them still locked away in our cabin.

The wind and snow whipped around us, but after about two miles I had enough of a feel for the machine and the terrain that I upped our speed a little. Sometimes when the wind blew snow into me, I'd catch the image of people moving in the dark. Like some odd second sight, it shadowed at the edges of my vision every once in a while projecting another image on the opposite side of my sight. I tried to keep from jerking the sled every time I saw it. And since Jamie wasn't demanding to drive yet, I figured I must be doing okay.

We wove through miles of trees, and the snowpack lessened, like the storm hadn't reached this far. When the station finally came into sight, a huge sigh of relief echoed through my whole body. Hope could do that. We'd get help and go home. I wouldn't suggest another winter vacation anytime soon.

The parking lot was empty of snow and vehicles. The building looked like an older wood cabin, with heavy-duty windows and a couple of generators. One level with a giant tower of solar panels and a satellite off to the right. The station was meant to be self-sufficient, even in the winter months. But it looked abandoned. Was anyone here? Why would the rangers leave the station in a storm?

Jamie was nudging me, motioning me to park around the side. I eased to a stop and looked back at him. "What?"

"No smoke in the chimney. And no hot air waves coming up. We should park the sled out of sight and come back on foot. Hopefully no one will steal the sled."

I nodded, running the sled a little farther away before stashing it in between some snowy mounds of baby pine trees. We both approached the station cautiously. Jamie shoved me behind him. I shook my head, grabbed an axe from the woodpile, and made my way to the door while he was peering in a window.

Weapon in hand, I knocked on the door. No one answered. I shoved the door open, kicking it wide with my foot, happy to find it unlocked, but nearly puked when the smell hit me. The cabin must have been warm at one time, since Ron the maintenance guy hadn't smelled like that.

"Shit," Jamie muttered when he shone the flashlight inside.

"The rangers?" I asked.

"Probably. Isn't pretty. You should stay out here."

"Whatever." I pushed my way inside, scarf pulled up over my nose to filter out some of the stink. The scattered bits of bone and flesh looked like something out of a graphic video game. If I thought of it that way, I wouldn't lose my breakfast. The floor was dark brown with dried blood, and the number of pieces strewn about seemed to mean there had been more than one person here. A skull, half the skin still clinging to it, lay off to the right by another doorway.

I gagged. Fuck, okay, I was going to lose my breakfast. I leaned out the door to lose it in the snow instead of inside with the bodies. It took a couple minutes and some deep breaths before I could make myself go back inside. "Think video game," I muttered to myself. "Just a video game. Not people. Don't think about the fact that these were people..."

Jamie handed me a small container of VapoRub. I raised a questioning brow to him.

What other interesting items did he have in that Mary Poppins bag of his?

"Helps with the smell," he said. He also pulled out a small jar of Vaseline. "This will help with your chapped skin." He pointed to his cheeks and the glistening under his lips. "Vaseline first so the menthol doesn't irritate your skin. Then the Rub."

I dabbed some on, surprised that it really did kill the smell and felt good on my wind-burned face. Then I grabbed the light from Jamie and checked the room for the radio. It was there, turned off. *Damn.* This was the closest station in a two-hundred-mile radius. There was another over the border in Canada, but they were almost seventy miles north of the lodge.

"Look for a working phone. Yours still has no signal, right?"

I pulled mine out and sure enough, still no signal. "Yeah, nothing."

"Maybe they have something else. A working satellite phone, CB, something," Jamie told me as he began riffling through drawers.

"What do you think did this? Animals?" I tried not to think about what I was stepping in. But there was no way to avoid it.

"With the door closed like that? Nah. I'd say vampire. Probably bent on destruction instead of feeding since there's so much blood. They get a lot of good PR, but a psychopath is a psychopath. Whatever did this enjoyed it. No reason to tear them up so much otherwise."

"Shit."

"Yeah, we need to get back to the lodge before dark. Most vampires are like Gabe, limited during daylight hours."

"Except Andrew Roman."

Jamie's frowning nod told me he'd had the unhappy thought of what vampire might have done this. "We get back to the lodge, Gabe and Sei. Get them out. That's priority."

"We may not have enough gas for that."

"Then we'll walk."

"In a snowstorm."

"Snow's died down a bit. Lots of wind, not as much water." He glanced at me and down to my arm where the old tracker used to be.

"You think the tracker had something to do with it?"

"No way to tell. Better safe than sorry. If it was a spell, it probably won't be that easy to break."

"They would have been able to trace me to the cabin, then," I pointed out.

"Which is why we aren't going back to the cabins."

My heart hammered in my chest. Was it a spell? Something had been on the trackers that pulled power from us? Used me? Could they still have control of me? I shivered at the idea.

I carefully moved around the dead until I found the plug for the radio. I flipped it on and it roared to life, though the chatter wasn't coming from the lodge. It was coming from another ranger station.

"Beaver Creek, please respond. Over."

"Beaver Creek, I think. Over," I said. Was this station Beaver Creek? I yanked a map out from the drawer next to the radio and studied the dots that marked all the stations. Yep, we were at Beaver Creek.

"We've been trying to reach you for days, Beaver Creek. Over."

"We're travelers from the Pinecrest Lodge. The rangers are…" I didn't know how

CONVICTION

to describe them. Finally, I settled on the truth. "Dead? Over."

"Pinecrest, do you have a medical emergency? Over."

Jamie took the radio from me. "Two fatalities—the rangers, we think. Possible rogue vampire at Beaver Creek. Travelers trapped up at Pinecrest. Will run out of food and water soon. One dead. Sleds and vehicles incapacitated. Over."

"Can you make it to Rabbit Five, Pinecrest? Over."

Jamie and I searched for Rabbit Five. It was the station over the border in Canada. "Maybe. But we only have one sled. Over."

"When the storm lets up we can send a chopper. Over."

"What if it doesn't let up?" I asked Jamie. 'Cause the storm was not normal.

"Rabbit Five, do you have sleds? Over."

"Yes. Over."

"They won't take those out in the storm. And we can't send random people out on sleds in the middle of a blizzard," I pointed out to Jamie, then kicked a gum wrapper with my shoe, irritated by our lack of options. If the storm didn't stop, we'd all be dead, and it didn't seem to be stopping. Even if the tracker had somehow been tying it to my power, there was enough moisture in the air to keep it snowing for days.

"Rabbit Five, we will try to get some of the travelers to you. We're headed back to the lodge now. Over."

"Understood. Be careful. Over."

Jamie put the radio aside. He almost looked indecisive as to whether to take it or not, but it was just too big to carry. I found the kitchen area and took what food I could that didn't look spoiled. Jamie examined the bodies while I continued to pretend they weren't there.

"They've been dead a few days. Blood and tissue is pretty dry. Try to find keys. There should be a storage shed here with extra sleds, maybe some gas."

"We'll never make it to Rabbit Five. That's too far. We can't get four people on a sled." Though it was our best shot at getting help.

"We will go back to the lodge." His tone left no room for a challenge.

I sighed, not wanting to start an argument again. One blow job did not marital bliss make. A set of keys were shoved under a cup left on the counter. Water still beaded around it, like the glass had spilled but someone had turned it over to hide the keys. I touched the water tentatively, not really expecting anything, but felt a warm rush of fear fill me. I'd been seeing a lot of unusual things lately.

Someone glanced my way as though seeing me through the reflection in the water. He was young, dark hair, Asian eyes, and a sad expression. I felt his exhaustion, realized I'd been dreaming of him for days. He didn't have much time left before this whole misadventure killed him. The storm would die when he did. He couldn't force himself to let the cold misery of winter take him though he'd longed for it. He'd even tried goading the other to rip out his throat when he fed. No such luck. And when the young man thought of the other, it was just glowing dark eyes and fangs. Vampire.

I sucked in a deep breath. If that was truly a vampire, then Gabe wasn't showing us his true face. *Fuck.* The young man seemed to echo my sentiments. He sighed tiredly. I trembled at the feel of his despair and the shocking clarity of the vision.

Who was he? I tried to send the thought through the water, but it just rippled and distorted his image. Finally it refocused and showed me the shed behind the station and the Ski-Doo inside. Heavy cans of gas lined the walls. Finally, I caught the image of Sei, sick and retching while Gabe held him.

My head spun as the images faded. I didn't even notice Jamie behind me until he wrapped his arms around me in an awkward hug. "Okay?"

I huddled in his embrace for a minute, let his touch reground me. Maybe Sei could figure everything in the vision when we got back. Who was the guy? And the vampire? Was that Andrew Roman? "Something's happened to Sei. We have to get back. There's another sled and some gas in the shed." I held out the keys. "We have to get back."

He nodded and stared at me for a minute before saying, "Let's check out the shed, then we'll head for the lodge." We walked out to the dark wood mini-garage behind the station, closing the station door to keep the animals out.

The only remaining sled worked fine, though it was a little old. We filled it with gas, and Jamie brought the other around, refilled that one, and we made our way back in silence. He didn't ask what I'd seen or how I knew something was wrong with Sei. But he was moving like there was a demon on his tail.

We passed the cabins as the sun began to set and kept on moving. I ignored my rumbling stomach and forced the old machine to keep following Jamie until he veered away from the straight path to the lodge. He slid up to a stop in a cove of treetops jutting from the snow. I parked mine beside his.

"We walk from here," he told me.

I got off, left the helmet under the seat, and followed him through the snow toward the lodge. His caution made sense. Someone had wrecked half a dozen sleds to keep us trapped. They wouldn't hesitate to destroy these two if they found them.

The late night sky disappeared beneath the heavy blow of snow and wind. Odd how the storm got worse at night and calmed during the day. I wondered if Jamie noticed it too as we trudged our way to the door, which was unlocked. There were no lights in the lodge. Had the power gone out?

No one seemed to linger in the main lounge, though the fire still raged a welcoming warmth. Jamie and I made our way upstairs to Gabe and Sei's room, moving quietly.

Jamie knocked lightly on the door. It took a few minutes for it to open. I felt vulnerable in the dark hallway, like someone could come any minute and see us. Though why it mattered, I didn't know.

Gabe opened the door and silently ushered us in. Sei sat curled up in the middle of the bed, wrapped in a pile of blankets, looking pale and shaky.

I stripped out of all my snow things, leaving them in a heap on the floor, and shoved myself under those blankets too as my own shivering began. *Damn.* Was this what he felt? The never-ending cycle of power that kept rolling through the storm? No wonder he had a severe anxiety disorder. The pulsing waves of energy that rolled through me pushed around by the storm made me nauseous. If this was being "plugged in" to the power, no wonder he was always distant.

Sei smiled at me and practically crawled in my lap for warmth. The kerosene lantern gave us light, but the room had begun to take on a chill. If it got much colder, we'd have to chance going down by the fireplace just to keep from freezing to death.

"When did the power go out?" Jamie asked as he took off his gear.

"Late last night." Gabe glanced back at Sei. "Shortly after Sei was poisoned."

"What?" Jamie demanded. His eyes went to me and then to Gabe before falling on his little brother.

"I got it out of his system. But we can't trust anything that's in the kitchen."

"I'm so hungry," Sei whispered to me. "Threw up all the bad. Now I've got a grumbling tummy."

Jamie threw the bag of supplies on the bed and pulled out a half a loaf of bread and some jerky. "Eat. It's safe. I promise."

We shared the supplies, rationing things from what we'd stolen from the ranger's station. Jamie filled Gabe in on our trip and the dead rangers. "You should take one of the sleds and head to the station in Canada," I told them.

"This whole thing feels like an elaborate trap." Gabe paced the room. Sei rested his head on my shoulder and just watched his lover like it was lulling him to sleep.

"Why would you say that?" I asked. "The trip was my idea." Though Gabe had chosen the location, lodge, and means of travel. Were they still blaming me?

"I got an e-mail about this lodge just before we started making plans. I liked the distance from the rest of the world. I thought it would be good for Sei to get away from everything. Never thought it'd be the death of us all." Gabe ran his hands through his hair, making the curls fly in crazy directions.

"We'll be okay." Sei smiled like nothing in the world could bother him.

"Did you get a little nookie before we got here?" I whispered to him.

He gave me a dimpled smile and a slight blush. "Gabe tried to distract me from my rumbling tummy."

"Let's check the garage for more gas," Jamie said to Gabe.

Gabe glanced back at us. "Don't leave the room, and don't answer the door."

"Got it," I mumbled, happy now that I was warm and full.

"I'm good." Sei grinned at them.

The two he-men left, and I basked in the quiet time away from the storm with the guy I considered my best friend, only slightly bothered by being left behind like I couldn't fend for myself.

Chapter Fourteen

Jamie

Our march to the garage was a quiet one. Gabe said nothing, but I could feel his eyes boring into me. Could he tell that I was a pervert? That I'd had sex with a man more than fourteen years my junior? But in that moment in the cabin, there had been no other option. I had to touch him and watch the pleasure cross his face.

I'd tromped through the snow as fast as I could, praying the whole way that Kelly would make it, that he'd be alive. The smoke from the chimney had been the first indicator. If I hadn't been afraid of the tears freezing on my face, I would have cried. And then when he told me in earnest how he had to save our family, that he would rather be hurt than have any of us go through the pain again, I could hardly breathe. Not touching him would have killed me.

Watching him writhing in pleasure had made me so hard it hurt. Yet I felt okay about not coming. He deserved better. He was young, handsome, and smart. He needed someone his own age who would take care of him and make him smile. But the thought of someone else touching him and making him laugh or moan made me want to growl and kill something.

"Want to talk about it?" Gabe asked as we began sorting through gas cans.

"Kelly's power is growing." I knew that wasn't what he was asking, but we weren't talking about me anymore. "He saw that Sei was sick by touching some water that was on the counter at the ranger's station." I explained about the gruesome remains of the rangers, and Gabe listened quietly.

"So there is a vampire at play. We suspected that."

It was the only option that made sense.

"That doesn't explain how Kelly's power would increase. Not unless he became Pillar of water, and last I heard, Water lived in Cancun." Gabe leaned against the wall and pinched his nose as though his head hurt, which was almost impossible for a vampire. A Pillar was the most powerful witch of the element. Sei was Pillar of earth, but Kelly didn't have enough training to even know the words to speak to become Pillar. Would water even accept him if he tried?

"Maybe Roman got Kelly and made him his focus somehow?" I wondered if that was possible to do without Kelly knowing.

Gabe shook his head. "Not even a vampire could increase a human's power like that. And he'd have to say the words. Make a choice. The bond won't actually work if it's forced. I've known vampires who've tried."

"Maybe he's hitting some height of power? Didn't Sei's abilities increase as he got older?"

"Yes, but becoming Pillar is really what changed him."

I really didn't want to contemplate what would happen if Kelly became Pillar. Our fishbowl would shrink even more, and if someone threw harassment Kelly's way, I'd flip out. Gabe wouldn't have the chance to buffer my anger. I thought of my gym buddies and wondered how much of a pounding they'd taken from me each time Sei had gotten some nasty attention. Padding and referees only helped so much, but one problem at a time. "Do you think it's Roman?"

"The Tri-Mega believes he's dead."

"But you don't."

"No."

That he was alive was something that terrified me. He'd almost taken Sei from us once, and if he was after Kelly now, I wouldn't be able to keep myself from tearing him apart. But I was no match for a vampire. That bitter sense of helplessness filled me again. What good was being strong and smart if you couldn't protect the ones you cared about most?

Kelly

"THIS STORM blows, Sei."

"Figuratively, you mean?" The wind howled around the lodge.

The fury of the water being tossed about had me bundled in the blankets, shivering. "Do you still suspect me?"

Sei tore off another piece of jerky for me and shuffled the cards. We were on our fifth round of War. We'd both won twice. But then neither of us were all that competitive when it came to cards.

"Never did." He glared at the closed door for the fiftieth time. "The sun will be up soon. I'm worried."

"They'll be okay. They're he-men. Here to protect us weak men."

"Huh?"

I gave Sei a lifted eyebrow stare.

"Gabe's not like that."

"Jamie sure is."

"He's a big guy. Used to being in charge."

"Does it ever bug you?"

Sei shrugged. "Sometimes, I guess. But I yell at him when I see a lot of it. Then he gets all mad and brooding. Puffs out like a peacock. It's kind of funny. It's when he goes quiet that it bugs me."

I sighed. "I've been having some weird dreams, visions, whatever. Maybe stuff from the snow. I dunno," I confessed, figuring there was no time like the present. Might as well lay it all out there. "I had a vision while I was at the station. I touched the water, and it showed me a young man who looked sort of like you, in a tower, and he was dying. Then I saw the image of you being sick. That's how I knew to come back. But the other guy, he's part of the problem. The spell. Or whatever it is."

"A young man like me? Was he Asian?"

"Yes. He had slanted eyes, so I assume so."

He was silent for a minute and seemed to be thinking hard. Then he said, "Why was he dying?" Sei didn't look at me; he just flipped through his many sketches as though searching for something.

"I saw a vampire. Not like Gabe. But red eyes and fangs. The stuff they never show us. The guy's thoughts were that he'd tried to provoke the vampire to kill him, and that the storm would die when he did. Something drained him. He was tired, wishing for death." I paused, thinking of the pain in his arms. "He'd tried to kill himself, but the vampire won't let him die. It must be a crazy strong spell."

"Hmm," Sei mumbled. For the first time ever between us, the silence felt awkward. It stretched into a few minutes until I did the only thing I could think of to restart the conversation.

"Jamie blew me," I blurted out, waiting for the outrage and anger I was sure to receive.

"What?"

"Oral sex."

Sei tilted his head. "My brother? I thought Jamie was straight."

"So did I, but he had—" I coughed lightly. "—skill."

"Oh!" Sei frowned. "Does this mean you don't want to be my friend anymore?"

I examined my friend's face in confusion. "No. Why the hell would it mean that?"

"You said it could get weird on both sides."

Oh. I had, hadn't I? "I don't want it to get weird. But you're my best friend, and I really like Jamie."

"So go for it."

"Seriously?"

He shrugged. "Why not? Jamie could use a boyfriend. Maybe he would spend less time stalking me, then. You both like working out, and maybe being around you he won't be so afraid to eat where someone might see him."

"You do know he only stalks you 'cause he loves you so much."

"Yeah, but it's weird. Gabe likes to know where I am but he doesn't get angry if he isn't the one to take me there. And he doesn't freak if he doesn't hear from me right away."

Actually he did, but I sighed, not wanting to argue. We so had to work on Sei about the whole trust your family thing. "So if you came home one day to find me and Jamie on the couch making out, what would you do?"

"Other than watch a little, you mean?"

"Sei, I'm being serious here."

"Me too. You're both hot. Why can't I watch?" He frowned. "Is that a weird brother thing? I'm not supposed to watch 'cause Jamie's my brother? I guess that *would* be a little weird."

I shrugged and said, "Probably won't matter anyway. He didn't let me return the favor, and he hasn't been all that lovey-dovey since then anyway. He admitted he was trying to distract me from going out at night in the snow. It was nothing."

"So jump him. I'm all for that."

"Because you don't want a babysitter anymore."

"*Because* Jamie is my brother, and I want him to be happy too." He flipped through his notebook, which was more sketches than notes on his medication. Sei was a really good artist. One of the sketches toward the front caught my attention. It looked like the guy I'd seen through the water and in my dreams...

"Who's that?"

Sei flipped back and stared at the picture, a bunch of different emotions crossing his face. None of them good. "That's Sam. Is he the one you saw in your vision? Is he dying?"

I sat up straight, gut churning. *Shit!* "We should go find Gabe and Jamie. Yes, that's the guy from my vision."

"Then we have to help him."

I jumped off the bed and grabbed my coat. "You have to come with me. I don't want you here by yourself."

His eyes widened, but he got up and started pulling on his snow stuff. I packed a bag full of his and Gabe's stuff, adding as much food as I could, along with Sei's meds and notebook. If Sam was involved in this unwillingly, then it could only mean Roman was controlling him, and they were both after Sei. And that was so not happening again.

Once we were both bundled up, we snuck down to the garage. The snow kept the early morning very dark and cold. No one seemed to be moving about, which was eerie. What about the other guests? Had anyone else been poisoned? Was anyone else even worried?

We hurried across the snow-covered lot and ducked into the garage. Gabe and Jamie were going through gas cans. They both looked up when we came in.

"What's wrong?" Gabe asked.

"You guys should be inside where it's warm," Jamie protested.

I handed the packed bag to Gabe. "Did Jamie tell you where the sleds are?"

"Yes, but it will be light soon."

"If you move fast, you can stay in the cover of the trees until you get there. You need to head to Rabbit Five. Take Sei with you. Neither of you are safe here."

"What are you talking about, Kelly?" Jamie demanded.

Gabe just stared at me like he was trying to read everything I wasn't saying. But I was pretty sure he couldn't get that deep into anyone but Sei. "Okay," he finally said.

"Gabe!"

"I packed as much food as I could, and Sei's meds. The map is on the top." I pulled the map out and showed him how I had it folded to show the route to Rabbit Five. With the map, I had also tucked a note that told him about seeing Sam in a vision in the water and how he felt like he was dying, but that he'd led us to the extra sled and left the keys behind. Maybe Sam's power was water too and that's how he was connecting with me. I didn't know.

"You and Jamie should come," Sei mumbled through his heaps of coverings.

"We have to stay. Let people believe the two of you are still here. At least for a while. Get to Rabbit Five. Make them send help. We'll follow as soon as we can." Someone at the lodge had to be helping them. After all, Sei had been poisoned here. A few days sneaking about might give Jamie and me the time to flush them out while Sei and Gabe got help. I watched several bits of comprehension cross Sei's face. He looked at Gabe, then Jamie, then me.

Finally he turned back to Jamie and said, "Listen to Kelly, okay, Jamie? Keep him safe for me. Be safe too. We'll send help."

Gabe grabbed two helmets and the bag I'd packed, then led Sei out into the snow in the direction of the hidden sleds. For the first time in weeks, I felt the same crushing fear I'd felt when I'd watched Matthew take Sei from the parking lot of our building. That day Jamie had been shot and the whole world had come crashing down on me while I held my shirt to his chest to try to slow the bleeding and to wait for the paramedics.

Watching that car drive away with Sei in it had been one of the hardest things I'd ever done. Now, letting them go would probably be for the best. But it didn't stop the sense of dread that had already begun to rise. I hoped they made it and Gabe wasn't too injured by the coming sunrise.

Jamie grabbed a few heavy gas cans, and we snuck them out to our hidden snowmobile. Gabe and Sei were already gone, headed through the stormy night toward safety, I hoped.

Jamie and I returned to the lodge, took any remaining things of ours from their room, and retired to ours. It wasn't until he was inside and had eaten a sandwich that he spoke. "Tell me what's going on."

"Other than the fact that someone's trying to kill Sei again, you mean?"

"It could just have been food poisoning."

His glass-half-full attitude was seriously starting to piss me off. Didn't he just live the same few weeks that I had?

My look must have said something because he dropped down on the bed and sighed heavily. "Will it never end? Why can't he have a normal life? Or even a life where people just leave him alone."

The reason was pretty simple. And solvable. "Andrew Roman is alive."

Jamie said nothing. His expression said he'd suspected it all along.

I told him about the visions I'd been having of Sam in the tower. "Sam has been trying to do the right thing. What if someone, like a vampire, was making him do otherwise?" Sam had been bitten by a vampire before and forced to harm Sei. In the end, he had actually helped Sei escape with Gabe. "Maybe Roman controls him now. I saw him in the water on the counter at the ranger station. He was tired. Dying. He said the storm would die when he did."

"But he shouldn't have any power. His family isn't Dominion. We checked."

"The Dominion has been wrong before. In the visions he's thought about books. That only so much can be learned from books. And he's fueling the spell. So he has some sort of power. Even if it's just power to tie us together."

Jamie sat in brooding silence for several minutes before he flipped the lock on the door, then stripped out of his clothes. He went into the bathroom and checked the water, which was still running. "Cold, but it's better than nothing." He shut the door.

I guess we weren't going to talk about it anymore. I sighed, stripped out of everything, and dug out a pair of flannel pajamas. The lack of heat was already chilling the building. I did not want to freeze to death when I could have prevented it by not sleeping mostly nude.

When Jamie came out, he was wearing just his boxers, though it was a different set than what he'd worn last night. Had it only been last night? I began to shiver again. The storm hadn't been nearly as bad, but there was still a lot of fury to the blowing wind. "It will really suck if we freeze to death," I told him.

"Not gonna happen." He stacked the blankets he'd stripped from Sei and Gabe's room on the bed before crawling in beside me. He didn't bother with modesty or distance. Instead he pulled me close and rubbed my arms, using his body to warm me. "Get some sleep."

"I remember how you made me sleepy last night." He was close enough to kiss. Would he push me away if I went for it? "It would be a nice distraction."

He laughed. The sound was sexy as hell. "This time I'm just too tired to get it up. Sorry."

I sighed and curled up against him, glad I had the human furnace to keep me warm. Once my head hit the pillow, instead of dreams, I walked into a world that I now recognized as Sam's. He struggled through the snow. The storm stole energy from him like endless nips of blood. And though he never showed me Andrew Roman, he nodded his agreement that this was all part of that greater scheme. Sam did what he had to because he had no choice. Free will had been taken from him. He reached the wooden steps of a tower and began to climb, heart pounding sluggishly, telling him that death was coming soon. He longed for it. Kept hoping for the end. He was so tired.

The dream shifted. Just before I awoke again, I saw a sled moving through the rising morning light, ducking around trees and flying at top speed. I knew it was Sei and Gabe because I felt the snow pelting them. When I saw them reach the large outpost of Rabbit Five, I wanted to cheer. But the sun was up, and Gabe needed shelter. Sei ushered him inside, and once the door was closed to the blowing snow, I lost all sight of them.

I stretched and shifted. Jamie was a solid mass around me. When he slept, he was down for the count. The pale light in the room from the nearly snow-covered window made him look younger than I knew him to be. I wondered if age was an issue for him. Or if he just wasn't willing to do more because his brother and I were friends. Or maybe he really was straight.

I'd always felt protected by him. After the last attack on Sei, when I'd gone off to find him, Jamie had yelled at me for it afterward telling me I could have been hurt. His words had been harsh, but felt more like concern than actual anger and distrust. This trip had them both. Maybe I just really didn't know how to read him. Did anyone? The better question might have been would he *let* anyone?

The man needed someone to keep him from stressing so much over his little brother. There were four of us now. We could share the responsibility. And contrary to popular belief, I was no pushover. I decided at that moment to take Sei's advice and jump him.

I shoved the blankets down a little and reached for Jamie's stiff body. He was always tight and firm like a brick wall, solid muscle, bulky and big. But I would almost bet my subscription to *Surf's Up* that he would be one huge knot of tightly wound nerves. Beginning with his large calves, I began massaging the stiff muscles like that was all that mattered in the world.

By the time I'd gotten to his lower back, he'd rolled onto his stomach and was moaning with pleasure. "Where the hell did you learn that?" he asked, though it came out sounding like "Wad a he d u urn tat?"

"I have an older sister who's a massage therapist. She used to practice on all of us, and I was so intrigued, I asked her to teach me. Plus it's a great way to seduce dates. Give a guy a little shoulder massage and he's putty in my hands."

Jamie snorted. "Somehow I don't think you have trouble seducing anyone."

I shrugged, knowing he couldn't see me. "Most guys want a quick fuck. It's the rare few I need to seduce that I really want."

He sighed. "I shouldn't be doing this. I have to make sure Sei is safe."

"How are you going to do that? No radio, no phone, remember? He's fine. I saw him through the snow. They arrived at the station about an hour ago."

"That's some crazy power you have there."

I kneaded his beautiful shoulders, pulling another moan from him. "I don't get what's going on at all. My powers have never worked like this before. They were so far away I shouldn't have been able to see them. Plus I barely put any energy into it. That's never happened before." I tapped him on the side. "Turn over so I can do the front."

"Not a good idea," he told me.

"Just do it."

"You're really bossy."

"Look who's talking."

Finally he rolled over, cheeks flushed, and I immediately saw his problem but swallowed back the smile. His cock was hard beneath his boxers. In fact, the fabric strained to hold it, forcing him to curve and almost letting it poke out the top. Damn, I so wanted to taste that. But I ignored it, like any good masseur would, and began again with his ankles and worked my way up.

"This is really embarrassing," Jamie said, though he didn't try to pull away or move more than what I told him to.

"It's supposed to be relaxing."

"It feels good, but I don't think I'm relaxing."

"I'll just have to work a little harder, then."

He groaned when my hands skipped from his huge thighs up to that sculpted eight-pack that was chiseled out of his stomach. I gave each muscle its due, counting in my head the time before moving on to the next. When I reached his pretty pecs, I worked my palm into the flesh. The hair rubbing beneath my hand went right to my cock.

"You need to stop waxing. You can't be that hairy." I wanted to roll against him, feel that hair tickling my chest.

He frowned. "I'm a bear. Seiran would think it's gross."

"How often does Sei sleep with you?"

Jamie looked offended and lost for words all at once.

"Right. Stop waxing, please. I like a man with hair."

He closed his eyes and seemed to sink into the feeling. I even massaged the muscles of his face and scalp. When I finished he almost seemed to be sleeping again, since his breathing was so deep and slow.

Finally, I bent over and did what I'd been waiting to do since that night in the cabin when the storm first hit. I sucked one of his mocha buds into my mouth. Swirling my tongue around it, I tasted the salty sweetness of flesh and man for a while before moving to the next. The pebble hardened, and Jamie moaned lightly beneath me.

"You shouldn't," he said. "*We* shouldn't."

I wasn't turning back now. I had to see the whole deal. If all I got was to suck him off, that was just fine with me. His amazing bronze skin was chiseled into amazingly decadent lines and sweet planes. I couldn't help but be drawn farther and farther south.

The boxers had to go. "Please tell me you don't go full Brazilian?"

He flushed.

Damn. I eased the fabric off his hips, watching his cock break free in a hard triumph to nearly reach his belly button. Wow. That was going to be hard to swallow, literally. Like his arms, the veins jutted in heavy lines down his shaft. The whole thing looked more like man art than any cock I'd ever seen.

I began with the tip, figuring I'd work my way down. The bulbous head barely fit in my mouth.

Jamie made a protesting noise. "You don't have to."

"I sure don't, but I'm going to." He was almost as wide as my fist, dark bronze in color, like always-flushed cheeks on a suntanned face. Though there were no tan lines, so the color had to be natural.

His balls rested against him like a huge apple, darker in color than his cock, tight and obviously ready for more. I reached down to feel the heavy weight of them, juggle them in my fingers, applying soft pressure and soothing caresses. He groaned, making me smile and lick around his huge dick.

He was uncut, with a thick foreskin, which was odd because the Dominion were religious about circumcision. They were always about controlling men when they could.

"Your mom didn't…"

"No. It was my father's one demand. If he had been alive when Sei was born, Sei wouldn't be circumcised either."

I teased the skin, enjoying the salty, male taste. Having never been with an uncircumcised guy before, I didn't know if it was a good thing or not, but Jamie's hips twitched. "Good?"

"Mhmm."

Exploring the whole breadth of it had him writhing beneath me. I watched his body tighten and gripped him to deliver strokes in time to the play I gave him. The way that thick flesh slid over his head and back again was erotic enough to nearly make me come. Damn, what was I missing out on?

The sound of the slick flesh moving smoothly with the help of his precome and my spit made me want to jump him. He growled at me when I eased back just before I was sure he would come.

"I think we should come together this time."

"Then you best get up here."

"I won't last long." Shimmying out of my pajamas in a hurry, I hoped this was really going to happen. I crawled up beside him and he turned toward me, pulling me tight against his warm flesh and pressing us together. Surprisingly, he kissed me, tongue delving deep as he wrapped one hand around both of us. I'd never noticed how large his hands were before. Now the feel of them on me made my cock leak and twitch with need.

We broke away from the kiss, both panting and thrusting against each other. The friction built up fast, like a geyser getting ready to bust. His chest was hot against mine, both of us slick with sweat despite the chill in the room. His short hairs teased my skin and made my nipples ache. My cock was so hard it hurt, almost too sensitive to be touched.

He yanked my hips against his hard enough to hurt, but it added to the grinding friction. He gripped one of my ass cheeks to press us together.

"Jamie—"

Our precome mixed and helped lube the way between us. He finally let us go, grabbed my other butt cheek, and mashed our bodies together. I writhed against him, pleasure welling up and spurting between us, like some kind of liquid fire. He gasped and shot too, still humping me and pressing us together.

Finally we lay in the sticky warmth of each other, both breathing like we'd run a marathon, arms and legs tangled, but relaxed. "You really have done this sort of thing before, haven't you?" I mumbled against Jamie's chest.

"Long time ago. College." He paused, then said, "The first time around."

"I'm the jealous type. Don't tell me."

Jamie laughed, which made me hard again.

"Jeez." How that little sound could make me hard so fast was unbelievable.

"Youth."

"Not up for another round, old man?"

"Not right now. Maybe later." He put some space between us and glared at the drying come. "I haven't come that hard in years."

"Blue balls."

"I hardly think they're blue." He took some tissues off the side table and cleaned us both up before tossing them in the basket.

"Not anymore." I winked at him and rolled over to my side of the bed to grab the blankets. "Nap with me."

Jamie sighed but wrapped himself around me. "You're sure Sei and Gabe are all right?"

"Yes."

"Okay." And we both went back to sleep.

CHAPTER FIFTEEN

I AWOKE wrapped in Jamie's arms like he was holding on to me for dear life. It was amazing. But the room was sweltering. I looked up and realized the light in the bathroom was on. Did we have power?

"Jamie?" I nudged him. "Hey." I couldn't hear the sound of wind or feel anything from outside. Maybe the storm had stopped. A glance out the window brought the realization that it was daytime, and if it was like most days, the storm would lessen during the day and grow worse at night.

Jamie finally roused beside me. "It's hot in here," he grumbled, not opening his eyes.

"The power is back on."

That got him to wake up. He glanced at the side table, rolled over, and reached to flick on the light. When it worked, we both nearly leapt from the bed in the direction of the bathroom.

"Share a shower?" I asked him.

"No, we need food. You go first. I'll go find out what's going on downstairs."

I tried not to show my disappointment and bent over to turn the water in the tub on to test for warmth. By the time the temperature was right and I pulled the lever for the shower, I realized Jamie hadn't left yet.

"Invitation is still open," I told him and wiggled my bare ass for his benefit.

He groaned but left the bathroom. I watched him hopping into his jeans while I stepped under the warm spray and tugged the curtain closed. After the door to the room had opened and closed, I jerked off to the memory of this morning's escapade, unable to keep the smile off my face.

The happy feeling that almost made my feet float lasted until I got to the kitchen to find Jamie and food. Cat was all over him, feeding him bits of a cut-up apple. Didn't he get that he should be wary of everyone? Someone had poisoned Sei. Maybe they were after all of us. I guess our one little interlude didn't make us a couple. He could at least act like I hadn't been an "only option" at the moment.

I stomped across the room, grabbed a spare bowl, and an unopened box of cereal that sat on the counter. Jamie shot me a raised-brow look while I poured myself a bowl and began eating it without milk. The jug was open and half full. What if someone put something in that?

"Did you or Con get sick at all Cat?" I asked curiously.

"No, why? Are you not feeling well?" She stepped back, putting some distance between herself and Jamie. "Are you coming down with something?"

"What was for dinner last night?"

"We had vegetable stew with pasta salad. The cook made it."

Jamie seemed to catch on. "Did Seiran eat that too?"

"Both he and his *friend* were down for dinner, yes."

I ignored her comment about Gabe, wondering if she had a problem with vampires or homosexuals, which made me think she might not like Con much either. "Who brought him food?"

"We all ate at the table in the main dining hall. The food was already out." She looked between Jamie and me, then cut another piece of apple for him. I chewed on the dry cereal and tried to focus on the issue at hand rather than my irritation.

Cat dropped a piece, and Jamie scooped it up and fed it to her. Her tongue lashed out to lick his fingers. His deep chuckle said he wasn't upset about it.

I growled at him, grabbed the box of cereal, and headed back to our room. So much for a good morning, though it was almost noon.

Mrs. Gossner stopped me on the stairs with a hand on my arm. "I haven't seen the little one yet. Is he coming down for breakfast?"

"No. He's not feeling well, so he's getting some sleep. I'm going to bring him some cereal, though." I held up the box still in my grasp. "We'll make sure he eats."

Her smile was tight, but she nodded. "Do you want me to send up some milk? Now that the generators are running, we can use the fridge again. I don't think any of it spoiled."

I didn't want to touch anything that was open, but telling her that would be rude. "Nah, it will just sour his stomach. He'll probably be fine later anyway. What time is dinner?"

"Six, in the main dining hall."

"We'll be there." I nodded to her and continued up the stairs.

Constantine waited outside my room. I couldn't contain my sigh, but maybe if we just rehashed some shit, he'd get the point and leave me alone. I opened the door to my room and held it for Con. His eyes widened, but he followed me inside. Not like he had a chance to beat me up unless he had chloroform in his pocket. More than three years of martial arts training could do wonders for a man's self-confidence. I was so going to be teaching Sei when we got home.

I grabbed a handful of the cereal and handed it to him. He took it and munched absently. With the door closed, he seemed nervous. "We heard that you left."

"Just forgot something at the cabin. No biggie."

"The gym bunny followed you. Are you a couple?"

"He's all over your sister right now. You tell me." I put the cereal box down and shuffled through my things for a magazine I hadn't read. Maybe the storm really was over and we could just wait for rescue. I certainly wasn't a super sleuth and wanted to just go home. We'd file a police report, tell them about the rangers who were dead and the attempted poisoning, maybe even the sabotage of the snowmobiles.

Con crossed the room and sat beside me on the bed. "So why can't we try again? We were good together. I felt like a real person when I was with you."

Yeah, I remembered that about Con. He had sometimes been sweet but almost always manipulative.

We'd spent most of the weekend in the woods, mostly naked, pretending to be wild men and fucking as much as we could. The last day, I stood in waist-high water, bathing and fishing all at once. Con wore shorts and bent over the fire near our campsite, coaxing the coals to flare back to life. The dragon tattoo had color now and made him look so hot in the midday light.

"You going to catch anything or stare all day?"

I felt my face flush and looked back into the water. Curious fish darted around me, some large enough to feed us both. Staying still was key. Their big mouths would dart up for air, and if they were close enough, I could grab one or two.

Movement on the shore brought my attention up. Con peered into the woods, and a moment later his dad stepped through the shrubbery. We were on their land, but there was acres of it. I wondered how he found us. He and Con exchanged a few words, then he turned around and left the area. The stiffness of Con's shoulders made me think that something had gone wrong. Maybe something had happened to his mom.

I waded toward the shore, thinking we'd get through it, whatever it was. We had each other. "Everything okay?"

He turned back my way and gave me a tight smile. "We should head back."

"Okay. Give me a few to pack everything up." I tugged on my shorts and a shirt and stuffed everything in my bag. He doused the fire and tied his bundle of things before we headed into the heavy woods.

The tension ate at me the whole way. He said nothing, didn't even look at me, just hiked a few feet ahead. My heart raced in fear. Had his family found out about us? We already snuck around a lot. I couldn't imagine having to take further steps to hide from them.

"Con? Talk to me, please."

"It's nothing."

"Did they find out about us?"

"I said it's nothing."

"Maybe it's a good thing. We don't have to hide anymore. That would be great, right?"

He stopped, swung around, and snarled at me, "It's none of your fucking business."

I couldn't keep from flinching. "What the hell is wrong with you? I just want to help."

"You're what's wrong with me. I'm tired of toting your queer ass around, pretending to like all that shit. I'm done with you." He whipped back around and stomped down the trail toward home.

Stunned was hardly the right word for what I felt in that moment. Broken, maybe. Confused. Lost. And numb. We'd done so much together. Stopped using condoms months ago, spent endless days together, and he'd said he loved me a thousand times. Yet it all drowned out the truth like white noise, distant, unapproachable, and empty. He'd just been using me. My heart ached.

I don't know how long it took me to get back to the house, but I didn't bother going to the door. After throwing everything in my car, I hopped in and turned the key. The hum ran through my bones like a jackhammer. I backed out of the drive, and the tears didn't start until I pulled into the driveway of my parents' home.

My mom sat on the porch looking sad. She patted the swing seat next to her, and I all but fell beside her, letting my tears wet her shoulder. So this is what everyone meant about the doomed first love. His words rolled over and over in my head, while every bit of me kept saying "But I love him."

"Did he tell you?" my mother asked softly.

"He said he's not gay and doesn't want me." I fought back the tears now, dragging my T-shirt bottom across my face and cursing myself for the weakness.

"Ann is pregnant."

The words made it hard to breathe. Pregnant? He'd said he was just pretending with her, keeping up appearances. Hell, obviously he didn't care much for protected sex. God, I felt so empty and betrayed. My mom rubbed my back like she knew, and maybe she did. I damned myself for being so blind, but he wouldn't win. He wouldn't destroy me. I was stronger than that.

And I had been. Years of martial arts training, countless meaningless relationships, and pulling away from the world kept the hurt out. Until Brock introduced me to Sei. Sei, whose smile was honest and trust was so hard-won. We were two of a kind, he and I. And we weren't defeated.

Con rubbed my back like he had so many years ago. The betrayal still stung more than I thought it would have. I'd tested every two months after our relationship ended, fearing what he could have given me. Any encounters I initiated were practiced with a high level of caution. It'd been three years, I told myself; he had no power over me anymore. The ache in my chest now was all about Jamie, and that was different than what I felt for Con.

That day when Jamie was shot and Sei taken, I thought I would die. The world had become this dizzying spiral that threatened to pull me down into madness. And those days that I searched for Sei, I'd teetered on the edge of an abyss ready to drag me into endless despair. Jamie, barely breathing and stuck in a hospital bed, had begged me to find Sei. His heartbreak had been mine, and I did all I could to bring our little brother home.

I closed my eyes and realized it was really true. Sei was the brother of my heart. Jamie meant more to me than he should. And that feeling that had been infatuation for Con so long ago had vanished.

"Don't you want to try again?"

Was he for real? "You hit on Seiran! You haven't changed at all from the whoring bastard you were when we were teens."

"I was lonely. He's attractive. I think everyone has heard rumors about how easy he is. I didn't know you were here."

Excuses. Always. "Seiran and Gabe are exclusive. And I'm not looking to relive the hell of high school, thanks. I'd hate for you to have to tote my queer ass around." I pulled away from him and threw myself into the chair. Then something else occurred to me. "You're Dominion, right? You and your sister. Have either of you tested?"

"Males don't test. Cat has. She's a three."

"I tested. Sei tested. We're both level five. He's earth, I'm water. What element are you?"

"Air. Just like 80 percent of all Dominion families. Ordinary, dull, weak, air." He sounded more than a little bitter.

"Air can do some pretty heavy damage when combined with water." I gestured to the window and the snow piled up outside. "Like create a blizzard."

"I can barely make the wind blow. Cat could probably push around some clouds, but we've had five days of this blizzard. Neither of us have that kind of power."

Their whole relationship was a mystery to me. Most families weren't as close as

Jamie and Sei. "Why are you here with your sister?"

He shrugged and looked around the room as if it interested him. "She broke up with her boyfriend. I thought the trip would get her mind off him. He was bad for her anyway. A cop. So always away and kind of a rough sort of guy. My aunt and uncle said we could stay as long as we wanted for free."

"Aunt and uncle?"

"The Gossners."

"Are they Dominion?" I hadn't sensed any power from either of them, but if they weren't water, I wasn't likely to. They'd both been pretty nice to all of us, and I was becoming a paranoid bastard. Maybe Con had more details that Jamie hadn't already learned.

"No. Hans is my mom's brother. He married a non-Dominion girl."

And that meant he was no longer Dominion to some of the higher-ranked families, since he hadn't done his duty to bear a Dominion child. The laws were so messed up sometimes. Jamie was in the same predicament. If he married a non-Dominion girl, he would have a hard time doing anything with his very Dominion-focused brother and sister. He'd be the last chance the Browan family had to marry into a dynasty since Hanna was married to a non-Dominion girl and Sei was with Gabe. Hanna might still breed a reasonably powerful heir. Or the family could force Jamie into a marriage with someone of the first wave to breed a more powerful witch. I didn't want him to marry any girl at all.

Con seemed to be studying me. "We could be good again. Start over. Cat is happy around your friend. When she's happy, she doesn't cling to me so much. You and I can try again."

I got up and walked toward the window. How many years had my heart ached for him? How many scenarios had I thought of to get him back? And for what? To be some secret lover in a long line? "What happened to your baby? The one Ann was going to have?"

"It was a boy," he said quietly. "She aborted as soon as she found out."

Damn Dominion laws. "I'm sorry."

He didn't rise from his spot on the bed. I leaned against the wall.

"It's been a few years, so it doesn't hurt as much. I will probably never have children now. Catherine doesn't want any, despite what our parents say. So I can't even live through her babies."

Having discovered my homosexuality in my teen years, I'd had time to accept I wouldn't have children. And not being a part of one of the top families in the water aristocracy meant that I wouldn't be forced to have them since I had sisters, though I wondered if that would change now that I had tested as a level five. "I'm sorry. Sei is having a baby through a surrogate. I'll be happy if he lets me see the kid once in a while. Maybe I'll do that sort of thing in a few years."

"Were you and he lovers?" His eyes searched mine; there was pain there. Maybe he really had missed me.

"No. Just friends. He's my best friend. Seiran doesn't do anyone but Gabe now. They need each other." There bond was as metaphysical—magical—as it was love.

"Seiran Rou, the prince of the earth witches. I saw you on the news with him after the kidnapping and got so jealous. Never expected to run into you up here. In fact, I said yes to Catherine's request because I wanted to get away from the memories of what I'd fucked up. It was weird that she wanted to come up here all of a sudden. She's never liked Uncle Hans much. But it's good to see you again. Even if it's unexpected."

"You and I weren't meant to be." Shaping a new life with my new family was really making me anticipate what life had in store for me. I wondered if Jamie would even consider a relationship with me. He could have a baby through a surrogate like Sei had. We could work it out somehow.

"You left because of the baby?" Con asked. "I told you I was sorry for those things I said."

"I left because all you would give me was sex, and I wanted love."

He let out a heavy sigh.

"There was a time when sex was all that mattered. But I'm not a kid anymore. I have friends I love, my own little makeshift family." Did I love Jamie yet? Maybe. Either way, I was a careful guy, and I could keep myself from falling too hard. No need to be hurt again.

"And if I gave you all of me now? Told you I loved you?" Con sounded desperate.

"Too little, too late." I folded my arms across my chest and frowned at his sorrowful look. "You always told me you loved me," I pointed out. "It was only in the end that I realized you didn't mean it. It was just a means to an end. Empty words."

"I did mean it," Con insisted. "I never got over you. When you left and then they killed my baby, I thought I would die. Even checked into a mental institution for a few months." My expression must have been questioning because he continued. "I was cutting. The last time I nearly died." He pushed up his sleeves and showed me the myriad of scars that crisscrossed his arms. "That's when I went to rehab. Sometimes the need is still there. Like the pain will help. But I know it won't." He stretched and got up from the bed. "Then when Cat heard last month that her guy was not coming back, she began to do it. I was terrified she'd travel that same road I had. When my aunt offered this trip, I thought it'd be a way to save her."

"Has she done it while you're here?" I spent a lot of time studying psychology now that I'd met Sei. Issues inside the head were often more damaging than physical ones could be. His panic attacks were brutal and sometimes painful for everyone.

"I don't know. She rarely comes to our room. When we were at the cabin, she'd spend hours out by herself. I figured she just needed the time away. But I don't see any marks."

Just because he didn't see them, didn't mean she'd stopped. I thought of Jamie and wondered if he knew, but thinking of him fooling around with her just made a sharp pang of jealousy run through me. Why I figured jacking off with him gave me ownership in any way, I didn't know.

"Once we all get out of here, you should get her help. Real help. Not just half-assed attempts to get her to relax. Cutting is a serious mental disorder."

He nodded, looking miserable. I felt like an ass for being so mean to him before. Sure, we would never be lovers again, but that didn't mean we couldn't be friends. Not if he was out. He really looked like he needed a friend.

I grabbed his arm and pulled him to the door. "Maybe I can talk to her. Get a feel for it."

He looked indecisive for a minute, then said, "Okay. I'm just down the hall."

But I led him out of my room and headed in the direction I'd seen him go the other night. "Which one are you?"

He motioned to the one at the end on the left, then pulled his key out of his pocket. I watched him open the door and shove it open. He peered inside. "She's not here."

The room was empty, somewhat messy, but had double beds. He looked back at me again like he wanted to say something else. Then he just grabbed me and pulled me into the room, his arms wrapped around me in an awkward hug. The door banged shut, but he didn't let go.

When he eased up enough to free my arms, I hugged him back, patting his back and saying nice things like "You'll be okay" and "Everything will work out." He sobbed, hard and ugly. I just held him and let him release all the anguish. Unless he was a really good actor, the pain was real.

Ten minutes had probably passed before he finally let me go, sniffed, and looked away. "Sorry."

I held my hands up. "Hey, we all have our breaking point. Maybe you should let your sister know how worried you are."

"She never listens to me."

"Do they ever?" I had enough siblings to know better.

He chuckled lightly. "No, they really don't, do they?"

"We probably don't listen to them much either."

"No."

"I should go." I turned back to the door.

"Kelly?" He gripped my hand.

"Yeah?"

"Thanks."

"You're welcome." I left his room and headed back to mine.

Chapter Sixteen

Jamie

SEEING KELLY go into Con's room felt like a knife in the gut. I'd spent a lot of time in the kitchen playing up my role to Cat, trying to get her to talk. She knew more than she was saying, but I couldn't get much out of her. Then seeing Kelly and Con come out of our room and head to his made me want to punch someone.

The jealousy was new. But after that morning in bed, when I'd branded him with my come, I felt Kelly was mine. Gabe would have told me to suck it up and tell the kid. Kid, shit he wasn't really a kid was he? He would be twenty-one in a few months. I had to stop treating him like I treated Sei. Kelly hated the kid gloves. He didn't have Sei's issues. But any future we had together needed to be Kelly's choice, not mine. He was so young.

I paced the room, feeling like I'd been caged for days. The stink of Cat's perfume kept rising from my clothes. Usually those sorts of things didn't bother me. Sei was the one to complain, and he wasn't here. I hated the thought of her all over me. Women like her were what made the Dominion so bad. Her dislike for men was palpable. She tried in vain to mask her irritation whenever I brought up Seiran being Pillar. Despite my words the other day, she didn't seem to think he was strong enough to carry the title. Not even Tanaka was so blinded by the Code. Sei's mother, for all her weaknesses, fought for rights for her child, demanded the professors treated him like the powerful witch he was, and drafted laws to ease the entry of more males into the Dominion in the future. If she hadn't been such a cold bitch Sei's whole life, maybe they'd actually get along and he'd have been here with a coven of Pillar-supporting witches bonding instead of hiding with his boyfriend, best friend, and brother.

I sighed and stretched, my whole body aching from the fast trek to find Kelly yesterday. His massage had helped, but it would take a few days for the tension in my muscles to ease. I wondered how Kelly was holding up. He hadn't mentioned being sore, but his sports repertoire was more vast than mine. I know he went skiing with his father regularly among other things. Was Kelly in better shape than me? Was that even possible? I frowned at the thought. I had been a little lax lately.

I stripped out of my clothes as I walked toward the shower. I had to get the stink off me. It was hard to think with the ghastly perfume of fake flowers and chemicals drowning my senses. I needed to decide how to get us out of here. There was no telling how long it would take help to arrive. If Sei and Gabe couldn't convince the authorities of the plot to kill them, they'd wait till the storm was over.

I needed to think of a way to keep the situation from spiraling into further danger. The power was back on, and that was a plus, but it wouldn't be long before they discovered Sei and Gabe where gone. Would they turn to Kelly and me for revenge? Try to poison us too? If Cat was involved, Con probably was too, and I'd need to keep an eye on him as well. First and foremost, this storm needed to end. The only solutions that were coming to me were all suicide missions, but if that's what it took...

Kelly

THE SHOWER was running, and Jamie's clothes lay on the floor. Had he done something with Cat? Was he washing away the evidence? Did they have enough time to do anything? I hated the jealousy that ran through me. Jamie wasn't mine. He never said anything that would even make me think he was mine. Fuck, I hated the idea that I'd been used again. Granted I hadn't demanded anything in return and the sex had been good so far, but still, I wanted to be something to Jamie. Not just a bit of distraction while we were stuck here.

I sighed and tried to stomp down that growing green monster. Picking up his clothes and folding them, I then put them in his bag, trying not to be creepy and sniff them for his masculine scent.

There was a tray of food: fresh fruit, cheese, and meat that sat on a platter. A jug of milk sat beside it, unopened. I reached for a slice of cheese.

"Don't touch any of that until I try it," Jamie said, stepping out of the bathroom, towel wrapped around his hips. He swabbed at his hair with another towel. "Cat ate some of the fruit, so that should be fine, but I haven't tried the cheese or meat yet. And I brought the milk for your cereal. It's unopened and was toward the back of the fridge, so should be okay."

I blinked at the water trickling down his chest and longed to lick it away, but the green monster came back when he mentioned Cat. "Was it necessary to flirt with her? Or are you searching for a baby momma?"

He frowned, a stunned expression crossing his face before anger took its place.

"And you conveniently went to Con's room to scratch that endless itch you have, right?"

Was he accusing me of having sex with Con? I was the one with my clothes still on. "Constantine was having a rough day. He's worried about his sister. I was just comforting him. In a nonsexual manner."

Jamie glared at me.

I sighed, realizing it was probably better to tell him now than let him find out later that I did in fact know Con. "He was my high school boyfriend. But I broke it off three years ago. Do you really think I want him back after all this time?" I shook my head at Jamie. "He got a girl pregnant and told me he was tired of me following him around, then tried to call me a few weeks later for sex. There is *nothing* between us."

He stood in silence, thinking, it seemed, until his expression was back to that calm mask he always wore. He reached around me and snatched up a piece of cheese, bit it in half, chewed, then swallowed. After a moment he pressed the other half to my lips. I let it pass, tasting the sharp bitterness of it and the saltiness of his fingers when he brushed his thumb across my lips.

When his hand finally moved away, I could hardly speak, but blurted out, "Shit, keep that up, and I'll be throwing you on the bed and having my way with you."

He laughed and dug out another pair of boxers, let the towel slide off, then stepped into the clean shorts. I watched every second of it like it was a porno on slow mode. He even turned his back to me, leaving the boxers low on his hips, and bent over to retrieve his brush from the bag.

"Are you torturing me on purpose?"

"Like your little ass wiggling by the shower did earlier?"

I sighed dreamily. "You can have my ass anytime."

"Don't say things like that."

"Huh? You think I don't mean it?"

He crossed the room to stand before me again, close enough to kiss. "You don't."

Was he kidding? I grabbed two handfuls of that long blond hair of his and pressed my lips to his. The mint of his toothpaste had faded, but his tongue was flavored with fruit as it dueled with mine. I traced the shape of his mouth, sharing the wet grace that had me breathing heavy and my cock throbbing. I pulled back to sample just his lips again.

His chocolate brown eyes were that half-lidded stare that I knew meant arousal, even if I couldn't keep from looking down.

"No protesting this time?" I asked him.

He shrugged. "I want you. You're not a kid. I know that. My brain keeps saying I have to protect you."

"Protect me from yourself? I'm not a virgin. Hell, I've had my heart broken a half-dozen times. There is nothing you can do to me that hasn't already been done."

Jamie frowned. "You deserve better than that. You deserve someone who cares, loves you, wants to take care of you."

"You volunteering?" I asked.

"Maybe," Jamie said after a quiet moment.

I kissed him again just for saying those words. This time he pressed against me, letting his erection grind into my hip and swaying slightly to rub mine with his thigh. This time had to be more. Blow jobs and masturbation aside, I wanted him something fierce, didn't know if I could take him, but if that's what it took, I was willing to try. "Condoms?"

Jamie gulped, his neck flexing in a hot swallow that made me want to follow the tight skin down. He reached back, pulling a small sports bag out of his larger duffel. Inside was a small first aid kit: liniment rub, lube, and condoms.

"Cub scout," I laughed, reaching down to rub the length of him through the boxers.

"It's my sports kit. I give the condoms out at the gym. Safe sex is important."

That it was, but the condoms weren't likely to fit his monster cock. "But they won't fit you." I picked up the lube and scanned the back; yep, we could use it.

"They'll fit you just fine." He glanced away, looking at the bed instead.

I blinked, trying to understand what he just said. "You want me to fuck you?"

He sucked in a deep breath, anger rising up like some hidden sea creature bobbing to the surface. "When you put it that way..."

No way were we stopping now. I closed the new distance between us and pushed myself against him, grabbing his hair again and yanking him close. It was amazing to have such a large, strong man at my mercy, willing to submit to me and be manhandled. Oh the things I wanted to do to him.

I reached around to stroke his hot ass with one hand and dip down the back of the waistband with the other. "I'm sorry. It's just most guys expect me to bottom. Will you let me make love to you?"

His expression spoke of uncertainty, but he nodded and pulled me toward the bed, a condom and the lube in hand. He flushed before he dropped the items on the table beside the bed. "Yeah. You I will."

It made sense. He spent so much time taking care of others, being the strong one. Maybe he wanted someone else in control for a change. "Lose the shorts."

They dropped to the floor, and he stepped out of them.

"On the bed, chest to mattress, ass in the air." It felt good to have that kind of power. That kind of trust. He did as he was told without question, turning his head to the side so he could look at me. And seeing that clean-shaven ass and beckoning hole nearly made me come. He was beautiful.

I stripped out of my clothes and caught him looking my way, lust and hope in his eyes. He watched me, eyes trailing down my chest over my thighs. "Like what you see?"

"Yeah."

I grabbed the supplies and crawled onto the bed behind him. He was already hard and leaking, heavy sac and thick cock twitching with the need to be touched, hanging heavily between his legs. But we wouldn't be doing that just yet. Instead, I let my hands caress the insides of his legs, starting at the ankle and slowly gliding upward, tickling his thighs and finally reaching his straining sex and that amazing round ass.

Just like the rest of him, those two muscles were strong, defined, and begging for attention. I bent forward, letting my cock brush his thigh, and kissed each of those cheeks. No tattoos on his ass. I smiled and blew a soft breath across each cheek. He shivered beneath my touch, and I was only beginning.

Starting at his taint, I lapped at him with my tongue, sucking little slivers of flesh into my mouth and nibbling lightly at the soft skin. By the time I got to that puckered hole, he was clutching the headboard, muscles rippling with the restraint, back and shoulders tense, and I could feel his heart pounding where my face touched him.

The first nudge into his hole had him nearly jumping off the bed. I pressed a hand to the small of his back, calming him and stroking his spine while his flesh seemed to twitch around my touch.

"Please," Jamie begged. "I'm used to hard and fast. You're killing me."

I grinned and scooped up the lube to rub some on my fingers, letting the warm slickness center me. Giving myself a few heavy pulls had Jamie swallowing again, eyes locked on my dick like he wanted that between his lips. "Soon enough," I told him, then let myself go to press one finger into him.

"You're really tight." Had he ever bottomed before? Scratch that, didn't want to know. The green monster flared its head for a second, and I almost missed the wiggle and press of his hips, forcing me farther into him. The sweet nub inside him was close, I was sure, but if I touched it, he'd come, and I didn't want us to be done yet. "Ready for another?"

"You..."

"Pretty sure I'm bigger than one finger." Bigger than three. Not as big as him, but I still didn't like the idea of hurting him.

"I can take it."

I frowned at him, but his eyes were closed, face peaceful but still turned my way. I decided then that we'd go slowly if needed, and I trusted him to tell me if he couldn't handle it. I slipped on the condom, added more lube, and lined my tip up.

"Look at me," I commanded, giving him the rough edge of my voice.

His eyes whipped open, meeting mine as I pressed inside. He gripped the headboard hard, knuckles white, but he didn't flinch or move away. In fact, he nudged his hips backward to engulf all of me. His heat made me pause and shudder. This wasn't enough. I let him adjust, though, felt him stretching around me, body fighting to clench up before finally relaxing. *Damn.*

I pulled out and slapped his hip. "Turn over."

He rolled onto his back and stared up at me with worry. I bumped his legs apart and sank into him. This time the entry was much smoother. His body relaxed around me, muscles twitching a little the deeper I went, and when I hit his prostate, he grunted, his hole tightening on my sex. He closed his eyes again, seeming to savor the feeling. I pulled back and slid in slowly, making sure to bump his sweet spot again. He let out a soft sigh and closed his eyes.

"Open your eyes."

He smiled and opened his eyes. I began to move, setting a slower pace. "Touch yourself."

Watching his big mitt wrap around his erection and match his strokes to my thrusts was almost better than being in him. His expression was seductive and relaxed. I wanted him writhing again. *Shit that was hot.*

I pulled back, shifted position, and slammed forward, repeating the motion in earnest. His eyes closed again, hand moving faster, sweat appearing at the edge of his forehead. I worked him hard, loving the sound of our bodies coming together, the feel of him against me, and the expression on his face as he spiraled to lose it.

"Eyes," I demanded. He struggled to open them again, finding me and holding my gaze as the final moment came to us both. His body clenched around mine, cock spewing forth long streams of spunk over his hand and chest. I let go inside him, filling the condom, feeling his body milk me of everything I had and spinning my brain into that peaceful satiated place that only a good orgasm could get me to.

Jamie wrapped his arms around me. I lay on his chest, breathing in the smell of us and feeling like I could conquer the world. "If only we didn't have to go kick Andrew Roman's ass, we could stay like this forever."

He looked at me, but instead of that sexy smile I was used to, he frowned, pushed me off, grabbed his brush, walked into the bathroom, and closed the door.

"What'd I say?" I asked the empty room. After tying off the condom, I threw it in the trash and cleaned up the room again before getting dressed.

When he finally emerged I was greeted with a stony silence. Had the last hour not happened? He dressed like he was going downstairs. "You want to talk about it?"

"No."

"It's not your fault he's still alive."

The look he threw me was a tired one. I probably shouldn't have brought up Andrew Roman. The guy was a madman who was determined to kill Sei if just to get back at Gabe for some imagined reason. But that wasn't Jamie's fault. He dug through his bag for clean clothes, his shoulders tense, posture reading: fuck with me and I'll beat you.

"Are you going down to dinner?" I finally asked.

"Yes. You should stay here."

That made no sense. "So they can poison you and not me? You're the nurse. Shouldn't we keep you healthy?"

Jamie looked at me, his expression an odd mix of anger and sadness. "If something goes wrong tonight, I want you to take the sled to Rabbit Five. Gabe will know what to do."

"What are you planning?"

He said nothing.

Damn him! "Stop treating me like a kid. I can help. Just tell me what to do."

"I did. I told you I want you to stay here."

I tried to keep from ripping the room apart. "Fucking A! Why can't you trust me?"

"How about you tell me what's going on in your head first," he answered coolly. "Andrew Roman is a psychopath. Neither of us need that trouble. What do you really want us to do? How can I convince you to stay here where it's safe?"

"There is no safe anymore," I told him.

He flinched.

"I keep dreaming of Sam. I thought maybe we can try to help him."

"Whatever Sam's involved in has got to be trouble. Neither of us need that."

"So we let him die?"

"We're not gods, Kelly. We don't decide those things."

"But shouldn't we help if we could? I knew that if it was Sei out there, you'd be on your way to find him and save him. Is it different because it's Sam? He has no one."

Jamie's expression was cold. "He kidnapped Sei. Hurt him."

"So he deserves to die? This is some sort of fucked-up karma? You're better than that, Jamie. Fuck. What if it was me? What if I had made the same bad decision? I was friends with Brock. I thought he was a nice guy. Didn't have any idea he was a psycho cutting people up. Does that make my life worthless too?"

Jamie's silence was deafening. Was that it? He didn't trust me, couldn't trust me because I'd known Brock? Brock and I hadn't even been all that great of friends, more we hung in the same circle of athletic guys. All of those guys had since abandoned me, though whether that was due to Brock's death or my acceptance into the Magic Studies program, I didn't know.

"Fuck me," I grumbled, tears stinging my sight. That was it, wasn't it? My irritation built for a few more minutes while I tried to ignore him. Finally, I gathered up my things, took Sei and Gabe's keys off the dresser, and headed for the door.

"Where are you going?"

"To Sei and Gabe's room. I hope you sleep well with your suspicions and distrust. I don't deserve that and you know it."

"Kelly..."

I shook my head at him, grabbed my box of cereal, and checked the hallway, which was empty. Then made my way to the abandoned suite. Jamie didn't try to stop me.

The room didn't look like anyone had been inside. I left the Do Not Disturb sign on the handle and turned the light on, then flipped the deadbolt so no one would be able to get in unless they broke the door down. My gut ached at the sheer echoing silence of the room, the loneliness.

Their room wasn't much different than ours, other than the heavy lightproof curtain that covered the single window. I turned up the heat and crawled into bed. The cold and weatherworn days were getting to me. The bed smelled like clover and honey. Seiran. It made me smile.

Conviction

I snuggled down into the sheets that smelled so nice and clicked off the lamp. Here I could imagine that I was home in my own bed. That I'd wake up and find Sei puttering around the kitchen. I'd hear Jamie wandering through the apartment grumbling about the lack of fire extinguishers or some other safety nonsense. Gabe would slide up behind Sei, kiss him, hold him close, and I'd flush with embarrassed excitement to watch two people so in love. Jamie would steal occasional glances at me that contained more heat each time. Then we'd go to the Y for a few hours of swimming and home for some pillow time with my lover. A guy could dream, anyway. I buried my tear-covered face in the pillow and prayed for sleep.

Chapter Seventeen

Jamie

MY ASS ached, a constant reminder that it had been years since I bottomed and that I'd let Kelly have complete control over me. It was self-loathing that had made me yank myself out of bed and later yell at him, treat him like a kid he obviously wasn't.

Every time I thought of Kelly with someone else I had a nearly irresistible urge to kill things. The years of Gabe threatening me if I bothered Sei suddenly made sense. The instinct to protect and shelter almost made me feral. I could feel the bear inside nodding its approval of Kelly, telling me to claim him.

Then Kelly had casually offered himself up as a sacrifice for a guy he'd never even met—a guy who'd kidnapped Sei and had been a part of a plot to kill Gabe. I was so pissed at him. And at myself. How could I condemn some poor kid who'd made a bad choice and now seemed to be forced into a life-or-death situation? Hadn't my years of RN training prepared me for that? Impartiality was impossible when it came to family. I couldn't separate the fact that it was Sam and Andrew Roman. Had Sam saved him from the fire? Why? *Fuck.* Did that mean there was a chance Matthew Pierson was still alive? If he was, I'd risk jail time just to off him myself.

I growled at the idea of Roman building a spell and an elaborate plan to trap us in the middle of nowhere. Sei was safe, but Kelly still needed me even if he insisted he could handle the situation. No average person could take a vampire. Hell, I was pretty sure *I* couldn't take a vampire. Just because I could bench-press 350lbs didn't mean I was stronger than the average vampire. And Andrew Roman was far from average.

A deep rumble welled up in my chest and the sound that reverberated was hardly human. I tried to breathe through the fear, anger, and self-loathing to control the beast within. Only one other time in my life had it demanded control so fiercely. That time had ended in a terrified Sei and a couple dead thugs. *Fuck.* At least I knew where Kelly was. I soothed the bear by assuring it he was just down the hall, feet away, inside a locked room, protected...

Did Kelly have any idea how much I wanted to create something more permanent with him? Was he even ready yet? He was so young. He probably still wanted to run wild and experience parties, tricks, and endless one-night stands. I shivered at the idea, the bear thundering through my blood with discontent. *Fuck.* I wasn't ready to let him go yet, and certainly wasn't about to let him go out and die for a guy he'd never met. We weren't fucking Marines. I'd never been mentally stable enough to enlist, spending most of Sei's high school years going from one eating disorder center to another. Kelly wasn't the warrior he claimed he was either. He was just a track star, a swimming guru who taught kids at the Y how to swim on Saturdays and watched over my little brother like he was the older one instead of Sei.

I sighed, knowing what I had to do. Kelly would only wait so long. He'd either sneak out or force my hand. I had to be ahead of him. Keep him out of trouble until Sei and Gabe brought help, or the spell ended. And if the spell would only die when Sam did, then I couldn't let Kelly be forced to make that decision. It would break his heart even if he didn't know Sam.

Fuck, I hated having to be the grown-up. Hated realizing the only way out of a situation was to hurt someone. Ever since they tried to take Sei from me, I'd been forced into this role over and over again. The bear could do it with little trouble. Bears were all about food, territory, and protecting its young. If I let it go completely, could I come back? I'd always been more human than bear in my other form, and it wasn't near the new moon, but I knew I could change. The beast ran through every pore, every vein, and tasted every breath. It wanted out. It wanted to claim Kelly, fight off the danger, and declare victory—dominance—over anyone who would try to take him from us. There was only one thing left to do.

I listened at the door to be sure he went to Gabe's room and didn't come back out. At least he was safe. Gabe would have help on the way by dawn, and whether I was here or not, Kelly would be going home. My ass throbbed as I moved, reminding me I'd let him closer than I had allowed anyone in over a decade. In that moment I'd thought he really got me. His orders were filled with a loving tone that said he needed to control as much as I needed to let go. Even the bear had settled, soothed by his voice and sweet mastery.

Maybe he did really get me. Because he was right. We couldn't leave Sam to die if there was something we could do. Sei would never forgive me, nor would Kelly, obviously. I probably wouldn't forgive myself either.

Grabbing a pen and a sheet of paper from the desk, I sat down to write a short note to Kelly. At least if I didn't return, he'd know what I felt. Gabe was right; I couldn't run from my feelings for him. Couldn't bury my emotions in my need for family. Kelly had blown that ship out of the water when he said he'd be willing to lay down his own life to save us. Gabe, Sei, and I were his family. And for some reason I had yet to understand, Sam had been added as well.

After I finished, I set the note on the pillow and grabbed up my things. Tonight I'd have to act, and since night had fallen and the storm rose again, I knew someone would be leaving the house to help the storm build. All I had to do was wait and watch. I nurtured the bear, keeping him close to the surface so I could change fast and at will the second danger reared its angry head. I'd never felt it so close before, and knew how easy the change would be. Maybe not painless, but fast enough to be deadly. Most people looked at me and saw a large man. None ever saw the beast within. Maybe it was time for that to change. If I succeeded in scaring the bastards away from my family, I'd risk just about anything.

I monitored the hall for almost an hour before I saw anyone. I'd hoped it would be Con because beating the shit out of him would have relieved some of the tension. But Cat headed for the stairs, decked out in a snowsuit and gear. I waited for her to get to the bottom of the stairs before following.

After tiptoeing down to the registration area, I followed her outside and around the side of the lodge into the woods a ways. When she stepped onto a hidden snowmobile and it roared to life, my heart nearly skipped a beat. Damn, I'd have to hurry to follow her. If I kept far enough back and left the lights off, she wouldn't notice my sled over the noise of her own.

I rushed back to the sled Kelly and I had hidden, praying I could catch up with Cat and stop the storm. If she was part of the magic, maybe just stopping her would help. Kelly said Sam was there and dying, though how this was all tied to him didn't make any sense. If Andrew Roman was really behind this mess, then it was a suicide mission. But I had to do something. Maybe I could get Sam and get out, be back at the lodge in time for breakfast and to show Kelly I really did care. Then Gabe would show up with the cavalry, and we'd all go on with our lives. Only that scenario meant that Roman probably survived and would come back to bite us in the ass another day.

Catching Cat's trail was fairly easy, as she didn't seem to care that the snow wasn't yet heavy enough to cover her tracks. Removing Kelly's bracelet must have made it harder for them to use his power because the snow itself hadn't been nearly as bad since

I'd tossed the damn thing in the fireplace at the cabin. The wind was still fierce, whipping up whiteout conditions with little effort, but there wasn't more coming from the sky.

I caught a glimpse of her lights in the dark and hoped that wherever she was headed, it would lead me to Sam. Gabe would have been more prepared. He carried a Glock in his suitcase and had it on him whenever he suspected someone might be after Sei. My only weapons were my fists and my head. And while I was a big guy, used to being stronger than others, I wasn't a fighter. No one looked at me and tried to start something, so I'd never had a reason to learn. My only experience came from sparing in the gym with my buddies, and most of that was just swinging meaty fists at each other rather than any skill. Somehow I didn't think my hours spent pounding a boxing bag would actually work with a real person. People didn't stand still, and vampires moved faster than humans. Though if I was really going to be facing who I thought I was, all the skill in the world wouldn't matter nor would a gun or any other type of weapon. A wood chipper would help. Vampires could only be destroyed by fire or total body destruction. But I couldn't imagine finding one of those laying around somewhere.

CONVICTION

Cat snaked around the river, flying across areas of water that didn't seem completely frozen with practiced ease, and headed for what looked like a dark shadow in the distance. The closer I got, the more I could make out the round barrel shaped tower with windows painted black. The earth around me cringed away from it because whatever was inside was so unnatural even the distance couldn't lessen the growing menace. This was death magic—something I hadn't even known existed until that moment—but the feel of the spell was clear, dark, a waiting pulse of doom. I prayed that whoever was dying up there wasn't Sam.

The tower so distracted me, I hadn't realized I'd lost Cat until I was almost on top of a cabin. I stopped the machine, shutting it off to listen for her sled, but the world was a cold, silent wind. Heat rolled in waves from the chimney of the cabin, and light flickered in the window. It was twenty feet away, and if anyone was inside they would have heard my sled. I cursed and slid to a stop, cutting the engine, parking it off to the side. Maybe I could play casual. Claim I'd just followed her out into the storm because I was worried. Pretend to be the rescuing hero...

The door opened, and Cat stepped out. Though her expression was blank, blood dripped from her lips. She almost looked like a broken doll, eyes vacant and detached, lifeless.

I never saw him coming, but Roman appeared next to me in nothing but tan pants and a stained long-sleeved T-shirt. I could only think that he didn't look injured at all from the explosion that had killed Matthew, just as he came at me, fangs glistening in the dark. I sucked in a deep breath, ready to let the bear loose, but I wasn't fast enough.

Kelly

SAM AND I seemed to have a lot in common. Each time I fell asleep, I dreamed of him. And like me, he dreamed of going home too. Only his home was filled with family, all speaking a different language and laughing at the babies that crawled around an already crowded room. He didn't have the same makeshift family that we had created for ourselves. But he was hoping to get back to his regular one even if he'd always felt like an outsider.

He opened his eyes to a worn little cabin. The fire was dying. He rushed to throw in another log. The flames rose again, but he didn't linger. He pulled on a hat and some gloves and stepped out into the cold. Night was falling; it would start again. The snow would once again become a blizzard. He was so tired. This would be the end. He promised himself that tonight he'd succeed, destroy the spell, end the storm, kill himself.

My heart ached for him.

Through his eyes I saw the dilapidated cabin and the watchtower that stood behind it. A frozen river wound its way around the area in a winding path that wasn't quite covered in snow.

Was it an abandoned ranger station?

Sam carried with him some trinkets: a lock of hair, a comb, and a watch. These things helped him keep connected, he told me without words. It wasn't all about the tracking bands we'd been given, though they had helped establish the first connection. He wasn't natural, and what he could do wasn't normal. I tried to ask him what he meant, but he didn't answer. Maybe he couldn't hear my question so much as see images from me like I could from him. And I didn't know how to ask questions I wasn't sure I had even formed yet.

He headed for the tower, where shadows moved through the windows like a monster waiting. I tried to shout, tried to tell him to stop, but he climbed a ladder, and when he opened the hatch to step inside the watchtower, I woke up, sitting up in bed, drenched in sweat, heart racing like I'd had the scare of my life. Yet I'd seen nothing other than an old cabin and a tower of some kind. Whatever had been inside the tower was still a mystery. A part of the spell maybe? More death? A monstrous vampire waiting? Getting up, I went to the window and peered beyond into the darkness, then glanced at the time on my phone, which still searched for a signal.

My stomach growled. It was after dinnertime. Jamie hadn't returned. Was he okay? He hadn't been poisoned, had he?

It was eerie how silent it got here at night. Mr. and Mrs. Gossner seemed to never be around. I never saw Con or Cat much past dark, and if there were any other guests, I hadn't seen them at all. Something about the place just gave me an eerie vibe, like something could be waiting around the corner to jump out at me. I hated it and couldn't wait to go home. If we made it home.

I wandered downstairs and, finding no one in the dining hall, grabbed a loaf of bread that appeared to be untampered with and ate a slice while I studied the large map pinned to the wall in the main lobby.

The map was a topographical close-up of the area. All of the cabins were marked.

Ten in all, spanning a four-mile radius. To the south, beyond all the cabins, a blue snake etched the map in a curling weave. Some sort of creek or river. Hadn't Sam been near a river?

I followed its path, tracing it with my fingers, searching the banks for anything that looked like it could be the old tower. When I found it, I could hardly contain my shout of glee. Less than three miles to the southwest there was a circle and a blip that could be the cabin. Though nothing was written to say what it was, I was pretty sure that was what we were looking for.

After grabbing a spare map from the main counter, I folded it and marked the location and made my way upstairs. I opened the door to the room I had shared with Jamie only to be surprised to find it dark and empty. My heart sank into my stomach when I realized all his gear was gone.

Had he gone off to Rabbit Five without me? For a few seconds it was really hard to breathe. I even took a few heavy swigs from my inhaler. Did he distrust me that much? Enough to leave me behind? I sank down on the bed, feeling like I weighed a million pounds.

"What about it?" Jamie had said about the first time we'd had sex. The fact that he

saw me as nothing more than a fling really bugged me. Was it wrong to have gotten my hopes up?

Sucking in a deep breath, I fell back against the bed and glared at the ceiling. Dreams of a happy family all popped like Zuma bubbles falling away into oblivion. Of course it didn't change the outlook of my life, because if I didn't get out of this frozen wasteland, I'd die. Sei was still my best friend. He'd promised me he'd send help. And there was no one more earnest about a promise than Sei. I could wait. Hide. Pray. Only Sam would die. Wherever he was, he was going to sacrifice his life to end it all. Somehow the idea of that sounded worse. If he died, would the spell actually end? Or strengthen? Fuck.

Something crinkled beneath my head. I rolled over and grabbed a note that had been on the pillow. Was it from Jamie? My heart skipped a beat. Maybe he hadn't abandoned me to escape. Maybe he was headed right into the worst imaginable danger. I sucked in a deep breath as I read over his words:

Kelly,

I'm sorry I had to do it this way. You're very young, and you deserve to find the love of your life and have a long and wonderful existence. I know how angry you are with me for not letting you go after Sam, but I can't let you. Sei needs you, and I need to know you survived.

I will do the best I can to stop Roman. Gabe will be bringing help, so wait for him, please. I know you'll be pissed at me. That's okay. But know I'm not going alone because I don't think you can handle yourself. I'm going alone because there's no way either of us can face a vampire and survive. I'd rather you lived. Take care of Sei. Know that I trust you, and I love you.

Jamie

Air left my lungs in a great whoosh that felt as though I'd been hit by a linebacker on the forty-yard line. I dropped the note, tears clogging my vision, and had to reach for my inhaler. It made me so mad and heartbroken at once. I didn't need a goddamned hero. Why couldn't he let me help? Maybe we would have a chance together. Thought of something to take out the vampire or slow him down. Anything other than this stupid suicide mission. The pain in my chest didn't ease even though the discomfort in my lungs did.

I lay there for a while, trying to pull myself together and debating my options.

Were there any? I couldn't leave him out there alone. But following was a death wish. Neither of us were armed, and how did anyone fight a vampire anyway? Without some C4 and a tactical team, I couldn't imagine there was much of a chance to beat him. Sei said Sam had shot Matthew point blank and then set the barn on fire. I didn't have a gun, but I did have fuel. Like he would somehow stand still long enough for me to set him on fire...

I took a heavy breath and stepped out of the room quietly, wondering what to do now. Go to the tower and find Sam? Getting Sam out would probably stop the storm. But I had no idea what I was up against. My magic training was minimal, and I was pretty sure whatever they were using wasn't in standard Dominion textbooks. The Dominion so needed to overhaul their training. Sam shouldn't have power, and yet he somehow combined the power of several witches to create the storm of the decade. That had to be magic worth studying.

The light on under the door at the end of the hall gave me a bit of inspiration. I knocked on Con's door, praying his sister didn't answer. He opened it looking depressed, with eyes swollen like he'd been crying.

"Everything okay?" I asked him, feeling more than a little awkward. It didn't look like his sister was around. Funny how she was gone in the middle of the night. I would have suspected her of being with Jamie, but couldn't imagine him running off with the rail-thin air witch. He'd even been irritated by the smell of his clothes after touching her, going so far as to wrap them in a separate bag so her perfume didn't linger.

"Yeah. Fine. Want to come in? Not like I'm getting any sleep anyway." He stepped back to let me in the room.

Walking in, I looked around further. No sign of Cat.

"She's not here."

"Is that why you're upset?"

He rubbed at his eyes. "I'm not upset. What are you doing here?" It almost sounded like what the fuck do you want? Con looked tired. His wrist was red around the tracker he wore. I groaned. If he was part of this, would he have been left behind like some battery, discarded until he was useful?

I had to stop doubting myself. Had to start trusting in others. I would have to be strong enough to hold Jamie up this time. And it was now or never, I supposed. "Can I trust you?"

"Sure." He shrugged like he didn't care either way.

What was the worst he could do, attack me? If he helped, I might have a chance. So I poured out the whole story to him about the bad storm not being natural and Sei's past and my current rocky relationship with Jamie. Constantine sat in silence, soaking it all up, asking a question here or there. I even told him about Sam and the tower I saw.

"It's an abandoned ranger station. Floods every spring. That's why they moved the station southeast," Con told me. "But I don't get it. If this Sam guy is trying to do the right thing, why doesn't he just stop?"

"I'm pretty sure a vampire is making him do it. The power of compulsion once they bite you is pretty damn strong. Matthew made Sei put a knife in Gabe's chest by just commanding him to. And Sei is crazy about Gabe. The whole thing almost killed them both." Sam didn't have a chance against a vampire as strong as Andrew Roman. "The rangers at the Beaver Creek station were dead. Jamie said he thought it looked like a vampire kill. They were just torn to shreds."

"Can vampires really do that? Control people? I thought that only happened in movies."

"If they take your blood and they are a powerful enough vampire, they can control you. Matthew kept having to feed on Sei to control him. He said it feels like someone else is pulling the strings of your body. Your brain gets no say. A stronger vampire may only have to bite you once. Gabe once said that the blood connection fades over time, but never completely. Like that vampire could come back years later and yank you around like a dog on a chain." It was an unsettling truth about vampires. Gabe always came across as polite, respectful, and very human. Only he wasn't. I think we all tiptoed around the idea that Gabe wasn't exactly what we saw. We wanted him to be human, and so he was. Did Sei ever see the vampire? Somehow I didn't think so.

"Shit."

"Yeah," I agreed.

"So what are you going to do?"

"Go to the abandoned station and try to get Sam out. Maybe that will stop the storm, and the vampire will give up. Destroying the spell would be ideal, but getting Sam out is priority. I think he's the one keeping the storm together somehow."

"But why does the vampire want us dead anyway?"

"Not you. He probably doesn't even know who you are. He wants Sei dead and Gabe to suffer because Gabe killed his lover years ago." I got up and went to the bathroom, searching under the sink and praying that some of the old staples were there. They were. I'd have to check in my room too. Maybe we had an option to get out of here. I don't know why I didn't think of it sooner. We'd had a Ski-Doo that had gotten water in the lines when I was a kid. My cousin had driven it into a creek not fully frozen over. He'd been crying and terrified he'd ruined the expensive machine. But I'd watched my dad drag it out of the water and patch the machine back up.

Grabbing the bottle of rubbing alcohol, I decided to have a backup plan for the sleds in case Jamie had taken our hidden one. "We'll need more alcohol, but we should be able to clear a sled." If Hans hadn't taken them all apart. I suspected they were somehow involved in this mess since they'd given us the trackers and had helped cut us off from the world. "You should head to Rabbit Five."

"My sister was dating a vampire," Con said after a quiet moment.

His words stopped me cold. "What vampire?" Hadn't he said before that his sister's boyfriend was a cop? *Shit.*

"His name is Andrew Roman. He's a detective in the cities. I only met him once. He seemed nice. Talked about a group for male witches. Cat didn't like it much, said men didn't have much power. Andrew didn't seem to like that comment much. In fact, he didn't seem to like her much."

"He's the bastard who wants Sei dead."

"Do you think he bit me? Maybe Cat?"

Cat for sure. Con, maybe. *Fuck.* Was talking to Con like telling Roman everything I was doing? I stared at him for a minute, exhaustion showing in every bit of his body. His eyes were ringed with dark bags, face almost gaunt, shoulders sagged, back bowed like he'd been defeated. How long had they been pulling power from him? *Fuck.* I grabbed the bracelet off his wrist and stuffed it in the side drawer.

He blinked at me in confusion.

"Trust me," I told him.

"Then I'm going with you to the abandoned station."

"No way. It's not safe."

"Look around you, Kelly. My sister isn't here. She's never here. That means she's probably out there with him. She means nothing to him. He's probably messed with her head. But she's all I have." Con began tugging on his snow things. "I can help you get the sleds working. There's more alcohol in the maintenance cupboard beside the lobby. It should be enough to clear out a sled or two."

I stared at him for a minute, wondering if I could really trust him. But it was everyone else's lack of trust that had been really eating at me. How could I ask them to do what I wasn't willing to do? So I took a leap of faith. "Fine. Meet me downstairs in ten minutes."

He nodded. I returned to my room to pack up my stuff and bundle myself up. Jamie had left most of his things, but so had Gabe and Sei. There just wasn't enough room on a snowmobile to carry luggage. I grabbed one of Jamie's huge warm sweaters and put it on before piling into my snowsuit. The journey was going to be long and cold, but I'd get there and end this no matter what it took.

Chapter Eighteen

Jamie

I came to in pain, my neck warm with blood and aching. It took me only a moment to remember what had happened and where I was. The cold blew around me. I could almost feel the spell trying to pull the earth from me, only the earth was a fickle thing, it only responded when it wanted to. That's why earth witches were some of the most powerful in the world.

The cabin was uninspired. Stained, dirty, smelling of unwashed human flesh and old blood. Cat sat in the corner, a vacant look on her face and the blood from her most recent bite gone. There would only be one reason for healing that fast since I was pretty sure Roman had no reason to heal her. She'd been changed.

I cursed to myself and turned my head carefully to peer at the rest of the room without trying to alert anyone to the fact that I was awake. I'd been bitten. I could feel that much. I was surprised he hadn't just ripped out my throat. Maybe that's what he'd left Cat behind for, since Roman didn't seem to be in the cabin anywhere.

The fire raged, so at least I was warm. I wondered where Sam was. In the tower? I closed my eyes and focused on the earth. I could feel the tower in the distance, pulsing like a thorn in the thumb of the earth. Mother Earth wanted it gone. She offered me strength, despite the sleepy prowess of the winter-laden ground, she crammed power into me.

I couldn't help my scream as the change rolled through me, ripping me apart, and putting me back together, until the cry became a roar. I barely noticed Cat vanishing out the door, locking it behind her as she went.

Kelly

CONSTANTINE WAITED for me by the front door. He'd packed up a bag of food and had an arm full of alcohol bottles. I directed him to the garage and went to check our hiding spot for the spare sled. Sure enough, it was gone. Another pain lanced through my chest. He really had gone alone, knowing he'd probably die. Damn him and his stupid hero complex. I was so going to break him of that if we made it out of this alive. If we moved fast enough, I could help. He'd be pissed that

I hadn't stayed safe at the lodge, but sometimes you had to just suck it up.

The snow was falling again, and the wind began to pick up. The ferocity of it sat just beyond my senses, like a cougar in the bushes, waiting to pounce until I'd almost made it back to the garage. The power hit me with the force of a lightning bolt flowing through my core. I dropped to my knees and barely kept myself from falling headfirst into the snow. There was no mistaking the power of the storm or what the spell pulled from me. My hands shook while I pulled myself toward the door and then up so I could walk inside and put the barrier between us. Now I would need Con. He'd have to drive the sled. I wouldn't be able to battle the storm and drive too.

He was already bent over one of the newer machines. I instructed him on how to clear the lines and sat on my knees beside him, struggling to breathe. He poured alcohol into the gas tank, then tried to start it, then added a little more. Until finally it kicked on, sounding like a sick chainsaw. But it ran. We let it run for a while to clear out some of the tainted gas, then added another few gallons of the fresh stuff. Hans had pulled apart most of the other machines, but maybe he didn't want to lose the newer ones. Maybe he was bitten too. I sighed and pushed the thought aside. The police could sort it out later if any of us survived.

"Can you drive?" I asked Con. "I'll try to keep the snow from pelting us." Though I knew how tired it was going to make me. I was already setting myself up behind the shield that Sei had been practicing with me before we came here. I'd never thought to need it. Never thought I'd be faced with a spell strong enough to pull power from me. Sei's shield worked a lot like the metal door wrapped around his heart. It only opened for certain people, though I know when he became Pillar managing the amount of energy had become a struggle. I focused on the memory of his lesson, how he pictured the barrier, something more metaphysical than tangible. I pictured mine more like a forcefield, wrapping it around me, tight at first, which eased some of the pull from the spell, then widening it a little to include Con.

"Sure." Con shoved the door to the garage open. "I used to play down there as a kid. I'd know the way in my sleep." He cursed when he saw how hard the snow was blowing and the wind whipped hard enough to shove us around. I put more force into the shield and searched far and wide for the strength of water. Found the creek, though it was miles away, topped with ice, but free-flowing beneath. It promised me strength, and I grasped for anything it would offer.

We loaded up the sled, he slid on, and I jumped up behind him. After making sure we were both covered up from the cold and had our helmets on, we headed out into the night. I pushed my energy into a large bubble that surrounded us, giving enough distance for him to see. Con drove fast, but well enough to take us around rocks or bushes that I couldn't see until they were upon us. I was too focused on the storm, the snow, the water in the distance, and the spell that beat at my shield. The closer we got to the creek, the stronger I felt. Maybe this would work after all.

The vibration of the machine and the raging blizzard gave me something to focus on instead of the loss of my new family. I refused to think about Jamie and the time we'd spent alone together. Those thoughts weakened my power. Without the bubble, the sled would be crawling along instead of flying through the darkness. And since I felt Sam in my head, losing more strength, I knew we had to hurry.

Con slowed the sled well before the tower came into sight. He pushed up into a heavy clot of pines and let the machine die. With a flip of his helmet, he was staring at me in question. Were we really going to do this?

Yeah. Yeah we were.

I jumped off and left the helmet behind. First we'd sneak into the tower and try to get Sam out. Con would take him back to the lodge, then come back for me. If Roman was around, he was going to die tonight. However, getting Jamie, Sam, and Con to safety were first on my list. And really, armed with only a kitchen knife and martial arts, if I ran into the vampire out here, I probably wasn't going home again. But I'd hurt the bastard really good before the hereafter took me.

We trotted along through the heavy snow, Con and I moving among the trees like ninjas or hunters trying not to scare a deer. Neither of us would point out that, if there were a vampire near, he'd hear our heartbeats long before he saw us.

When the tower came into sight, the darkness from the above windows lingered like a bad omen. The entire area pulsed of magic, dark and thick unlike anything I'd ever seen before. Evil. I sucked in a deep breath. Magic wasn't supposed to be good or evil. It just was. It was the intent that made it something, but this… I had no other word for it.

Only a small flicker of light from within led anyone to believe that someone might be alive in there. The cabin twenty feet away roared with light, smoke pouring from the chimney, a fire obviously raging within. Was Roman in there? He wouldn't need the heat. That would be more for Sam, maybe Cat, since vampires couldn't feel the cold.

Not that it mattered. We'd run into him sooner or later.

I tiptoed to the ladder to the tower, looked up at the closed hatch above, then started to climb. My hands tingled from the wind that wailed around us. Several rungs wobbled in my grip and made me cling harder going up.

"This place has seriously bad vibes," Con whispered. I barely heard him through the constant howl of cold.

"Stay here," I said to him and continued to climb. When I reached the top, the closed hatch loomed like something out of a horror movie. So much could be beyond that piece of wood. There had been a time when things like vampires hadn't scared me. They just hadn't been real. But the memory of the murdered rangers at Beaver Creek had ripped away that illusion.

Hell, the whole axis of my world had changed since meeting Sei. People really did hurt you just because they could. Monsters came in many different shapes, forms, and types. Some of them were human, and some of them truly just monsters.

With that thought, I pushed on the wood plank, felt it shift and slide back. The flicker I'd seen from the ground was a single candle that bounced light around the dirty corners of the tower.

The power of a spell drenched the room. Red stained the floor in intricate patterns, and the stink of blood made me cover my nose. I didn't know enough about spells to understand what I was seeing. But Sam sat curled in on himself, face gaunt enough to make him look skeletal and eyes hollow with heavy black bags around them. He looked like a skeleton. His dark hair was stained and dirty, his face marred with bruises, and what looked like frostbite trailed over his arms and fingers. Fuck, he already looked dead, but he moved, and I had to swallow back a gasp of horror at the realization he was still alive.

He shook his head at me, lips forming words that didn't make a sound. I rushed to his side and lifted him. He was so light, nothing but skin and bones. His mouth was still moving, trying to speak.

"How do I end the spell?" I asked him. "How do I stop the storm?"

"Kill me," he whispered, voice cracked and gravelly like he hadn't spoken in years.

"Not happening. Tell me how to end the spell."

He didn't answer and was little more than a rag doll in my arms. I searched the tower room for anything that made sense. Maybe if I destroyed the scrollwork. I dug the knife out of my pocket, pulled off the sheath, and scratched at the edges of the design. Sam writhed in my arms, blood welling up from a cut that magically appeared on his cheek.

Shit! He was attached to the spell.

"Only way," he whispered. "Kill me. I tied the spell to me. He doesn't know..."

I put the knife away and decided that I had only one choice—remove him from the situation. Shifting him to a fireman's carry, I made my way down the ladder and out of that horrible tower. Maybe if I got him away from the spell, it would weaken enough for me to free him. I headed toward where Con and I had left the sled, only to hit an invisible wall. Sam groaned in my arms, his body shaking so badly I struggled to keep a grip on him.

"Con?" I called quietly into the trees. When no response came, my heart skipped a beat.

"Kill me," Sam begged. "Please."

I touched the invisible barrier, and my hand went through just fine until I moved far enough to try to carry Sam across the barrier. Whatever it was wouldn't let him pass. But there was no way I was going to leave him here. I'd seen him come from the cabin in a dream, so maybe we just had to go around the barrier. Following the trees around the large gap of the river, the smell of the wood burning and the snapping of tree branches breaking because of the cold made me shudder.

Holding on to Sam seemed to be pulling the energy out of me. The wind had died down, but the moisture in the air grew. The spell ripped power from me at an insane force. It would have driven me to my knees if the river hadn't been right there offering an endless supply of new energy. I tapped into it, thanked it for the power, and tried to strengthen my shield. Only with Sam in my arms the barrier wouldn't go up. Was this another part of the spell or something to do with Sam?

The frozen river shimmered like something alive. I stared at it a few minutes while contemplating my options. And nearly jumped out of my skin when Con appeared in front of me. "Crap, Con. Give me a heart attack, why don't you?"

He didn't speak, and I didn't have enough time to react when his fist slammed into my face. Sam and I flew backward from the force. I tripped through the snow, trying to keep Sam from taking my fall, but we both landed on the ice. He just lay there on his side, eyes wide and fear-filled as Con jumped me.

Blood oozed from Con's neck, and a shadow leered just a few feet from us on the shoreline. Andrew Roman. Cat stood at his side, her expression so empty she looked dead. Her eyes glowed in the little bit of light refracting from the cabin. I heard a roar pierce the air. Jamie!

Something hit the cabin door hard, and the wood began to splinter. He must have changed. That could be a good thing so long as he didn't try to kill me too. *Shit!*

My brain churned, trying to think of a way out of this that didn't kill us all. But Con's hands wrapped around my neck, and he banged my head into the ice, making stars of pain flood my vision. I barely saw Sam reach out his hand to touch the ice as the darkness was pulling at me from lack of air.

The piercing crackle of ice brought me out of the black, fighting, kicking, punching, landing a solid blow to Con's face the second his hold faltered with shock. We fell in a slow motion of horror and cold. Water poured around us, yanking us into the frigid grip squeezing like a two-ton weight on my chest. The power of it pulsed through me with new strength even as it froze my lungs and made my heart sluggish. Con followed me down, his weight pushing us farther into the depths beneath the water.

I kicked, grabbing on to him, hoping to free him from the water before he drowned. Cat screamed from the shore and leapt toward her brother, ripping him from the water and me before bounding them both back to shore like she were some sort of incredible, agile jungle cat. Roman didn't move. And all the while I fought to catch another breath, each one colder than the last.

A little sound made me turn back to Sam, who closed his eyes as his body slid off a broken chunk of ice and into the water. No, dammit, I wasn't failing anyone today. Defying my already tiring body, I dove, cold stinging every part of me and freezing my eyes as I sought out Sam, captured him around the neck, and pulled him to the surface.

CONVICTION

The river swirled and churned around us. The break in the ice Sam caused became larger, letting the water speed its way south and rushing us farther downstream. I gripped pieces of ice, trying to stop us from being forced under the ice shelf, but they kept breaking away. The current pulled us under until I fought again to bring us back out, pounding at the sheets over our heads.

Struggling against the water, I caught sight of Jamie, bloodied, moving up behind Roman, his bear form huge and enraged. I floundered, gripping another hole in the ice and trying to haul us up, but nearly lost my hold on Sam. Jamie must have come looking for Sam but found Roman instead. Even with the distance, I could see the blood matting his fur. He looked like he'd been bitten several times, maybe beaten. He roared, a deafening sound, and ran, claws flashing. He got in one solid hit across Roman's chest, tearing into him and throwing him to the ground, where his strong jaws dug into the vampire's spine.

Andrew howled and fought, arms writhing while he tried to reach back and shove the bear off. Cat slammed into Jamie with enough force to tip him over, the two rolling away to fight in a fury of fangs and claws. Con sat up and blinked, looking lost and confused.

"Jamie!" I screamed for him, water choking me and making my lungs feel like icicles formed inside them.

I gripped a heavy root of a large tree and tried dragging Sam and I to shore. He was nearly lifeless in my arms. His small size, dark hair, and almond-shaped eyes made me think of Sei and how I'd failed them both. I carefully crawled up onto some ice, so incredibly cold I wondered if some of my limbs were still attached. How my arm was still wrapped around him, I couldn't guess. "Don't die on me, Sam. Please."

But the wind suddenly picked up, hitting me hard and knocking me back into the water. The chill poured over my head, taking me into the murky brown-blue darkness of the mud-caked water that wouldn't let me find my footing. But a hand grabbed mine. I fought to reach my other hand up too, saw Sam's eyes widen as he kept me from being swept downstream.

His lips moved, saying something I could barely hear. "Water is stronger than wind."

"What the fuck does that mean?" I asked, hoping he had some idea how to get us out of this. The ice began to break around him, and I fought to get him to release me so he wouldn't be dragged down too. Just as the crack ripped through the air like a cannon, he smiled apologetically, reminding me of how Sei had looked in that closet, lost, hiding from the world, afraid. Sam was just as broken. But unlike Sei, he was ready to die.

We both fell beneath the rising river, him not letting go and me feeling that terrible dread that had plagued me for weeks in my sleep. Only it wasn't Jamie dying in my arms. Cat had probably killed him—was a bear a match at all for a vampire? Now we'd never have a chance, since I was going to drown if the cold didn't burst my heart first.

The feeling of powerlessness nearly strangled me as the world began to lose focus. I had to save Sam, somehow. I closed my eyes and gave everything I had to the water, willing it to take my power and my life, just to save them all. For Sam and Con, who both needed a chance at life, for Cat, whose life had been stolen, for Sei and Gabe, who seemed to always be followed by demons, and Jamie, who I loved so much I couldn't imagine life without him. I gave up all that I really had—my life.

Chapter Nineteen

Jamie

CAT'S FINGERNAILS ripped like claws into my side, but I fought her anyway, trying to get to Kelly before the river stole him from me forever. She fought like the girl she was, shrieking, all nails and teeth, no skill. Brute strength was bad enough, since the ache in my chest said she'd cracked a few ribs. I got in several hard swipes, clawing through flesh and bone, making her scream, but not slowing her movement. Damn vampires.

She smashed me backward, throwing me a good thirty feet into the woodpile. The bear began to recede, and I gripped for the magic, begging for help. Without the claws and fangs, I was as good as dead. She glared at me, watching me change and bleed, but then looked back over her shoulder where Sam and Kelly struggled in the water. If they didn't drown, hypothermia would take them quickly. I needed to get to them.

I struggled to my feet, surprised that my arms were still furred and half bear. Roman was standing suddenly beside Cat, bleeding, shredded, and monstrous. Fucking vampires just didn't stay down.

CONVICTION

I tripped over the wood pile and landed next to the axe, yanking it free without another thought. Roman had turned, was reaching for Con. Maybe he hoped to make Con into a puppet too. Have a matching set. I didn't know or care, I just hurdled the axe with as much force and strength that I could muster, striking Roman square in the back.

The blow should have severed his spine. It would have killed any human. And Roman toppled over, but his arms flailed like he was trying to reach the axe. Fuck!

Cat slammed into me, forcing me back into the wood pile, fangs ripping into my now very human arm. It was the first time I'd ever wished I had Sei's kind of power. I wouldn't have to work to have the earth pulsing through me, or beg it to help. I kicked at her, limbs starting to tingle from the cold. My clothes were torn and only covered me in pieces from my transformation. I'd never gone back and forth so quickly, and I was tiring fast.

Con stood over Roman, confused and completely lost. Roman struggled at his feet, reaching for the axe handle like some flailing zombie. Cat fought like a wild thing, and even though she was probably only 115 pounds, she had more than double the strength I did. But if I could get by her to finish off Roman, she would be nothing more than a disoriented baby vampire who would need a new master.

"Con!" I screamed at the kid, hoping he wasn't as lost as his sister. "Finish him. It ends when he's dead."

But he bent over and pulled the axe out of Roman's back, then let it rest against his shoulder, losing the few seconds' window to strike down the root of all our problems. Roman rose, looking pained but having use of his legs again, even though I'd aimed well enough to sever his spinal cord. His dark hair glistened with snow, and those piercing blue eyes that had haunted Sei for so long glared daggers at me. He was healing. The torn flesh and rivulets of blood that I'd delivered were now just minor scratches. I cursed and kicked hard at Cat again, rewarded with the sick crunching of something breaking in her jaw. She didn't stop coming, but neither could she open her mouth enough to tear out my throat.

Roman didn't say a word, but Con moved behind him, jerkily heading my way with the axe in his hands. Just another puppet. *Fuck.* Cat stopped flailing and changed position to hold me down. Con approached as I saw Sam and Kelly behind him, on the river, fighting their way up onto some ice.

Holy shit, they were still alive! My heart flipped over in happiness and fear. If I couldn't take out even one of the vampires, we were all dead. Cat held me down, but Con seemed to be fighting the compulsion because his steps were slow and jagged, almost drunken. I slapped my hands into the earth and pulled like I'd never pulled before. I offered the earth every bit of me, promising I'd lay down and die if that's what she wanted, just to help. Save Kelly. At least save Kelly, I begged the power.

A strong tremor shook the ground hard enough to make Roman and Con stumble. Once again, Roman's hold on Con broke. Con turned away from me, looking back toward the river, seeking out Kelly. Cat growled at him and let me go to grab him, but he turned at the last second and buried the axe in her chest.

His pained expression didn't stop him from pulling the axe out as she fell. I jumped to his side and yanked the weapon from him just in case he went puppet again. He didn't try to take it back, just dropped to his knees, emotion overwhelming him as he stared at his sister's bleeding body. The blow couldn't have killed her, but maybe she would be down for a while.

I turned to the water to make sure Kelly and Sam were safe, but they were gone. The rushing water rolled through the area, spilling over the banks of the creek. My heart churned and I dropped to my knees, searching for any sign of them. Every moment I'd spent with Kelly flashed through my head in bittersweet memories of what I'd lost. How could life be so cruel? Years of searching, only to find the one I wanted and have him ripped from me. It couldn't be too late for me to tell him I was ready to try, wanted a chance.

An earth-shattering rumble shook the ground again, and this time it wasn't me. The water began to build upstream like some sort of tsunami, rising twenty, then thirty feet. I caught a glimpse of Kelly's blond hair when the water seemed to pour backward into the growing wave, and grabbed Con's hand, dragging him toward the river.

Pulling my own power from the muddy and newly awakened ground, I focused it into a current of energy. I let it flow freely from the earth, filling me and looping back through the ground. In the distance I could feel Seiran, his link to the earth unshakable. And he could feel me, approved of me, let the earth shove more energy into me than I thought a human could live through and still it kept coming. If burning me out was what was needed to save Kelly, then so be it.

When I reached the edge of the river a few seconds later, I heaved Kelly upward, releasing my own tidal wave of power into the ground and copied a page from Sei's book. Heavy roots pierced through the mud and snow, wrapped around us, cradling us in an almost deadly grip as the water hit with a crushing force.

I struggled to breathe in between the bursts of cresting and falling water. Needles of cold pricked at my skin and numbed me to the battering debris bumping around us. We fought to stay together, me holding Kelly and Con gripping us both. The booming crash of water brought the tower down, the evil magic it held washed away in the flood. I felt an almost cleansing pop as the spell vanished and the wind stopped blowing.

Not even Roman could escape the rushing power of the river. He vanished beneath the waves, struggling against the current. He would not get away this time. His time of haunting my family had to end here and now. I focused more power into the roots of the forest, directed them to grab him and hold him in a steel-like grasp. He wasn't going to escape this time. Not while there was any life left in my body.

The river finally calmed, and Kelly stirred in my arms. He sputtered and gasped, his body shaking so bad if it weren't for Con, I would have lost my hold on him. I dragged us to shore, exhausted and freezing, air turning my bare skin icy. I struggled to open my eyes, make sure they were still with me, but I was so damn tired. The buzz of a snowmobile roared toward us and I prayed it wasn't another enemy. I wasn't sure there was enough life left in me for another battle.

Chapter Twenty

Kelly

I WAS tossed around like I'd been put in a washer on the cold spin cycle. My stomach heaved, making me hack up icy, dirty water and some blood. That couldn't be good. Water whooshed out of my lungs as fast as it was sucked in, and I struggled to find air, even the smallest breath before being dragged back beneath the waves. Jamie's grip was like cold iron, unyielding and almost painful in its bite.

The storm stopped, and within a few seconds the moon appeared and glowed down on us. I'd felt the power of wind snap away when Sam had died. He'd died when the water hit the tower, destroying the spell. My heart broke and I couldn't hold on anymore, but as the water rocked us, it wasn't me who kept us together. Jamie dragged us from the water, his body shaking, frostbite starting to form on his naked flesh and nasty gouges covering his arms and chest. He moved slowly and deliberately, dragging, yanking, and not stopping no matter how pained his breathing until we were away from the water.

Con and Jamie curled around me, both shaking nearly as hard as I was from the cold. We'd die from hypothermia if we stayed out here. We were all wet, injured, exhausted. The magic rolled around us, water, earth, and wind. The elements almost seemed to dance in a tangible whisper of lights. If I'd had any strength I would have reached out to try to touch them. But all I could do was lay there and barely breathe. I'd lost Sam. His light wouldn't dance with the others.

Tears froze as they dripped down my face. I gripped Jamie, tried to wrap him in what was left of my coat, and buried my head in his shoulder. The water reassured me it had Sam, though it didn't understand the difference between him being dead or alive. The waves gently lifted him from the bowels of the banks and deposited him just feet from us. He lay lifeless. He'd been so battered, never had a chance to have a good life or fall in love. It was so unfair.

A snowmobile rolled to a stop a few feet away. I couldn't see well enough to make out who approached us. "There are helicopters on the way." The voice had Gabe's old-world accent. He unzipped his jacket and laid it over us, and a few seconds later I heard the rattle of a package and a thermal blanket wrapped around us.

Jamie nodded against my face and tried to get up, but his legs refused to work. He shivered so hard I knew he was going to go into shock. Gabe pulled a couple more thermal blankets out of a bag he'd been carrying and wrapped us each in one, huddling us together for warmth. "The helicopter is just behind me. I pushed the sled to the limit."

"How'd you find us?" Jamie asked through clenched teeth.

"Sei felt you ask for power. I was already at the lodge with the police. I had to get our stuff and they were questioning the Gossners. When they discovered both Con and Cat missing, they admitted to helping Andrew Roman." There was a pause, then, "Where is the bastard?"

"Water," I said. I reached out, shaping the power that coursed through the river into what nature intended. It refroze, crackling and shifting as chunks until finally the creek looked more like a large glistening skating rink. I'd never changed the temperature of water before. Never tried. But it was as easy as breathing. I sighed as the power began to relax around me, releasing its unrelenting grip on me.

Sam stared my way, eyes vacant, open. Lost. I wrapped myself tighter in the thermal blanket and cried. Why did he have to die? He was just a kid. Hell, he was younger than me by a year or so and had already been abused by two different vampires. Why? Because he had some kind of weird ability to cast spells even though he wasn't Dominion? It made no sense. I wanted to scream, cry, and sleep.

Jamie grabbed me and yanked me close, his trembling body quaking with me. It was unspoken, but I knew he was reminding me we'd tried.

Gabe stood over Roman on the newly formed ice, watching the man struggle against the roots and frozen river. He stood so silent and still, I wondered what crossed his mind. The flash of red in his eyes, I recognized as anger. His hands gripped at his sides, twisting as claws slid from his fingertips. Surely he didn't think Roman could walk away from this one. It had to end here.

He knelt down to meet Roman's gaze. "It's over," Gabe assured him.

"Not until you're dead," Roman sneered. He was all fangs and red eyes now, fighting with renewed strength. The roots around him tightened, and I realized that Gabe must be borrowing Sei's power somehow. The focus bond, maybe?

"You don't have the balls, Santini," Roman accused. "Never did. That's why Titus died, and your new little princess will die too.

I'll rip him apart in front of you and listen to your screams."

I pushed myself to my feet, legs more like rubber than what I was used to. Jamie's hand grasped at mine, but I shook him off. This was for Sei, Sam, and everyone who'd been hurt in Roman's baseless quest for revenge. I limped across the ice to Gabe's side, leaving Sam in Jamie's care. "He needs to die."

Gabe sighed. "Yes. Taking his head won't be enough. And I can't chance that he gets away again. I may have to call the Tri-Mega to oversee his execution. The very old are harder to kill."

"Not really." I agreed that total body destruction would probably be the only thing to work on a vampire as old as Andrew Roman. But vampires were essentially humans with special powers, which meant that, just like everyone else, he was 80 percent water. The power of the water still ran through me like an electric current, charging me up without even asking. I could feel the oceans though they were thousands of miles away. Every lake, pond, river, creek and stream answered my call. In that moment I felt like I could call up a flood of biblical proportions and wipe out the entirety of the planet. That was how connected I was. The rest was as easy as breathing.

Roman glared and cursed at me with those pretty blue eyes rimmed in glowing red when I touched his forehead, rolled the power through him until he sputtered, water coming from his lungs, drowning him from the inside out. Then with a single thought, a dangerous thought that at any other time would have me questioning my sanity, I changed the temperature of the water and froze him. It wasn't pretty. Not even as pretty as Hans had been, left out in the snow. But I got up and walked away when he stopped moving, knowing Gabe would take care of the rest.

A person shouldn't shatter, but Roman did. None of us watched as Gabe released every last bit of that calm, collected resolve he fought so hard for and lost himself in rage. The earth caught the bits, squeezed them, cracking the last of Andrew Roman into pieces so small even the fishes wouldn't bite come spring. The last remaining slivers washed away in the water under the thick ice shelf.

When the helicopter appeared at the edge of the river near us, there was no sign that Andrew Roman had ever existed. It was a medical helicopter. Which was good since I was pretty sure neither Jamie and I were going to walk out of there on our own.

I only vaguely remember getting rolled on a gurney into the loud machine and pulling away. Panic enveloped me just as I realized I was no longer with Jamie, and unconsciousness finally found me.

WAKING UP in the hospital was sort of creepy. The drop-tile ceiling and weird stand lights looked like something out of a TV show. A soft whisper of peace spread through my bones, easing the ache and telling me I was safe and warm. Wow did warm feel amazing or what?

I turned to see my best friend's smiling face staring down at me.

"Hey, sleepyhead," Sei said. He looked a little tired but otherwise unhurt. Water trickled somewhere nearby, filling the room with the soothing sound of a fountain. The running water rolled through me, making me dizzy for a moment. Sei gripped my hand. "Breathe through it. Don't hold it in, just let it flow," he instructed me. The nausea faded and I sucked in a deep breath, exhaling power and tension at the same time. "Like riding a bike. You'll get used to it and not have to work on it so hard after a few days."

Used to what? Shouldn't the power I borrowed from the creek be done? I blinked at him in confusion. Too tired to think of a million things I probably should have been asking. Instead I asked. "Is everyone okay?" Then I remembered Sam, who I'd failed, and closed my eyes. That stung worse than any physical pain I could have felt.

"Con left the hospital yesterday."

"How is he?"

"He's broken up about his sister. I think he feels really guilty for attacking you and Jamie. Though he couldn't help it."

I nodded. "We'll help him through it."

Sei smiled like that was what he was expecting me to say. "Gabe's at home since it's still light out. Jamie is recovering from some broken ribs, cuts, and minor frostbite. He had a fit when I told him I was taking over for a few hours, but he really needed the sleep. He pulled a lot of energy from the earth and I think is still trying to shake off the grogginess."

Jamie had been here? He was okay?

Sei laughed. He must have read what I was thinking in my expression. "Like a bear protecting his mate, that one. Gets all dark and brooding if the nurses kick him out to make him sleep."

Embarrassment burned a fire up my cheeks, heating my face. Did Sei know we'd had sex again several times? That I wanted to keep repeating that until the world ended? Did he get how badly I wanted to try to make a family with Jamie? Close the open end of our circle, and open the door to something I'd wanted for years—love?

"And you just need to get your feet under you, and then you'll get to leave."

My feet under me? The thought made me panic, thinking something had happened to my legs. But I wiggled my toes beneath the blanket, and everything felt fine. I even pulled back the blanket to make sure all my toes were intact and counted my fingers too. Everything was where it should be.

Sei kept talking. "So the ceremony will be after Solstice, with mine. My mom says we should dress up, but I don't think a suit will help either of us gain more respect. Jamie's already arguing that we both need covens for support. I don't get what the big deal is. I've been okay so far without one. Gabe is sort of my coven of one." He paused. "Though I can pull from Jamie too, so maybe a coven of two." Sei stared at the waterfall that poured water just inches away from my head. He ran his fingers through the water, and I felt every stroke like he had actually touched my arm.

"You're making no sense," I finally said when I could focus on him instead of being distracted by the water.

He looked back at me, serious worry on his face. "The Pillar of water is stepping down. Water wants you as its Pillar, can't you feel it?"

Good God, was that what the tingling waves meant? I gripped Sei's hand and felt a moment of absolute unity, like waves lapping gently at the shore. "I don't have a choice, do I?"

"The ceremony is just a formality. When you offered yourself in sacrifice, water decided to expand that bond. The earth sort of gave a nod of approval. I felt it. This is what the Pillars are supposed to be. Unity." Like the calm of a sunny day on the beach. His grip warmed me, and I could feel the whole world through him, from the deepest of oceans to the highest mountain stream.

I sighed, grateful for his touch, but had to ask, "I won't have to move, will I?" Granted, warm weather and blue oceans were great, but my family was here.

"Nope. Your training will intensify, though. Sounds like the current Pillar of water is coming up here to help teach you the ropes." He patted the back of my hand. "I spoke to her on the phone. She sounds really nice. More like Hanna than any of the other Dominion girls I've met."

That was a relief. I didn't know much about the water Pillar. Had never expected to get into the Magic Studies program or be on the road to actually serving the Dominion. My two years of business studies would be set aside for the change, and oddly enough, that was okay.

Sei checked his watch. "I have to go upstairs. Hanna is having her ultrasound. Wanna come?"

Since I wasn't hooked up to any machines other than an IV with fluids, I suddenly really wanted to go. Seeing the baby would help remind me that I still had my family, even if I'd lost someone I'd tried so hard to save. Even if Jamie wasn't here to discuss if we had a chance at a future. "Can I?"

"Let me go get a chair." He disappeared outside the room for a minute and returned with a nurse who wheeled a chair in and hooked my fluids bag to it before helping me to sit. Sei put a blanket on my lap and pushed me toward the door. "If you feel weird when we leave the room, let me know. You may not be ready to leave yet."

When we crossed the threshold, I made them pause as nausea and disorientation pulsed through me. "I'm okay," I told him after a moment. And I was. I let the little flares of power flow naturally, like a current would have, which eased the queasiness.

We rode the elevator up, and he pushed me down the hall to a room where Sei knocked before entering. My heart skipped a beat as Jamie opened the door for us, his smile sweet but worry etching his brow in lines he was too young to have. "Should he be out yet?"

"He'll be fine. He's already got the hang of it," Sei answered and left my chair for Jamie to push. "You are supposed to be resting."

"I couldn't miss this. It's bad enough Gabe has to." Jamie guided me around near the bed. Allie, Hanna's partner, smiled at me from her chair near Hanna's head.

Hanna was up on the table, shirt raised above her stomach, gel making the area look slick. The big TV was just dark fuzz until the doctor put the small paddle to her belly. Then things started forming. Small shapes and miracles that made me wonder what it would be like to someday have a surrogate and a baby for myself.

Sei's face was locked in a look of wonder while Hanna and Allie searched the screen in a mix of worry and excitement. He gripped my hand, and the small tremor that had already developed made me pray for good things. Sei deserved good things. And I could see a baby as a positive in his life. Someone for him to dote on, and worry about, and teach all his crazy cooking skills.

The doctor said nothing for a while, but Jamie leaned closer, as though he saw something on the screen he didn't understand. "Is that...?"

"I believe it is," the doctor said.

"What?" Sei asked, gripping Jamie's shirt. "What is it? Is the baby okay?"

The doctor moved the paddle back, tracing one outline and then another. Was that? Oh my God, it really was. The doctor switched to 3-D scan and everything became as clear as day. *Holy fuck!*

"Twins," Jamie whispered.

Allie and Hanna burst into tears at the same time. Sei seemed frozen next to them, staring at the screen, a mixture of terror and pain crossing his face.

"Are they both girls?" he asked so quietly I didn't think anyone but me heard. "Can you tell that yet?"

The doctor pressed another area, and it didn't look any different to me, but he shook his head. "Can't be positive yet. They are pretty close together, but I'm thinking one girl, one boy." He focused the paddle in one area and there was a tiny blip which could have been a baby peen.

Sei almost dropped into my lap. The chair was wide enough that he fit in next to me, curved onto his side. He gripped my hand. Jamie grinned at us while Allie and Hanna kissed.

"Can we share?" Sei asked. "Can both our babies have mommies and daddies?" I knew what he wanted. He wanted the normal life for his babies that he had never had a chance of. He wanted to live outside the norm of the first-wave aristocracy. He wanted to be a daddy, and let his babies have a mommy too.

"Yes," Hanna said. "Our babies will be blessed with mommies and daddies who love them more than anything."

Chapter Twenty-One

JAMIE WHEELED me back to my room a little while later, letting Sei marvel over the new babies with the girls. He would get copies of the pictures of the babies, and they were already discussing names. But Jamie hadn't said a word, even when he parked the chair and helped me back into bed. The running water calmed my fast beating heart. But his stony silence grated away at my nerves. After everything we'd be through, was he still gonna treat me like a kid?

He sat down in the chair beside me and handed me the romance novel I'd been reading at the lodge. "Sei said you might want to finish reading it."

"Thanks." I tucked the book aside and studied him. What would he say if I laid it all on the line? "You can do it too, you know."

"Do what? Read the romance? It's not really my thing."

No, he was health guides and medical journals. "Find a surrogate to have your baby. I know you want babies."

Jamie looked away. "Seiran will need my help. So I don't think that will be an option for a while."

"Hmm." I grabbed his hand, making him look back at me. "But someday, right? 'Cause I'd really like to raise a baby with you. Hopefully he or she will have your pretty amber eyes."

Jamie swallowed hard, his eyes burning into mine. "You're so young—"

"But I know what I want. And I swear if you use my age as an excuse again, I'm going to punch you."

He chuckled and looked away. I reached across the bed, pulling him closer and kissing his nose and then each of the scratches that marred his face. The wounds would heal, but it made me mad that someone had hurt him.

Someone cleared their throat. Jamie and I turned in unison toward the door. Gabe stood there, his eyes aimed above our heads, but a little smile tilted the edge of his lips. My heart skipped a beat when I saw he wasn't alone. It couldn't be possible, could it?

At his side was Sam, who was tiny compared to Gabe. But he no longer looked ill, his eyes weren't bagged in black, and he seemed to have put on enough weight to make him look healthy. Not dead.

How, in just a few days, he could not only come back from the dead but stand there looking perfectly healthy? Jamie held my hand and nodded to Gabe. "Sam is a vampire."

Did that mean Roman had made him? Did that mean parts of that bastard lived in him? My heart pounded in fear. Would he turn on us?

The door opened, and Sei walked in, carrying a handful of pictures of the babies. Sam wouldn't meet his eyes, but Sei hugged him anyway and began pointing out things in the pictures about the babies. Talking about how maybe one was a boy and you could sort of see the nose on the other and how it looked like his.

Jamie rubbed my arm, forcing me to look at him again. "It's okay," he said. "Sam is still Sam, and he has Gabe to guide him."

"What about Cat?" She'd gone mad. Nothing about that girl had still been human when she'd been changed.

"She's being put to death by the Tri-Mega. Her change was wrong. It happens sometimes. Sam is under watch by the Tri-Mega, and the Dominion is asking questions about his powers. They've never met anyone with the ability to enhance other people's powers before. They are denying that Sam has the ability."

Enhance? Was that how my powers had changed? Did that mean they would go away? "But am I really stronger than the former Pillar, then?"

"Yeah, it seems your powers evolved. And you're not the only one. Tanaka is asking me to test now as well. I've already refused. I have no interest in working for the Dominion. She tried to convince me that I could help change the way magic is taught, but that's not my battle. My family comes first."

I nodded. Because that was what Jamie did. Was. Family. He gripped my hand. Maybe my family. Was it really over? "Andrew Roman is dead?" I asked, just to reassure myself the end hadn't been a dream. I'd done something horrible to him, and Gabe had destroyed him.

"You did what you had to," Jamie assured me. "He's gone forever. No one is coming after our family again." He drew me into his arms. The hug was a pale shadow of his normally bone-crushing one, but it was sweet all the same. I don't know if either of us were healed enough for any real squeezing. Even the playful kind. I sighed and breathed in the smell of Jamie's hair, happy with the idea of watching my new little family grow by two more.

Gabe winked at me and led the growing crowd from the room. "Get some rest. I'll see about getting you released."

Once they were gone and I was alone again with Jamie, I rubbed his palm and studied the intricate lines of it instead of looking at him. "Do you know what I was thinking of when the water was pulling me down?" I asked, and he shook his head. "That I would let it all go to save you. That I loved you so much nothing else mattered. And you know that your family is my family."

Jamie closed his eyes for a moment, and when he opened them again, there were tears. His lips found mine, pressing his tongue inside to taste me and caress mine like it was all he wanted to do in the world. When he finally pulled away, I felt his heart beating beneath my palm. "When you told me back at the cabin that you wouldn't let our family suffer again, that's when I knew. Promise me you won't hide things from me anymore," he demanded. "If you're hurt or have nightmares or just need a fucking tow. Tell me."

"I'm Pillar of water now." Or would be once the ceremony was complete. It would bring more complications into our family. "I didn't ask for it to happen."

"I know."

"I was never trying to hide anything from you. You just always seemed to worry so much about Sei. I didn't want to add to it." My heart ached, fearing all the betrayal I'd suffered in my youth would come back to bite me. "They used me to fuel the spell."

"They used us all. Sam hasn't spoken much of it and the Dominion swept in to clear the cabin of any books left behind." He didn't look happy with that fact. "It was evil. Magic I'd never felt before. And hope to never feel again." He glared at the wall across from me instead of looking at me. "I'm sorry for trying to keep you out of things and trying to play the hero."

"Did Sei yell at you?"

He laughed and gave me a rare smile that nearly made my toes curl. "Yeah, but I deserved it. I should have told you a long time ago that I'm crazy about you."

I almost felt the world tilt. "I read your letter."

He looked away. "Sorry."

"I want you to say it."

"Sorry."

"Not that."

"Oh. Was it a surprise to you? I thought for sure you'd notice how I avoided being around you all the time because I was afraid to fall for you." He got up and began to pace. "When I thought you'd drowned... I thought I'd lost everything. I've been trying to talk myself out of being a pervert for a long time, but I can't help the fact that I love you."

The words reverberated through my spine, and the water of the room splashed around without me doing anything. Jamie eyed the room with a little apprehension.

"Sorry, you made me a little excited. You're not a pervert. I'm legal, out, and proud. Get over here and kiss me."

"You're really bossy."

"And you don't like that?"

"I think it's really hot." He perched on the edge of the bed and kissed me like he wanted to crawl inside of me. Probably someday soon he would, and I couldn't wait.

END

About the Author

Lissa Kasey lives in St. Paul, MN, has a Bachelor's Degree in Creative Writing, and collects Asian Ball Joint Dolls who look like her characters. She has three cats who enjoy waking her up an hour before her alarm every morning and sitting on her lap to help her write. She can often be found at Anime Conventions masquerading as random characters when she's not writing about boy romance.

OTHER BOOKS BY LISSA KASEY

Hidden Gem
Model Citizen
Evolution
Evolution: Genesis (Coming October 2015)

Other Dominion books: (Rereleasing 2015)
Inheritance
Reclamation
Conviction
Ascendance

Free Shorts:
Friction
Resolute
Decadence
Consequences
Devotion
Samhain

Printed in Great Britain
by Amazon